OLD GUY MUSIC

By the Same Author

Novels
Howell Grange (2019)
Gemini Day (2021)
The Densham Do 2022)
Diamond Val (2023)
The Judas Gene (2024)

Poetry Collections
Raised Voices (2014)
Kaleidoscope (2017)
The Huntington Hydra (2019)

Short Story Collections
First Flame (2013)
Odds Against (2017)
The Guy Thing (2018)
Fallen Eagles (2021)
Roxanne Riding Hood (2023)

Further details at:
www.bruceharrisbooks.com

OLD GUY MUSIC

BRUCE HARRIS

First published in Great Britain in 2026 by
The Book Guild Ltd
Unit E2 Airfield Business Park,
Harrison Road, Market Harborough,
Leicestershire. LE16 7UL
Tel: 0116 2792299
www.bookguild.co.uk
Email: info@bookguild.co.uk

Copyright © 2026 Bruce Harris

The right of Bruce Harris to be identified as the author of this
work has been asserted by them in accordance with the
Copyright, Design and Patents Act 1988.

All rights reserved. No part of this publication may be
reproduced, transmitted, or stored in a retrieval system, in any form or by any means,
without permission in writing from the publisher, nor be otherwise circulated in
any form of binding or cover other than that in which it is published and without
a similar condition being imposed on the subsequent purchaser.

The manufacturer's authorised representative in the EU
for product safety is Authorised Rep Compliance Ltd,
71 Lower Baggot Street, Dublin D02 P593 Ireland (www.arccompliance.com)

This work is entirely fictitious and bears no resemblance to any persons living or dead.

Typeset in 11pt Adobe Garamond Pro

Printed and bound in Great Britain by 4edge Limited

ISBN 978 1835743 539

British Library Cataloguing in Publication Data.
A catalogue record for this book is available from the British Library.

CONTENTS

PART ONE	Death of a Star	1
PART TWO	The Hunters and the Hunted	71
PART THREE	The Spreading Poison	103
PART FOUR	Patriot Man	131
PART FIVE	Back to the Present: Resolution 1	175
PART SIX	Resolution 2	217
PART SEVEN	Aftermath	245

PART ONE

DEATH OF A STAR

Raymond Oswald, aged sixteen, did not care very much for most versions of his name, including Raymond and Ray. To his schoolmates, he only answered to Ossie or Oss, and as he was quite a large boy for his age, this preference was fairly widely observed.

Oss was known, both on and off the football field, for a certain chutzpah. He was still well outside any deliberate criminality, not least because of his formidable mother, but he was, as his mates would have said, "up for it". His breezy, full-on way with girls caused admiration and embarrassment in equal amounts amongst his pals, depending on their own success or failure in this sensitive area. As a player, if it was a fifty-fifty ball, it would usually be Ossie's, and if there was any chance of having a go at the goal, even at optimistic distances, Ossie would give it a go.

A downside was Ossie's innate curiosity, which had already caused him to find himself in a number of difficult situations, including walking in on his older brother, Sam, when Sam's girlfriend, Charlene, was paying him a visit, which almost resulted in Sam setting about his little brother on the spot, had it not been for two problems, one being that Sam was almost naked at the time and two being Sam's awareness that Raymond would probably give as good as he got.

Ossie had also trespassed on a working building site and almost been brained by a girder being heaved about by crane, and interrupted two gentlemen in an obscure corner of the local park, who were doing what Ossie could only describe as "shagging", the first time he had realised that some men did that to each other.

Mr and Mrs Oswald remained constantly anxious about their second son, with an inevitable suspicion that Ray would one day find himself very much in the wrong place at the wrong time, and if they had known what Ray was doing on this particular day, their anxieties would have intensified.

Ossie was going home from football training, and the journey was taking him longer than the twenty minutes or so it would normally take him. A clumsy tackle from an inept defender had done something to his ankle, and now he had seen, at a distance, something which wakened his constantly curious nature.

A few hundred yards on the south side of the housing estate where Ossie's family lived was a group of buildings, known locally and loosely as "Reynolds' Farm", though no one seemed to remember who Reynolds had been and the place had long since ceased being used as a farm. The main building might loosely be described as a bungalow, but it was much larger than most bungalows anyone had ever seen and was surrounded by a number of mysterious outhouses, including a barn and several long, large, low-slung huts.

To give Ossie his due, his curiosity about the place was shared by many of the estate children. Everyone knew it had been there long before their housing estate was built, and the original owner had fought tooth and nail to get the housing estate built somewhere else. All the kids also knew the place had long connections with pop music and pop stars, not as they were now, but back in the day – as far as the kids were concerned, the Middle Ages, though it was more accurately the eighties and nineties. The group most connected with the place were called the Cougars, who had recorded several big hits and used Reynolds' Farm to record much of their output. It was the Cougars' original member and lead guitarist, Bill Massiter, widely known as Cougar Bill, who still lived in the place. At the time of the Cougars' greatest success, Reynolds' Farm had been widely used as a recording studio, where the bands and the people making the records could all be accommodated in the place away from remorseless public scrutiny.

That would probably have been enough in itself to excite Ossie's interest, but there was another, less legitimate reason. There were widespread rumours that certain kinds of illegal substances had been, and possibly still were, being kept on the premises, especially when the Cougars were at the height of their fame, but perhaps afterwards and perhaps even now. The persistent rumour in the young circles which Ossie frequented was that, if you knew the right people, obtaining a few so-called recreational drugs at Reynolds' Farm would not be too difficult. Ossie had never, as yet, used any illegal substances – his mother had made her views on the subject abundantly clear – but he was of an age when anything dodgy and possibly illegal had a certain inevitable magnetism.

However, as far as anyone in the locality knew, only Bill Massiter now lived there, and he was of too advanced an age for any of the local kids to really believe him capable of illegality. Even so, as much in jest as in any other way, they usually called him "Wild Willy", and while he seemed amiable enough when people saw him around in the town, most kids had been warned off by their parents. Some said he was a "junkie", some said he was so immoral and promiscuous that he used to have girls going to the place in an endless stream, and the air of decadence and degeneration which many people seemed to associate with him was, to estate kids, both a magnet and a turn-off simultaneously.

From time to time, so much noise emanated from Bill's place that people talked about calling the police. On two occasions so far, the police had actually been summoned, but as far as the estate could tell, they'd just been welcomed, given a drink or two and sent on their amiable way.

The more liberal "live and let live" inhabitants of the estate, outnumbered though they were, maintained that Massiter was simply living the lifestyle more or less as he always had done, that his house and its surrounds had existed long before the estate came along, and Bill Massiter was known to be willing to help out local charities when he could. They also pointed out that Massiter, as an ex-big pop star, "put our town on the map", and his willingness to make personal appearances in the neighbourhood, even if they were becoming increasingly rare, had ensured a good deal of local goodwill.

Even the adults who generally didn't approve much of "Cougar Bill" were prepared to make allowances, and this group included Ossie's mother, Angela, or, more usually, "Ange".

'He's trying to live his rockstar lifestyle for as long as he can, and who can blame him for that? What's he got left when all that's gone, up there in that sprawling place on his own?'

Ossie sat down for a moment in the long grass, partly to look at his ankle, which he suspected had already swollen, and partly to hide, because it was also rumoured that Wild Willy had security guys with dogs watching the perimeter of his house sometimes. The ankle was swollen, not particularly badly, but bad enough to need resting for a while, and Ossie thought about just hobbling off home as quickly as he could. But then he glanced towards the rambling house again and realised that his eyes hadn't been deceiving him. He was looking at a human form, or at least the lower half of one, and it was not where it ought to be; it was as if someone had their head poked through the roof and left the rest of them dangling underneath.

He remembered, after the building-site incident, that his mother had come as near as she ever had to clouting him round the ear, and after she'd stopped his money for a fortnight, he rather wished she had clouted him round the ear and had done with it.

'When will you learn, Raymond' – she resorted to Raymond whenever she was annoyed with him – 'to mind your own business and keep your nose out of everyone else's? We could be visiting you in hospital now…'

Then a few tears, which really did crease Ossie up. He could just imagine what would happen if some seven-foot-tall security guy took him by the scruff of his neck and delivered him to his house. The clout round the ear would just be the start of it.

But, as the boys were fond of saying, "no balls, no action", and he found himself creeping closer to the house, limping slightly and letting the long grass hide most of him.

Soon, he reached the wall around the large spaces of Wild Willy's garden, if such a large patch of grass and scrub could really be called a garden. As walls went, it wasn't one which would normally have caused Ossie any problems; it was only about four-foot tall, meaning he could put one hand on it and vault himself over, though how easy the landing would be on his ankle remained to be seen – and felt.

Without stopping to dwell on it, he duly vaulted, and the stab of pain through his ankle and up his calf as soon as he landed made him wince and nearly cry out, but this was the Ossie Oswald who was seriously in line to be captain of the school team and he didn't shout out for the sake of a twinge in the ankle.

All the same, he could now only hobble and he was beginning, not for the first time, to realise that his bravado had a price to be paid. He was also taken aback at the nature of his own curiosity; what did he care about druggies and getting into all that, which would certainly finish his long-shot dreams of professional football? He almost turned back but that would mean another vault over the wall which he didn't care to risk; he was just going to have to leave Wild Willy's by the front gate, and if he got caught, he got caught. He could always say he was looking for help with his ankle injury, and the way things were going, it probably wouldn't be much of a lie, if a lie at all.

Then he looked towards the house again, and he froze to the spot. No, it wasn't anyone with their head poking out of the roof. No, it wasn't anyone standing on a ladder painting or repairing something. It was a man with a rope around his neck, hanging from a beam on the roof, his legs dangling lifelessly below him.

Ossie's face, he knew, had gone deathly pale, and a slight trickle had started in his pants which he had to make a very serious effort to stop.

He realised he was gasping and he had an urgent need to piss. Moving behind one of the outbuildings he relieved himself while he thought desperately about what to do.

He had to phone, he realised, as the panic ebbed away. Yes, they would all be asking what he was doing there; yes, there might be clouts, or money stopped, or whatever other unpleasantness they could think of, but he couldn't leave the guy, who looked a bit like it was Wild Willy himself, just hanging there with his legs dangling. And if they all started on at him about why don't you mind your own business, Raymond, he could say, well, how long would he have been hanging there with no one helping him if I hadn't gone there?

He zipped himself up and realised, for the first time, that the building he'd been leaning up against was actually an indoor swimming pool, for all it was contained in concrete walls looking more like a prisoner of war hut. Swimming was a passion of Ossie's, occasionally in summer skinny-dipping at various quiet spots along the river meandering out of town, but more usually at the local pool, which, of course, he had to pay for and share with more other people than he would really have wanted to. To get his head round the idea that someone had their own indoor pool, sitting there in the middle of their garden for them to use whenever they chose, was difficult enough, but to also take in that this was probably the guy now hanging from the roof seemed to Ossie genuinely incredible.

A sudden wave of fear and doubt stabbed through him; he was, he knew, out of his depth with all this, but an answering voice insisted that he needed to do something, and quickly. It suddenly occurred to him that the hanging man might even still be alive, and he might also be getting ever closer to death, even as this daft lad who had found him was humming and hawing about what to do.

There was nothing else for it. He had to phone his mother.

An hour and a half later, the phone sounded in the office of Detective Chief Inspector Max Bellamy, who was in a rare, depressed mood after a particularly bad road accident in his "patch" had resulted that early morning in three deaths. Road safety wasn't usually Bellamy's department, but the junction where the accident had occurred had a previous record of disasters, and he was concentrating on what might be necessary to ensure the layout of the place was changed, as rapidly as possible.

In his tieless immaculately white shirt and neat jacket, forty-one-year-old Bellamy looked like a male model relaxing between takes, the cool blue eyes resting on the papers in front of him and his neutral expression no great clue to the emotions he was feeling; one of the dead had been an eight-year-old child.

Bellamy, with his Labour MP wife, Louise, and a sizeable private fortune inherited from his father, was an unusual policeman in not only the most obvious respects. Only those who knew him well remembered that he had been a journalist before he joined the police, and one of the aspects of the morning's dreadful accident he was contemplating was the likely reaction of the local press, whose opinions on the subject of Albury Junction, a three-way crossroad, had been aired on several previous occasions. Even the junction's name, Bellamy thought gloomily, would give them ammunition enough.

As he picked up the phone, pessimistic trains of thought were still occupying his mind, and he had to adjust quickly to the eminence he was now talking to, in the easy tones of Assistant Chief Constable Tom Hollins.

'Detective Chief Inspector Bellamy?'

'Speaking.'

'Oh, right. Hi, Max. I thought you would have delegated some young PC to answer your calls by now.'

'Hi, Tom – I mean, sir.' Hollins and Bellamy knew each other all the way back to journalistic days. DCI Hollins, as he was then, had been instrumental in persuading Bellamy to join the police force.

'It's OK, Max, I don't mind Tom when we're one to one. We've known each other for a long time, right back to when you were a young hack plaguing the life out of me. How are you getting on with being a DCI these days?'

'Well, the main difference seems to be spending more time in the office, oddly enough. Did you find that?'

'Yes, it's inevitable, I'm afraid. The higher you go, the more you've got to delegate; if you're permanently charging around like a blue-arsed fly, you'll wear yourself out soon enough, and that's no use to anyone. Anyway, we've got a difficult situation which has just arisen, and although it's not actually in your county, I've spoken to the relevant brass and they don't mind you taking it on. In fact, I think they're rather grateful for the suggestion.'

'Sounds a bit ominous.'

'And so it might be, Max. But first, let me get my facts right. Did your dad once have connections with one Bill Massiter of the Cougars rock band, more commonly known as Cougar Bill?'

'Yes, he did. He was the Cougars' agent for a while, before he got into the bigger stuff of managing gigs and venues.'

'Right. Well, I'm afraid Cougar Bill has just been found hanging in his own backyard, so to speak, that sprawling ex-farm which was used as a recording studio back in the day. It looks like suicide, and that was the first thing that prompted me to think of you, because you've got form with things which look like suicide, haven't you, after the Manningham case?'

'Yes, I suppose so, though I should probably mention that the Manningham case could probably be said to be the exception which proved the rule. Most cases which look like suicide are suicide.'

'Fair enough.' Bellamy detected a certain weariness in his old friend's tone, and wondered whether his now exalted rank was proving more than he wanted to take on. He heard an almost imperceptible sigh on the other end of the phone, and then Hollins pressed on.

'But, after that put you in mind, I then remembered the connection with your dad, and also the likely media frenzy which this whole thing is likely to generate. So far, we've been able to keep things pretty quiet. Cougar Bill was found by some kid who was on his land, for reasons we're not sure about, though the kid is saying he was just curious about seeing a hanging figure from a distance. We've still got the kid in custody, but of course, we've had to send people to the house, and with police all over the place, it won't be long before it all gets out, then all hell will break loose. The Cougars may be a fading memory for a lot of people, but the hacks will be all over themselves to know what went on anyway, and since you're the classic case of poacher turned gamekeeper, you'll be able to keep them in line.'

'My father once said of the Cougars that they were a kind of fusion band, mixing heavy metal and pop. He liked Cougar Bill, but he wasn't so keen on the rest of them, especially Rory Blaze, as he called himself, aka Tony Richards.'

'So how about it, Max? Are you willing to take it on?'

'Yes, sir. It does seem to be up my street, well, me and my dad, that is. But I'd like the assistance of Elaine Price again, as in the Manningham case, if you're happy with that.'

'I'm OK with it, but I'm not going to order her, Max. She's an inspector now; if she doesn't want to run around after you, that's her prerogative. I'll contact her. If you do, she'll feel too polite to turn you down.'

'Maybe, maybe not. If she was determined about it, she'd say so.'

'OK, let's do it like this.'

Such were the benefits of high rank, thought Bellamy, as he was finding out himself. People can chat around you as much as they like, but you're the one who makes the decision.

'You head over there now. The local guys are there, and I gather they've managed to cut poor Bill down and put him on some packing cases without disturbing the scene too much, and they've blacked out the windows to avoid any more curious kids, or whatever else that kid might have been up to. Apart from that, they've touched nothing, as I've told them to, and they won't until you get there. A post-mortem will be needed, of course, but I wanted you to have a look at the scene as it is. And if any keen hacks are already hanging around, put the fear of God into them, because I'm not having this turn into a circus.'

Hollins's voice suddenly softened. Yes, he's good at that, Bellamy remembered.

'How's Mrs Louise Bellamy, MP?'

'Enjoying it, but spending half her life in London. She seems to be getting on pretty well with the chief whip. She might even get a sniff at being a junior minister.'

'Bloody hell, Max. Are you going to finish up as a latter-day Mr Thatcher?'

'Who knows? She's a clever girl.'

'Good luck to her. I'll get on to Elaine Price while you head over there. If she says yes, she'll either be there when you get there, or she'll arrive shortly afterwards. If she says no, someone else will be there as your number two. Probably a sergeant. Call me when you get there, Max. Alright?'

'Yes, sir. I'm on my way.'

Somehow, the local force had managed to keep things low-key. A few curious people were standing at about thirty yards' distance from the large front garden of Cougar Bill's place, but there didn't seem any sign of media presence yet. However, Bellamy was not naive enough to believe that would carry on for much longer.

Before he entered the building where the suicide, or whatever it was, had happened, Bellamy could see that in the adjoining place an angry and exasperated woman was sitting next to a red-faced boy, pretty obviously her son, who looked as though he had already been on the end of a fairly uninhibited talking-to from his mum.

Bellamy entered the long, hut-like building which looked as though it was kept as Cougar Bill's office, with reminders everywhere of the Cougars' golden days – posters on the wall, some with huge pictures of various members of the band, most particularly, of course, Rory Blaze, lead vocals and frontman, and some advertising gigs at momentous venues, including football stadiums and rock festivals. But, judging by the presence of several cupboards and filing cabinets, this was also the heart of Bill Massiter's business empire, because it was well known that he had several fingers in a number of pies, not all of them directly connected to the music business.

Max could connect Cougar Bill back to his own childhood and he was now reminded, by a sudden unmistakable surge of déjà vu, that he had been to this place not once but twice, and on both occasions, with his father. In fact, the very room where poor Bill had been found had been one of several recording studios at the time.

The sergeant currently in charge of the scene Bellamy knew vaguely from police federation conferences. Now in his early fifties and looking to fairly imminent retirement, Sergeant Matt Freeman was solid, if these days quite stout, and wholly reliable.

'Matt, how are you?'

'Fine, sir, fine. I could have done without this lot, though, I really could. I first bought a Cougars record when I was about sixteen. It really creases me to see Cougar Bill like this.'

'Yes. I came here with my dad a couple of times.'

'Really? Was your dad in this business, then, sir?'

'He certainly was. For a while, he was the Cougars' agent.'

'Struth. Well, we've touched nothing, sir, except cut down the poor guy, of course, though leaving the noose loosely around his neck for the moment. The forensic boys had a look at him before we cut him down, and then we laid him out on a few packing cases the lads dragged out from somewhere; my lads were careful to use gloves. I've started the ball rolling regarding the post-mortem, and we'll be ready to send him when you say so, sir.'

'Yes. Forgive me for asking what might be obvious here, Matt, but have we established when he actually died?'

'Not exactly, sir, though he'd clearly been dead for some hours when we cut him down. We thought the exact time would be taken into the post-mortem.'

'Yes, OK.'

Bellamy trod carefully. Strictly speaking, someone medically qualified should already have had at least a cursory look at the body, but there were different interpretations of these procedures and it was no use giving grief to an old hand like Freeman.

As ever, he knew that he had a duty to overcome his instinctive preference when visiting the scene of a death to get away from it as soon as possible. He'd never been able to totally overcome his dread at the brutal finality of the whole business, some human being's hopes, loves, ambitions and longings suddenly and mercilessly cut down. Unfortunately, as a professional investigator, it made much more sense to linger in the place as it was at the moment of the death. Tom Hollins had mentioned the Manningham case, when the attempt to portray the event as a suicide had been so amateurish and clumsy that he had seen through it relatively quickly, but had he not bothered to stay on the scene for more than a few minutes, suicide would inevitably have been the conclusion he would have arrived at. At least, he thought, this situation was so obviously a suicide that the investigation probably didn't need to jump that particular hurdle before making further progress.

Then he looked at the rope still around Massiter's neck, and an alarm bell sounded somewhere inside him. Bellamy had spent some time in the Boy Scouts, more in defiance of his father than because of him; the Scouts came into the category of what Richard

Bellamy defined as "paramilitary organisations". The young Max had always felt that the uniform part of it served more as a leveller than an enforcer of military mentalities. His Scout training had involved quite a lot of work on knots of one kind or another; there was even a badge to be won in the efficient understanding and execution of knots. The knot tied around Cougar Bill's neck was undoubtedly a right-handed knot, and Bellamy wondered why that should strike him as in any way inappropriate; the great majority of knots were right-handed.

A forgotten scene returned to him, of entering this room when he was about seven or eight; the exact timing was difficult to recall. The whole picture suddenly appearing in front of him was awesome to his young mind; all these guys, normally only seen at gigs from quite a distance, or up on a poster, were right there in front of him, and greeting his father as if he was an old friend. They had just completed a long recording session, and three of them were holding guitars, while Doug Lane, the drummer, sat amongst his percussion empire, with more drums than Max had ever seen in one place. They all still had earphones on.

But what particularly struck Max, even then with his symmetrical, detailed methods of observation, was that Cougar Bill, the lead guitar, was pointing his guitar to the right, while Manny Orestes, bass guitar, had a guitar pointing to the left. It looked, at that moment, bizarre. Had they been playing them, the noise would have been the aspect of the scene which most took Max's attention, but they weren't, and the conflicting guitars pointing at each other impressed itself on him. It meant that Manny was using his right hand as his main playing hand, while Cougar Bill was most definitely using his left.

So it seemed that what he was expected to believe here was that Bill Massiter had tied a noose around his neck with a right-handed knot, when he had spent all his playing days on a left-handed guitar, a detail which whoever did this, because the clear implication was now that this was murder, had either forgotten or didn't know about in the first place.

Max had also noticed on a few of the small packing cases in this room, supposedly of coffee, tiny but identifiable print of addresses based in Colombia, in South America. Yes, it was possible that Bill was so serious about his coffee that Colombian beans were a rich man's indulgence, but it could also mean that Cougar Bill was receiving illicit drugs concealed amongst the coffee. Perhaps the boy wondering about the premises might have had some inkling of that, and Massiter or someone operating on his premises was selling drugs to under-age kids. If that was the case, the repercussions would have an immediate and considerable impact on the seriousness of the case. For the moment, Max kept his suspicions to himself.

'OK, Matt, let's get him off to post-mortem, and I'll talk to the forensic boys when we get the post-mortem results. I'm particularly interested in what prints they might find on that rope. Now I'm going to talk to this boy. Do we know whether he has any previous?'

'No, we didn't find anything, sir. Judging by the way he's practically shitting himself, I'd say he's no villain, whatever else he might be. You'll have more bother with his mum.'

'Fair enough.'

Bellamy made his way into the adjoining room, which was clearly no more than a storage space now, though he suspected it had been another studio at one time. He noticed a few more significant addresses on some of the cases. The boy's mother looked up at him as he came in, and he could see both fear and indignation in her eyes. She was a well-built woman, probably in her early forties, Bellamy guessed, who had undoubtedly been pretty in her younger days, but the cares of motherhood appeared to have taken their toll, and the lines under her eyes added an impression of tiredness to her obvious anger.

The boy himself was already an inch or two taller than his mother, meaning he was quite a hefty specimen for a sixteen-year-old, and Bellamy immediately considered that this probably wasn't the first time by any means that his mother had had trouble with him. However, he looked more expectant and worried than displaying the curled-lip contempt which Bellamy tended to associate with die-hard teenage criminals. He suspected this boy was in the situation not uncommon at his age that his physical growth outpaced his mental.

'Mrs Oswald, isn't it?' Bellamy said, as mildly as he could.

'Yes, it is, and who might you be, may I ask?' The edge in her voice was evident enough.

'Detective Chief Inspector Bellamy. And this is your son Raymond.'

'Yes, for my sins. As if I didn't have better things to do than sit around cleaning up again after what his nibs here has been up to.'

'Has your son been in trouble with the law before, Mrs Oswald?'

She glanced quickly at Ossie and seemed to realise that she might do better to tone things down a little. The boy himself was determinedly staring down at his feet.

'No, no, nothing like that – er – Chief Inspector. He's not an evil boy or anything, he just will keep shoving his nose into matters which don't concern him.'

Raymond, it seemed, had kept quiet for too long.

'The man was hanging from the roof, Mum. I was looking to save his life.'

'You were trespassing where you had no right to be, Raymond, that's what you were doing. It wouldn't surprise me if the police officer here didn't stick you in a cell all night to teach you a lesson—'

'I've done nothing!' The boy raised himself up. Bellamy grabbed one of the chairs stacked against the wall, and sat down facing both of them.

'All I'm interested in is establishing the facts of what happened here. We know that a man has died, and that's the most important thing we're concerned with at the moment. And it so happens that the man we're talking about was Bill Massiter, the founder member of a prominent band of the past known as the Cougars; Massiter himself was widely known as Cougar Bill. I should make clear to you, Mrs Oswald, and to you, Raymond, that it's only a matter of time before the media get wind of this and start gathering round here to get a sniff at a story. If we do what we have to do as quickly as we can, then with luck we'll avoid either of you getting your names in the papers, which might sound glamorous at first, but may mean your life won't be your own for weeks to come; Bill Massiter was still a famous man.'

The full realisation of their position was now dawning on both mother and son. Mrs Oswald's frustration was causing her to stare fixedly at her son, while the boy himself, try as he might, was not far from tears.

Bellamy found himself in a position familiar enough to him, though it never failed to be problematic, that of having to make a complicated decision with not enough time to do so. He knew some police officers prided themselves on being able to make decisions on the spot, but he instinctively distrusted such rapidity. Perhaps, he thought, one of the perks of higher office was the ability to arrange things so that you could have time to look carefully at the pros and cons.

He exercised his right to temporise. A wrong decision at this point could be extremely counter-productive, and when dealing with a murder case, which he had already decided this probably was, caution had a great deal to be said for it. Bellamy concentrated on sounding cool and composed.

'I'm going to ask Sergeant Freeman to look after you for a few minutes, Mrs Oswald and Raymond. When it comes to asking questions of people in this kind of situation, the first need is to get the questions right; if the questions aren't right, the chances are the answers will be misleading. I'm going to take another look at the room where Mr Massiter so sadly died, and then I will be clearer about what I want to ask you.'

Mrs Oswald seemed to flounce with frustration, but Bellamy was already on his way. Freeman was still in the room, though the corpse of Cougar Bill had already been sent on its way to post-mortem.

'I know we'll get a forensics report shortly, Matt,' Bellamy said, 'but did they say anything useful before they went?'

'No prints anywhere but Bill's, sir. His prints on the body, his prints on the noose. No one else's detected.'

Meaning, it seemed, either that Bill Massiter tied a noose around his neck with his wrong hand and jumped off the case underneath him, or someone else wearing thick gloves tied a noose round his neck, hauled him up, and then kicked the box from under him. So this appeared to be either a bizarre and illogical suicide or the work of a cold-blooded, very professional killer or killers.

Bellamy could see what Matt Freeman thought, and what most people would think, and he wondered whether his memory, at the age of seven or eight, was accurate enough to be reliable. He could easily envisage the defence lawyer's question: "If you can't remember exactly how old you were at the time, Chief Inspector Bellamy, can we really trust your memories of which hand Mr Massiter was using to play his guitar?"

But, he recalled, it would be an easy enough matter to check on photos and videos of the Cougars. If Bill was ambidextrous, some pictures would show him playing the guitar with his right hand and some with his left. If he was entirely left-handed, this did look, despite all appearances, like a planned murder, not a suicide.

As he walked back into the fresh air, Bellamy knew he still had a decision to make, and now was the time to make it.

He knew that this situation gave him every right to order the boy to be strip-searched. He was trespassing on Massiter property; if he was carrying illegal substances on him, and Bellamy knew from past experience the very intimate places young people could put their drugs in an attempt to conceal them, he could not be allowed to get away with it and announce to all the other young people he knew that stuff could be had on Reynolds' Farm if they had the nerve to go and get it.

It was also not impossible that the boy was carrying a weapon. Bellamy knew the frequency with which young boys now carried knives, and Raymond was big enough to allow for the possibility that he could have been seeking to get hold of illegal drugs by menace if necessary, now it was fairly widely known that Cougar Bill lived on his own most of the time, and presumably the budget no longer stretched to the elaborate security arrangements that used to be in place at Reynolds' Farm.

If the boy was guilty of either of these criminal attempts, to let him off by default would be an open invitation to other young bucks to have a go, and how long it would take to sell Reynolds' Farm, assuming that whoever inherited it, presumably Bill's wife, Josie, decided to sell it, was impossible to estimate. The premises could become a law and order nightmare for some time, and Bellamy knew well enough where the finger would then be pointed; he had no illusions about his ex-colleagues in the press.

But he had taken part in strip-searches before, usually on someone else's orders, and he had always found them profoundly distasteful and often futile. That, in itself, would not be enough to dissuade him if he really considered one to be necessary, but he had come across young drug addicts and dealers on a number of occasions, and he would lay odds that Raymond Oswald was not one of them. They tended to be pale, skinny, undernourished individuals, while Oswald was a strapping young footballer, tall for his age and athletically built. They also tended to be too cool for school types, monosyllabic and contemptuous of the police, and that wasn't how Oswald acted. He also seemed at least as afraid of his mother as he was of the police, and with that kind of parent in their lives, young people were generally less likely to go off the rails.

And Bellamy knew from personal experience the deep-seated resentment which such humiliations in younger years could create in people. Free-thinker and cool dude as he generally was, Bellamy's father, Richard, had accepted his wife's argument about sending Bellamy to a "good" school, i.e. a fee-paying boarding school, which Beverley Bellamy believed made it a good school, and Bellamy had found himself, at the age of fifteen, in a very difficult situation when he and two other boys were caught smoking during a period when the young Max was open to various kinds of experimentation.

Taking the resulting detentions on the chin was no problem; he had been caught breaking school rules and the price needed to be paid. But when the teacher concerned said that the only way Max could avoid a letter being sent home to his parents was if he agreed to being thoroughly searched to establish whether he was carrying any more cigarettes on his person, Bellamy felt he had no choice but to accept. Worrying his parents had no part in his experimental turn of mind at the time.

He knew well enough that this teacher had ulterior motives. Bellamy had come to reluctantly accept, on the basis of a few unsubtle comments from boys known to be keen on homosexual activities, that he was a good-looking boy; the blue eyes were well in evidence, as was the body cultivated by swimming and other sports.

To the accompaniment of the teacher's reddening face and heavier breathing, Bellamy was stripped all the way to naked and examined in the most searingly intimate ways. The whole incident was etched on his memory with great vividness. On the day at the end of the sixth form when he left school, the teacher concerned tried to say an amiable goodbye. Bellamy looked contemptuously down at the offered hand and walked away.

If it could be avoided, he didn't want to be a lifelong resentment for Raymond Oswald, and he needed to have a strong suspicion of the boy being guilty of something or other before he would seriously consider putting him through that. Yes, he could exercise the privilege of rank and order Matt Freeman to do it; the sergeant was a seasoned professional and he would make it as painless as he could. But Bellamy, however high in the pecking order he rose, still didn't believe in getting other people to do his dirty work for him.

Decision taken, Bellamy returned to the boy and his mother. He knew, nevertheless, that to get at exactly what the boy had been up to, he would have to put pressure on him.

He returned to his chair in front of the boy and his mother. By the look of them, they had had a frank exchange of views and, predictably, Raymond had got the worst of it.

'Mrs Oswald, I wonder if I could speak to Raymond alone for a few minutes.'

She looked at him, her anger still evident, and seemed about to start saying something, before changing her mind and sitting back.

'Yes, please do that, Chief Inspector, and maybe you can talk some sense into him.'

She crashed her way out of the room.

Bellamy allowed things to remain quiet to begin with. His searching blue eyes had discomfited much bigger and tougher people than Raymond, and it was clear soon enough that the boy was wilting, a sure sign that he was not used to this sort of thing.

'Why were you trespassing on Mr Massiter's property?'

Ossie seemed to gasp at the question but, Bellamy noticed, his eyes still connected with those of the man before him.

'I saw someone through a window, someone who looked like they were hanging up.'

'Was that all?'

'Yes, sir, honestly.'

'Were you looking for illegal drugs? Did you think there were any on the premises?'

'I'd heard rumours, sir. But that wasn't why I went in there.'

'Make sure you tell me the truth, Raymond. You were undoubtedly trespassing on someone else's property, and you must understand that if you do that, you're liable to being questioned and searched.'

The boy took a long intake of breath.

'Search me if you like,' he said, his voice raising. 'I was only trying to help.'

He stood up and started unbuttoning his shirt. Still, Bellamy noticed, the eyes kept contact, even as they were moistening and the boy was hating himself for it.

'No, sit down, Raymond. We haven't got to that point yet.' Bellamy's tone softened.

'As you've probably realised, Mr Massiter is dead. On balance, I think you were probably right to do what you did, though if you'd decided to contact someone as soon as you saw the hanging figure, it might have been wiser. You also seemed to me to be limping when you came in. What's that about?'

'Some clumsy sod – I mean kid – clunked my ankle in football training. I can hardly walk on it now, sir. That's what's got up Mum's nose. She thinks I've been fighting. Whatever else happens, she can't stand me fighting.'

'No,' Bellamy said quietly. 'And very right, too. The hospitals are full of boys who can't stop themselves from fighting, and sometimes it's knives they're fighting with. Every mother who cares about their children will hate the idea of them fighting. Your mother obviously cares quite a lot about you, Ray. I believe you've given your name and address to Sergeant Freeman, have you?'

'Yes, sir.'

'Well, it's possible that we may need to call you as a witness in some future legal proceedings. But in the meantime, Ray, go back to your mother and you can both go home, but please remember what I've said. There's nothing wrong with being willing to help people who look like they're in trouble, but you always have to remember that there are laws when it comes to going onto other people's property.'

Ossie sniffed and sighed, then got to his feet.

'Thank you, sir. Some kids have never heard of Cougar Bill, but I know the name well enough. They can call it old guy music if they like, but what if it is? I like old guy music.'

Bellamy could not stop the grin spreading itself over his face, and the answering grin from the boy had a warmth and spontaneity about it which was the precious province of the very young. They shook hands, and Raymond left to tell his mother the good news.

Almost simultaneously, the sound of a loud and powerful car drawing up deprived Bellamy of the chance to spend a few thinking minutes. There were already aspects of this case which were shaping up to be bizarre and contradictory; so far, either a convoluted suicide in which the man killing himself had tied the noose the wrong way round, or an even more convoluted murder, with the murderer taking great pains to ensure that he left not a single trace of himself, even as much as a fingerprint. Violent crimes, in Bellamy's experience, were generally hot rather than cold-blooded, spontaneous rather than calculated; this one was an enigma, and someone had set out for it to be that way.

The car's arrival was followed almost immediately by a loud, assertive voice, as if the man and the car were made for each other. And Bellamy recognised the voice, a sound from long ago and far away. Unless he was very much mistaken, it was a man who some of his fellow hacks had described, back in the day, as a legend in his own lifetime, among a whole batch of other exotic journalese; the lead singer of the Cougars, the one and only Rory Blaze.

Bellamy's feelings included apprehension as well as curiosity. He remembered his father, not a man generally to disparage people behind their back, describing Rory Blaze, aka Tony Richards, as "a human iceberg, in so far as nine-tenths of him is below the surface", which could, in some interpretations, actually be seen as a compliment, though Max thought it wasn't really how Richard Bellamy meant the remark. Hidden depths could mean a good deal of intellectual ability not always seen; it could also mean a propensity for evil of various kinds, not always obvious superficially.

The ex-rock idol was now in his sixties, but he still seemed able to let loose a kind of jamboree merely by his arrival. Rory Blaze had always been recognisable by his magnificent mane of hair, some of it descending down his back, and the fans loved it when he danced around the stage and set the hair flying. Tony Richards' hair was still longish now, but rather pathetically so, with the predominance of grey like an unkind caricature of his former self.

He'd arrived in an unfeasibly large BMW, with a uniformed chauffeur now standing beside the car like a guardsman on duty. Blaze himself had already attracted a small crowd of locals behind the police lines, and Bellamy realised with an inner sigh of resignation that his brief sabbatical from the media was already coming to an end.

However, as the old rock man was lapping up the attention of the small crowd, one or two of whom clearly didn't know who he was – the Cougars were quite far in the past now – someone much more welcome to Bellamy was also arriving, in a more modest vehicle. It was his old partner, now Inspector Elaine Price, arriving with two uniformed police constables, and Bellamy noted that Elaine had once more anticipated the needs of a crime scene rather better than he had himself, with her constables as reinforcements against the coming media scrum.

Elaine, he had noticed in the past, was not a habitual smiler; few people who had been serving police personnel for some years were. It wasn't a job which exposed people to the best of their fellow human beings. But the smile she wore now, as she walked up to him with her hand out, was broad and beaming enough to reassure the always self-doubting Bellamy that she really was genuinely pleased to be working with him again.

'Thanks, Elaine. I'm going to need you for this one.'

'Yes, sir. It already seems to have hit the airwaves; a radio bulletin I heard on the way here reckoned that Cougar Bill had "topped himself", in their less than elegant phrase. I don't know where they got that from.'

'No, neither do I. We haven't issued any statements of any kind. Where the hell do they get hold of these things?'

They turned to see Tony Richards looking at them, his face expressing disapproval, as if someone in his vicinity had the temerity not to be primarily interested in him.

'Well, you've managed to get behind police lines and start chatting to each other, so you must be important or something. Don't mind me, will you? I'm just the guy who worked with poor Bill all those years in one of the greatest bands in the world.'

Bellamy took a step towards him, with Elaine at his shoulder, and framed his words so as not to acknowledge acceptance of Richards' easy assumption of seniority.

'I'm Detective Chief Inspector Bellamy, and this is Detective Inspector Price. I take it you, sir, are Mr Tony Richards.'

With a sigh of resignation at having to tear himself away from his adoring public, Richards shook hands with the police officers.

'A DCI and a DI? Well, it's good to see this is being given proper importance. Can I see poor Bill now, please?'

'No, sir, not yet, I'm afraid. The body is to be taken for post-mortem.'

'The body? For God's sake, Mr Plod, have a little respect, will you? We're talking about one of the rock legends of the twentieth century here. And anyway, he topped himself, didn't he? What's all this forensics stuff?'

Bellamy fixed the man with his eyes for long enough to communicate a warning, and even the great rock star wilted a little in the gaze.

'Can I speak to you in private for a moment, sir? We really don't want to turn this into a circus; we are dealing with a man's death.'

Bellamy turned away, and Elaine accompanied Richards to the room where the last interviewee, younger and simpler than the present one, had recently sat. Signalling the man to a seat, Bellamy sat in front of him. Richards started to speak, but Bellamy got in first.

'Firstly, sir, do not ever address me in public, or in private for that matter, as Mr Plod.

Secondly, do not make statements, either in front of the general public or the press, making assumptions about the nature of the case.'

Richards, at close quarters, was altogether a smaller and more subdued individual. As Bellamy had calculated, his ego fed largely on having an audience. Their eyes met once more, and again, Bellamy's got the better of it.

'Alright, alright! Give me a break, Chief Inspector. I've just discovered that my long-term partner, a guy I love, and I mean that, has just topped himself. I'm hardly going to be at my sunniest, am I?'

'Whatever the media may already be assuming, I am not entirely convinced that what happened here was a suicide, Mr Richards. Arriving at premature conclusions about cases is generally not very helpful to anyone.'

'Not a suicide? I'm told he had a rope round his neck, for God's sake. I'm no detective—'

'No, Mr Richards, you're not. I am. And we have both been around long enough to know that things are not always as they seem. People with evil intentions are perfectly capable of making a scene look the way they want it to look. I think it was widely known that the Cougars didn't get on with each other very well in their later years, but I seem to remember you all made sure that none of the differences was aired in public.'

Richards' fierce eyes continued to glare for a moment, but then some kind of warning sign, some sudden inhibition, seemed to arrive within him, and his tone changed.

'Well, yes, that's true enough. Bill had acquired some habits, let's just call it that, which I didn't much care for, and neither did the other lads. However much you try and keep the media off your tail, some of it gets out.'

'Yes. I was a journalist for some years myself so I know what you mean. Rumours also abounded about your sexuality, as I recall, Mr Richards, presumably equally without foundation; my own paper heard them without acting on them. Allegations against rich men can have consequences, as you probably know yourself.'

Once again, Richards' expression suggested he was assessing and deciding on the spot.

'Oh, yes, that stuff about my preference for young guys. Well, we can say that now, can't we, Chief Inspector? I'm now out, as you may or may not know; coming out is not the media big deal it used to be. A few characters in the gutter press tried to pin it on me as a taste for young boys, but, as you say, we had plenty of money and good lawyers, and nothing under the age of eighteen had any chance of getting involved with me. Do you ask to look at their birth certificates, some scumbag once said, and I told him, as a matter of fact, scumbag, that's exactly what I did do sometimes; other times, I asked for the identity card a lot of them carry about so that they can get served in pubs. Sometimes I could work it out from where they were in their education; if they've left school or college now, they have to be eighteen. I always found out or worked it out, so what are you going to make of it? Nothing, it turned out. But my brief already had a letter ready to send.'

His eyes suddenly hardened, and Bellamy saw the side of Rory Blaze which some of the music press had consistently hinted at.

'So underneath that cool cop exterior, some kind of rabid homophobe is living, is it? Rory Blaze is a potential murderer because he likes shagging males rather than females? Is that what you're saying, Chief Inspector?'

One of the golden rules, Bellamy thought, is don't play to their agenda, however much your carelessness has got you into such situations in the first place.

'Don't interrogate me, Mr Richards. If we arrive at the stage of interrogation being necessary, which we haven't as yet, I'll be doing it. I thought I was agreeing with you about the tendency of the media to get hold of the wrong end of the stick. It isn't for me to approve or disapprove of your sexuality; that is none of my business, nor is it theirs. Perhaps the media have made you hypersensitive on the subject?'

Bellamy noted the interesting effect his words had on the other man. In the back of his mind, he could remember rumours that Tony Richards had aspirations in the direction of acting before his persona of "Rory Blaze" came along. If so, he probably chose the better course with the Cougars, because his reaction to Bellamy's words made clear enough what an act his indignation was. Such manufactured tantrums were, Bellamy guessed, the way that the lead singer of the Cougars exercised some control over the media around him day after day. Within twenty seconds, anger had been replaced by an ingratiating smile.

'Yes, of course, Chief Inspector. As you have so rightly perceived, it's an old wound, easily aggravated. I have been living openly with one of my ex-fans for some time now, and the media are no more interested in Sean and me than they would be in any average Joe in the street. But you're quite old enough to know that attitudes haven't always been like that. We must concentrate on pinning down what has happened to poor old Bill.'

At that moment, Bellamy realised that someone else was with them. A very well-dressed, tall, clean-shaven man seemed to have entered the room, without having announced himself. Bellamy wondered what Elaine had been doing to allow this to happen.

'Who are you, and what are you doing here?' he said.

'My name is Giles Ransome, I am a solicitor, and if Mr Richards is being questioned about anything connected with these recent events, I am legally entitled to be here.'

'Not before time, Giles, is it?' Richards boomed at him. 'I could have been thrown in the bloody caboose by now.'

'I'm sorry, sir, but your call didn't make clear to me that you were being interviewed by a senior policeman. Could you please tell me, sir, why Mr Richards is apparently being subjected to some kind of interrogation without any opportunity being offered to him to have his lawyer present, as is his right?'

Almost as soon as he'd finished speaking, Elaine burst in, and her first words to the newcomer showed her irritation clearly enough.

'What on earth are you doing in here, sir? You assured me that you would wait until Chief Inspector Bellamy came out of here before you approached him. I do not take kindly to being deceived in this way, especially on a crime scene—'

'A crime scene? Interesting. I am not under any obligation to explain myself to you, madam, whoever you might be.'

Bellamy had had enough. He got slowly to his feet, and that action, compared to the now fierce glare of his disturbing blue eyes, was enough to quieten the people around him.

'This lady is Detective Inspector Elaine Price, and I am Detective Chief Inspector Max Bellamy. You have absolutely no right, sir, to break in on a private conversation I am having with Mr Richards. I have not arrested or cautioned Mr Richards, nor am I interrogating him; we are simply discussing how we view what has happened in this place today, which, I will remind you, has involved a man's death. If and when I am taking actions against Mr Richards which entitle him to have a lawyer present, you will be informed; otherwise, either do what Inspector Price has told you to do or I will arrest you for wasting police time and obstructing a police officer in the execution of his duty.'

Ransome's well-scrubbed face paled even further, and he beat a retreat. Bellamy turned to Richards.

'That will do, thank you, sir, for the time being. When we have further information concerning what has happened here today, we will talk again, and if you choose to have your lawyer with you, please do, but I reiterate that I am not, at this stage, accusing or interrogating anyone.'

Richards left, and could be heard entering into an animated discussion with his lawyer almost as soon as he'd left the room. Bellamy and Elaine sat down.

'Sorry, sir, I was quite specific with him. He looked so respectable—'

'Yes, lawyers can manage that. It's not your fault, Elaine, if the guy enters into an agreement with you and then ignores it. If he tries it on again, I will arrest him. I take it we now have the media all over us like the plague?'

'We do, sir, and some of them have already got hold of the idea that this might not have been suicide. Is it not suicide, sir, as far as you can see?'

'Cougar Bill was left-handed. I can remember that from when I came here as a kid, and in any case, the footage of him will show him playing his guitar with his left hand. The noose around his neck was tied with a right-handed knot. I'm an ex-Boy Scout, I know this stuff. I can't believe that any man, at the extreme of having decided to kill himself, is going to deliberately tie a knot around his head with the wrong hand. I also strongly suspect that the fingerprints found on him – they only found his fingerprints on him – won't conform to the movements he would have made to hang himself, unless he'd become a contortionist.'

'Right, I see, sir. It means someone must have come in here with clear intentions to do what he did. It also means whoever has to have been wearing gloves right through doing whatever he did. I'm saying he, because a woman wouldn't have been able to haul Bill up on that noose.'

'No. But even if we accept that Bill did kill himself, why would he tie a knot the wrong way round? And why in here, when he must have known he could have been seen from those windows from a good distance away?'

For some time, the two of them sat brooding quietly; as ever, police work needed thinking time. Then Elaine spoke first.

'Do you want me to talk to the media lot, sir?'

Bellamy smiled.

'You would too, wouldn't you? No, since they know I'm here, it needs to be me or their conspiracy theories will start. It's not so long ago that I was a hack myself. I know their language, and usually I know how they think. When they think at all, that is. I'll go talk to them now. What I want you to do, Elaine, is find Bill's intimates, particularly any of them he's still in touch with. Find out whether he had any obvious enemies. I seem to recall that he had a wife and he was pretty young when he married her. We also need to track down the other members of the Cougars. It's pretty well known that Bill had an uneasy relationship with Rory Blaze; I want to know how well he got on with the other guys.'

They both emerged from the room and headed in separate directions, Bellamy towards the now quite large group gathered behind the front gate of the property, with three burly constables standing immediately behind the gate. In the background, a few locals had emerged from their houses to watch, including some children.

Bellamy approached the media confidently enough. Many police personnel would write down what they wanted to say and say nothing but it, but Bellamy preferred to play these occasions by ear. He could and sometimes had cut up rough with media people who had quoted words he didn't say, and he knew they knew him well enough to realise that.

Bulbs flashed in his eyes, but he was used to that, too. He stopped about ten feet short of the gate, and raised his voice.

'Max Bellamy, hack turned sleuth,' someone said.

'Yeah, right enough. And don't forget it. You fuck with me, boys and girls, and I'll do likewise. Don't quote anything I didn't say, or next time around, you'll get nothing.'

This seemed enough to impose the necessary silence.

'I can confirm that Mr William Massiter, aged sixty-four, widely known as "Cougar Bill" after being the founding member and lead guitarist of the Cougars rock band, was found dead on these premises this afternoon. In spite of the widespread rumours that Mr Massiter took his own life, there are circumstances, which I'm not going to discuss at the moment, causing us to treat his death as suspicious. We will be carrying out further investigations, and that's all I'm going to say at the moment, so you can stand there shouting the odds until you go blue, but that, for the time being, folks, is all you're going to get.'

At which point, Bellamy turned round and walked briskly away, to a background of various shouted questions which everyone knew were not going to be answered, but journalists needed to demonstrate to their bosses that they were doing their best.

Bellamy left Elaine to make arrangements with the local police for the twenty-four-hour security of the site, knowing very well that Elaine did not cut any corners when such arrangements were necessary; no more inquisitive schoolboys were going to wander their way in, under any pretext. He made his way to his office in divisional HQ. His general opinion was that this current office, reflecting his now senior status, was as good as offices could be. They weren't rooms he generally favoured for anything other than routine administrative work, but this one, functional but also airy, comfortable and properly furnished, was much the best he had ever had in either his journalistic or his police careers.

Elaine, as she eventually approached the office, expected to see him in his typical pose, his chair swung away from his desk towards the window or towards the wall, while he mulled over whatever he had to mull over. But, in fact, she saw a confidential phone call was going on, and by Bellamy's unusually deferential manner, it looked like he was talking to someone senior to himself, which excluded the great majority of the local force.

She hesitated, but he saw her and beckoned her in. She settled herself in an armchair facing his desk; Bellamy wanted people who came into his office to be as comfortable as he was. Unusually, there seemed to be a trace of anxiety in his manner; the legendarily laid-back Bellamy had been made at least a little uneasy about something.

Eventually, he put the phone down. He looked across at her and sighed, following the sigh with a kind of fatalistic smile.

'Good and bad news, Elaine. That was no other than Jack Henshaw, chief constable of the county.'

'OK, sir. Hit me with the bad news first.'

'His nibs Henshaw has fingered me as a policeman who's good with the media. Meaning, after this case, which he expects to "attract a good deal of media intrusion", he wants me to consider taking on lectures at the Police Training School on "dealing with the media". This is on top of my MP wife saying to me that she would like to put my name forward as a guest speaker at party meetings to talk about how politicians should deal with the media. Suddenly, I'm everybody's media man. How I'm supposed to find time to do such stuff is not a question either of them bother themselves with.'

'And what about the good news, sir?'

'The good news is that we're getting the same arrangement as we got with the Manningham case, which is we do nothing else until this case is sorted. The difference is that this time, it's not the politicos, it's the senior echelons of the police, as represented by Chief Constable Henshaw, who want it like that. "The media are going to be all over this, DCI Bellamy," he says, "and they'll carry on being all over it until it's sorted. And you seem to have made yourself the go-to expert on cases which look like suicide and aren't." As in one previous case. Henshaw is famous for getting bits between his teeth, and he's got one about this. It's like the Manningham case, but only in so far as the knobs don't want to finish up buried in the smelly stuff, except this time it's police knobs rather than political knobs. If it does turn out that it was a suicide, whatever the explanation for the right-handed knot, then all that smelly stuff is going to descend on me.'

'Well, CC Henshaw is right about the media, sir. By the time I left, they were already flocking in; not just the press, but the television cameras. I thought most of the world had forgotten about the Cougars; their last hit, which never got higher than number eight, was in 1997. But the whole thing was meaty enough to start with: "Rock Star Tops Himself" stuff. Add to it the extra bit, "Top Cop Says Rock Star Didn't Top Himself" and they've got enough to sell copies for a week.'

'OK, Elaine, it's now a question of where we go from here. It's not going to be easy with the hacks on our case every step of the way, but we managed the Manningham case and we'll manage this. In the Manningham case, the attempt to make it look like a suicide seemed so pathetically inept, it didn't take long to shove it away, and as it turned out, no one was actually trying to make it look like a suicide in the first place. This one's different. If it hadn't been for the coincidence of me having seen the Cougars in their rehearsal room here when I was a kid, a scene containing a man hanging with a noose around his neck would have been about as obvious as it gets. But, try as I might to think about some reason why Massiter would tie a noose round his head with his wrong hand, I can't think of anything that makes sense. But then again, the supposed coffee cases scattered over his storeroom suggest he might have been doing cocaine, possibly in generous quantities, and we don't know what effect that was having on him or what other issues there were in his life. Why was he taking it up his nose in the first place? It could be a legacy from his rock career, it could be some secret in his life – massive debt, maybe, but probably unlikely in his case, given the kind of money the Cougars must have made in their heyday. And if I'm right, and it was murder, who would have it in for Cougar Bill? He had a reputation for always being courteous and prepared to put himself out for the fans. We know now that Rory Blaze, as he called himself, was and is gay, but I doubt whether that would have bothered Bill or any of the other Cougars very much. How do we go about this, Elaine? Any thoughts?'

'Well, I have to say, sir, much as I regret it, that one of us is going to have to spend quite a lot of time on media and crowd control. It's a classic tabloid case, and they are going to want big, fruity bits of it. It's not just at Bill's place that they'll be hanging around; they'll be after everyone associated with him. I heard some of them talking about Massiter's wife because as far as they know they are estranged but they never divorced. One of the Cougars, Manny Orestes, has already left the country, though I gather that's not too unusual; he has dual British and Spanish citizenship, and businesses in Spain. A press guy I recognised, Tom Allston, reckoned Manny and Bill were big mates, but neither of them got on too well with Tony Richards.'

Bellamy smiled.

'You pick up a lot, don't you, Elaine, just listening? There are two good leads there. Well, it seems to me that we don't have too much choice in how we divvy things up. If I'm the one looking after the media all the time, they will give me a lot of grief along the lines of "why aren't you out there finding out who did it, since you think it's murder?". I also don't think I'm as good as you are at picking up on what they're talking about.

'CC Henshaw said something else, as well. He's attaching a sergeant and a constable to us for an initial two weeks so we can, in his words, "put the case to bed as soon as possible". That's how they are in the police stratosphere – if it's a case with heavy media attention, they want it sorted quickly. What happens if we haven't sorted it in two weeks, Henshaw is not saying, but we'll cross that bridge when we come to it.

'So this is how I want to divide it, Elaine, but please, if there's anything you're not happy about, say so. I want you and our two recruits to look into the background of the four members of the Cougars, including their partners, associates, business interests, the lot. We need to get hold of whatever might be crucial before the hacks do, and we must remember that, while we're not under any obligation to tell them anything, they are obliged by law to tell us if they've discovered blatant breaches of the law, whether they print the stuff or not. The imbalance between those two is one of the reasons why I left the media and joined the police. I think we must work on the theory that Cougar Bill was murdered, and murdered by someone in a calculated, clever way to flag it up as obviously as they could to look like a suicide. But that doesn't mean we should forget altogether that it was possibly a suicide, carried out in a cack-handed way by a guy coked out of his mind.

'The Cougars lived for years in the public gaze, and if there were tensions between them, it shouldn't be too difficult to track them down. While you're doing all that, I'm going to track down the obvious people to talk to – Cougar Bill's wife, whether she's ex or not, any members of his wider family close to him, the Cougars' manager or ex-manager, etc. Well, I've banged on for a while, Elaine, what do you want to say?'

'I've got no problems with any of that, sir. But I did wonder…' Elaine hesitated momentarily, which Max saw as a sign that she was about to enter what might be termed personal territory. 'You mentioned that you came to see the Cougars in their recording studio at Reynolds' Farm when you were about seven or eight. I just wondered if your dad had any connections or experience which might be useful.'

Bellamy was silent for a moment, and Elaine had started thinking that she had trespassed into a difficult area, but, typically, Bellamy just needed time to think.

'Yes, I am going to look at that. I'm not usually too keen on mixing the professional and the personal, but in this case, it could actually be negligent to avoid that area. My father was eventually an arts lecturer, but earlier on, he made a lot of money in the music business, managing various bands and venues; it was very lucrative, but also twenty-four hours a day and very demanding. He also wrote reviews and articles for the music press, operating as a freelance journalist, which is maybe where I got it from. He wasn't too wild about me going into the police, and he was surprised when I specialised in crime as a journalist rather than music and the arts. But his links with the Cougars were not just professional; he was at school with one of them – if I remember rightly, it was Doug Lane, the drummer. I have all his diaries – a lot of them are dates, times, quick notes about what he needed to do, that kind of thing, but he did sometimes put in material about the people and experiences he had in the business. Before he got ill, he was talking about publishing his "memoirs", as he called them, and while his health held up, he was preparing material for that.'

Elaine found herself intrigued by his words. One of the few frustrations she'd had in working with Max Bellamy was his self-contained detachment, his reluctance to enter into the personal areas which would flesh out the person he was and make it easier for those working with him to understand him. Now here he was opening up on the subject of his father, who had never had any more than the occasional oblique reference before.

Elaine wondered whether she dare push her luck, and decided she would.

'When did your father die, sir?'

The Bellamy eyes settled on her for a moment, in that cool examination mode they were so good at, but perhaps he'd already decided he knew her well enough by now.

'In 2013, when I was thirty and he was sixty-one; not long after I'd decided to join the police. I would have more of a conscience about it if I didn't know that his condition had advanced by that time beyond the point where it could be retrieved. I've always had a feeling that using his memories for police work would, in a way, be adding insult to injury; he didn't like the idea of me becoming a police officer at all. All he said was, "you must do what you think best, Max", but I knew what he felt.'

For a moment, Bellamy swung his chair away from Elaine and she wondered whether such memories still caused him pain. But then he swung back and smiled.

'There again, he liked the Cougars, all of them, including Bill Massiter – maybe especially Bill Massiter. I think he found so-called Mr Blaze a bit artificial – and I don't doubt that if he was still alive, he'd want to do whatever he could to help Bill. However different our priorities were on occasions, he was a good-hearted guy. So yes, I will refer to his memoirs if I need to, but that won't stop me doing the rounds concerning the people I need to talk to. Anyway, Elaine, the way this seems to be working out is that you're going to be stuck most of the time in here, while I'm on my travels. Are you sure you're alright with that?'

Elaine was feeling oddly privileged, as if she'd just been allowed to join someone's exclusive club. But business still had to be business.

'I don't mind that, sir. I do enough charging about a lot of the time. But I will need to make regular trips to Reynolds' Farm. I'm not sure we can just leave the whole security operation to the local police. Remembering the Manningham case again, they were trying on all sorts of stuff around Houghton Hall and its grounds, and Reynolds' Farm, while it's not as big as the Manningham estate, is big enough for them to fool around in, especially with all those outhouses and barns scattered all over the place. And while I'm visiting, I can pick the brains of a few of them; I know some of the better ones by name.'

'Yes, absolutely, Inspector. In any case, if we've got a decent sergeant and a willing constable – and if either of them are not that, I'm not having them, Henshaw or not – then they can be doing the phoning and internet-delving stuff a lot of the time. OK,' he said, getting up, 'let's start getting it sorted out, Elaine.'

By the afternoon, the team had acquired a sergeant, DS Mary Stanhope, who was widely known for her ability to research the wider backgrounds of suspects and known criminals, or "dish the dirt", as the more direct phrase had it, and a constable, DC Dean Matheson, who, at twenty-two, was a fast-track graduate entrant on the basis of his computer competence, and was known to have hacked into the sites of some fraudulent so-called "traders".

Bellamy knew the media frenzy was already breaking, and the pace of it put the more leisurely progress which he favoured already out of the question. Requests were received for a press conference to be held not later than five o'clock, to make whatever "story" the media wanted to make of it available for the six o'clock news bulletins.

The public relations room had been set up by half past three; it was a rather dark room, with only one window available, but in addition to the general seating, the three desks it contained were equipped with computers and each one also had a phone, for both internal and external purposes.

Elaine checked everything in the room was working, and sent Stanhope and Matheson to introduce themselves to Bellamy.

Looking at the younger faces sitting facing him, Bellamy found something reassuring about both of them, even though Matheson in particular looked, to him at least, ridiculously young.

The DC was a tall, blondish, slim young man, but something about him, his apparently innate confidence, perhaps as a result of having graduated very well quite recently, reassured those who met him that his youth did not imply either naivety or incompetence. Bellamy chose to talk to him first, because he preferred to have a one-to-one with Mary Stanhope.

'Now, DC Matheson, let me tell you the kind of information I want, and then you can tell me how long it's likely to take you to get it. Firstly, I want you to root out all the footage available on the internet, both new and old, about the Cougars generally and about each member of the Cougars individually. I don't just mean the news stuff, I mean anything in the way of documentaries, any individual activities each member has got up to since the Cougars split up, and anything relating to physical or mental health issues – medical records will be covered by confidentiality, but there might still be correspondence or news material.

'I also want to know about drugs. We believe Cougar Bill might have been using cocaine on a regular basis, probably right up until the day he died, and if he was doing so, there's always the possibility that the rest of the band were doing so as well. We also want to know about the Cougars' partners and lovers, with particular reference to any grudges or general differences the rest of them might have had with Bill Massiter, or he with them.

'One detail I'm going to need to know quickly; it's my recollection, when I was a child and went to the Cougars' recording studio with my father, that Cougar Bill was left-handed. This is important, Matheson; if he was ambidextrous, on the basis of all the footage you can find of him playing, I want to know quickly, because it could make the difference between this case being treated as murder or suicide. Now, tell me how easy you think it's likely to be to get hold of all this information.'

'The most difficult, sir, is likely to be the sources of their drug supplies. The dealers have various methods of throwing obstacles in the path of anyone trying to track them down, but with the authority given to us to access police records both nationally and internationally – and I think I can hack into some of the international ones even when they don't give us authority – I should be able to find out what supplies they've been buying, where they're buying them from, and whether or not there have been any financial problems arising from that use. Likewise, medical records, though that's an area where hacking could get me into trouble without backing from high places.'

'OK, well, come back to me if anything looks interesting enough on the medical front for us to seek that backing. Sometimes it will be there by implication; for example, if Bill has been using drugs for a long time, there are likely to have been medical issues arising, depending on how heavy his use has been. He's a rich man, and he could afford quite a heavy level of abuse if he wanted it. Thanks, Dean. Now, go and make a start, and get back to me if there's anything there that you need and you haven't got, but don't do it for at least the next fifteen minutes, because I want to discuss things with DS Stanhope.'

Matheson departed, and Bellamy turned to Mary Stanhope.

'Do you know DC Matheson at all, Sergeant Stanhope?'

'I've met him in passing, sir, but I know him by reputation. A superintendent I know refers to him as "Dean the Hack"; he's a bright boy, by all accounts.'

'Good. You will be spending a fair amount of time working with him, and your investigations and his might be overlapping each other at some points. I gather you and I share a certain media connection, do we not? I was a press journalist, but you did a stint with local radio, didn't you?'

'Yes, sir. I spent some time being what I suppose you could call a radio agony aunt. It was the extraordinary range of problems and issues people came out with which persuaded me to join the police, because many of the problems were direct or indirect results of criminality, and in most cases, criminality done to them rather than committed by them.'

'You have a reputation as a listener, Mary. You worked for a while in rape counselling, didn't you?'

'Yes, sir. Demanding but very rewarding, perhaps as you'd expect it to be.'

'Well, it's that kind of area which is the one which I want you to particularly look at in this case. When a very rich and successful man can't live without taking drugs, and is apparently estranged from his wife, even though she is still his wife, as far as we know, it doesn't strike me as too fanciful to suspect some kind of sexual issue might be involved, or something connected to mental health issues. The Cougars were not exactly a boy band, but they were a bunch of young guys with a large fan base; we know at least one of them, Rory Blaze, is gay, and the other members of the band would have reactions to that, I would imagine. They would all have had frequent offers of sex from young fans all over the place, and that would be likely to have had repercussions on them all. You might find that you could be talking to boys as well as girls. Would you be OK with that?'

'Oh, yes, sir. Not all of the rape victims I counselled were female.'

Bellamy paused for a moment's thought, and the chance to arrange his words.

'I know you couldn't really do what you do, DS Stanhope, without respecting people's confidentiality when you have to. I assume that when you talk to people, you make clear to them that if they tell you about something which is a crime, you are professionally committed to doing something about it.'

'Yes, sir, but it's often the case that the reason why they're talking to me is that they want something done about it.'

'Of course.'

Bellamy paused again. Mary Stanhope was an experienced officer, and he had heard nothing about her but good reports.

He suspected he was in danger of being rather over-cautious, and perhaps disparaging of her professional ability by implication. It was time to get the whole operation up and running.

'OK, Sergeant Stanhope, I'd like you now to start finding out what you can about the later history of the Cougars concerning their relationships, with particular reference to Bill Massiter, of course, and including what we can find out about health issues, both mental and physical. If you find access to health records has become necessary, I will seek the proper authority to obtain them. Please keep me informed of anything which you think might be even vaguely relevant.'

'Yes, sir.'

Bellamy watched her depart, and immediately picked up the phone, dialling a familiar number. The pathologist Colin Thurston was not exactly a friend; Bellamy privately doubted whether Thurston had many friends in the conventional sense, since his occupation was hardly the most suited to small talk and after-dinner conversation, and Thurston himself was blunt to the point of rudeness, on occasions. He was, nevertheless, very good at his job.

'Could I speak to Dr Thurston, please?'

'Speaking. DCI Bellamy, I presume, now speaking from your exalted status, no doubt. A big posh office, I'm guessing. Is it comfy?'

'Not too bad, Colin, thank you. Doubtless you are all mod cons in your morgue, are you?'

'Yes, I suppose so. The bodies all over the place spoil the ambience just a touch. Anyway, enough badinage. What do you want to know, specifically?'

'I want to know whether the deceased was definitely left-handed, and whether there are any marks on the body which indicate some kind of struggle had taken place.'

'What you're getting at, Max, is did he kill himself, I suppose, aren't you? Well, he's bruised around the neck, of course, but that's more or less it. There are no other signs of a struggle or an outright fight. And yes, he is indubitably left-handed. People who have always written with the left hand tend to have smaller wrists than they have on their right hand, and the difference with Cougar Bill is very noticeable. You noticed something about the noose, I believe?'

Who told him that? Bellamy thought, with a pang of insecurity. But he might have worked it out for himself, of course.

'Yes, it was a right-handed knot.'

'Well, sure as hell he didn't tie it, then. But I have to say, in my experience, which is not inconsiderable, if someone else tied it, one might expect signs of some kind of struggle, and there aren't any. Mind you, he wasn't in very good shape, to be honest. I suspect he'd been taking cocaine for some time, perhaps before the Cougars hit the big time. He was probably not far away from some big problems, particularly with the heart and the kidneys, but whether he knew that yet, I doubt. You got any aches and pains, Bellamy?'

'None I'm going to tell you about, Doctor Thurston. Thanks, anyway. There's a lot of useful stuff there. I'll have a good look at the written report.'

'You do that. It's your business more than mine, Max, but I'd lay good odds that this one was no suicide.'

Bellamy noted the remark, filing it away in his memory banks as he finished the phone call. He had been aware, ever since his early teens, of what he had come to regard as his particular gift. In boyhood, he had tended to shy away from it, with a boyish reluctance to identify or acknowledge in himself anything which would set him apart, or lead, as he sometimes suspected and dreaded, to other people regarding him as some kind of freak. He had a phenomenal memory for detail, so good that he could organise his mind like a computer bank of recall. When he came to the various stages of schooling and the inevitable examinations, he found, to his great satisfaction, that he could deal with them relatively easily because he was already operating his developing memory banks. Finally emerging from school and adolescence, he realised the value of what seemed to have landed in his lap without him having to do much about it.

An incident early on in his working career as a journalist was the first time he'd allowed someone to see just how remarkable his gift was. He worked under the auspices of the editor Ed Mowbray, who taught him most of what he knew about journalism and who once found him sitting at his desk, apparently doing nothing but staring into space. Mowbray came to know his self-contained, slightly withdrawn young recruit much better, but at this time, when Bellamy had only been at the paper for a year or so, he was still a probationer, and subject to Ed Mowbray's well-defined ideas of inculcating discipline and a work ethic.

'Haven't you got anything to do, young Bellamy? For God's sake, son, if you're going to spend all day sitting there in a fucking dream, you might as well go home and do it.'

Startled, Bellamy realised that, however reluctant he might be, he had to reveal something of himself.

'I was just reviewing what I now know about Sanderson,' Bellamy said, mentioning the name of a local trader suspected of various kinds of criminality, who the paper had identified as worthy of investigation. 'The more I know about him, his contacts, his past and his likely activities in the future, the better the chances are that we can pin him down and judge the point where he's likely to give himself away.'

Mowbray did what he rarely did in his restless wandering about the newsroom; he grabbed a chair and sat just a few feet away from Bellamy.

'OK then, big-thinking boy, you tell me what you know about the guy. All of it.'

Bellamy then launched into an exposition on the subject of Sanderson. This took in his schooling, his parentage, his commercial trading record, his associates, his family, his trips abroad, his likes and dislikes, etc., etc. After ten minutes, Ed Mowbray was listening open-mouthed, apparently entranced by the calm, relentless tones of his cub reporter. After twenty minutes, three of the occupants of desks nearby had stopped what they were doing and were listening to Max Bellamy. After twenty minutes, Bellamy had reached the stage of describing where he thought the subject of his investigation would be in the forthcoming two weeks and how best the investigation could be brought to a productive close.

He stopped, and the newsroom had been plunged into a most uncharacteristic silence.

'Fucking hell, son. You've done your homework, haven't you? You didn't, in all that time, look at a single piece of paper or book. You carry all that in your head?'

'I've always been like that, sir. It just seems to be how I am.'

'Well, if that's how you are, young Max, you're going to be alright in this business. You need time to think it all out, right?'

'Yes. Then I can work out what to do next.'

'Rock on. You do it your way, kid. When the bastard gets sent down, I'll – well, I don't know what I'll do. I might even buy you a pint.'

'Bloody hell!' said an undiplomatic voice a few yards away. Mowbray was notoriously shy when it came to opening his wallet. He fixed the source of the comment with a glare. Bellamy was hugging the editor's comments to himself. Maybe, he thought, he was a freak in some ways, but it was a useful freak to be.

Now he exercised one of the perks of his new senior police officer status, and told the lady on the phone exchange to hold all calls for the next half an hour.

'And no calls means no calls, Jane, please. If it's the chief constable, tell him I've gone to interview Bill Massiter's missus, which is what I will be doing in half an hour anyway.'

Bellamy occasionally amused himself by remembering police

officers he had known who, in his opinion, never seemed to think about anything very much; there were a disturbingly large number of them. As there were in journalism, for that matter. People who either believed in the creed of spontaneity, or more probably, were intellectually lazy.

Recalling his father came with baggage, of course. Max had always suspected that he had been something of a disappointment to the old man. However, what stayed with him as a consolation were the many times they talked, particularly in Max's adulthood, when Richard Bellamy obviously felt more at ease with saying what he thought. Now Max's memory banks opened the file marked "Cougars" and started to search for whatever he could recall. He knew Richard Bellamy was more likely to talk about people than he was to write it down; his diaries would be more relevant for knowing where and when his meetings with the Cougars, individually and collectively, took place.

File One centred on the Bellamy family home, which, at the time Max was remembering, was a comfortable detached place in the south London suburbs, where Max's room overlooked an almost rural patch of wooded land on the edge of the estate where the family lived.

Max's imagination would occasionally run riot about what might be happening in the wood at night, though he knew well enough the most likely answer was nothing at all.

At the time he was remembering, he would have been about twenty, and spending some time at home during a holiday from university.

Richard Bellamy's old school friend, Doug Lane, the drummer of the Cougars, was paying them a visit. Max's twenty-year-old mind imagined drummers to have some kind of wild eccentricity in their make-up which led them to enjoy pounding the living daylights out of things to make a living, and in that respect, the Doug Lane of 2003 was a bit of a let-down. Out of his gig gear, he was a very average-looking guy in smart casuals, then in his forties, with the Cougars' greatest days behind them.

Bellamy's mother, Beverley, had taken the opportunity to visit her sister for the day; she knew the kind of in-talk which her husband would get into with his friends in the music business. Both of his parents, Max remembered, had friends and relatives of their own, and neither of them seemed to have any problem with that.

'We're going to the club for lunch, Max,' said Richard Bellamy, as his son had withdrawn to the garden rather than, as he saw it, inflict his company on two old school friends. 'Would you like to come?'

'Sure, Dad,' he said, getting to his feet. 'If you're sure I won't be intruding.'

Richard Bellamy, as a university lecturer, could eat and socialise in the academic club at his university, and two guests were usually the maximum allowed. Max was not a student at the university where his father lectured, that situation having been carefully avoided by both parties for various largely practical reasons.

Richard leant over and lowered his voice.

'To be honest, Max, I'm using you quite blatantly. Even in the club, someone will recognise him, and while he's doing his "rock star at leisure bit" I will at least have someone to talk to. And, to give him his due, he's always taken an interest in what you're doing.'

So the three of them finished up in the fairly sedate atmosphere of Richard Bellamy's club, restricted to members of the university's teaching staff and their guests, and at least at first, there didn't seem to be any immediate recognition of Doug Lane.

Even Bellamy's memory didn't stretch to remembering every word spoken, but he could recall specific conversations across considerable distances of time, and he could trace the way the tones and emphasis of them changed.

During the meal, Doug Lane, already beginning to acquire a middle-aged midriff, consumed wine at, Max estimated, about three times the rate his father did, partly because Richard Bellamy was also drinking water. Max sipped diplomatically at halves of beer.

Lane was not a man most people would immediately see as a rock star. His hair was cut short and neat, he remained clean-shaven, and he dressed quite conventionally. Max almost felt disappointed, until the intake of alcohol started to move the conversation away from the uncontroversial territory of the older men's school days and Max's university progress, to the inner politics of the Cougars. The more wine he drank, the less inclined Lane was to be charitable towards the other members of the band.

'Bill and Tony can hardly stand the sight of each other now, to be honest. Between you and me, boys. I hear you're aiming to be a press man, Max, but you're not doing articles yet, are you?'

They all laughed, but Max sensed the question was far from entirely frivolous.

'No, Mr Lane. Though the college rag would see you as quite a scoop. But no, I don't tell tales out of school.'

Laughter again.

'Good boy. The Cougars' time is done anyway, to be honest. What with Bill's habits, which his missus, Josie, chews his head off about, and I'm not surprised, the amount of money it costs him, and Tony's – what shall we call them? – proclivities, neither of them is in good enough shape to carry on for much longer.'

'The boys still love the Rory Blaze thing, then, Doug?' said Richard.

'Yeah, all that leather cock rock crap, they lap it up. By the end of most gigs, he has a few outside his dressing room, half out of their minds and ready to do whatever he tells them to do. Which is just about anything you could think of, and a few you probably couldn't.'

He roared with laughter and drained his wine; that, Max noted, was the second bottle finished.

'We have separate rooms now, one for Tony and one for the rest of us. If they can't do us two decent dressing rooms, we don't do the gig. To give Tony his due, which I suppose I ought to do, he's careful with the age thing. It's easier with lads, generally; if they're not over eighteen, they don't look over eighteen. A lot of them carry identity with them anyway, so they can drink in pubs. With the girls, it's easy to get into all kinds of trouble; I've known fourteen-year-olds, physically almost fully grown-up, and when they get all their warpaint on, they could pass for twenty at least. In our main days, we got the girls, Tony got the boys. It's amazing how the fans just got used to it. They would line up, like they were going to separate loos. Mind, the girls wouldn't get much more than an autograph, which is all the lads would get, if Tony didn't fancy them; he is quite particular. Bill was very married, with Josie to deal with; Manny had a missus as well, and me, well, I preferred to stay single, but usually, at the end of a gig, I was too knackered to do anything but have a drink or two and go home.'

'So what does Eric think about it all?' said Richard Bellamy.

'Sorry.' Max made his first intervention in the conversation. He liked listening to these men, both successful in their different lines of work, but he didn't like getting lost along the way. 'Who's Eric?'

'Manager of the Cougars, Max. "Captain Storm" they used to call him, notorious for his rages if anything went wrong. But his real name is Eric Irwin. I suppose he's a bit quieter these days, isn't he, Doug?'

'Oh, he still has his moments, Rich, believe me.'

Now, Bellamy thought, it was about now that Lane came up with one of the essential points of the conversation, one of the central reasons why Bellamy was making this effort to remember as much detail as he could.

'Eric was the one who came up with the idea of the band's "house", a big, comfortable place in an isolated area where the band could get together with their "admirers", as Eric called them. So they weren't doing whatever they wanted to do in hotels, pubs, restaurants and clubs, where the hacks could be all over them if they weren't very careful. Eric was thinking mostly of Tony, of course, but he was worried about Josie as well. Rumour had it, and rumour still does, that Eric and Josie had a thing going on which was about more than sniffing a line or two. Rumour also has it that one of the Cougars' biggest hits, "The Ecstasy Train", was Bill writing about Josie and Eric's activities. Bill's always denied it, but then he would, wouldn't he?'

Ding, ding, ding. The bells went off in Bellamy's mind one by one. But there was one more essential recall he needed at this stage. He struggled to remember whether it was he or his father who asked the question, but he could remember Lane's answer readily enough.

'Cavelcombe House, they called it. South Cornwall coast. Just about as isolated as you could get without moving yourself onto a rock in the fucking Atlantic. Eric tried to rename it Cougar Mansion, or some such thing, but it never caught on; it had been Cavelcombe House since about seventeen-something. God, there was some weird shit went down at that place. We sold it eventually. Josie was involved somewhere along the line, too.'

By the time they reached the dessert, which for Lane meant a generous glass of old brandy, several club members were already asking for autographs, and what Richard Bellamy wearily said later was the familiar pattern took over, with Doug Lane holding court about "great gigs" he'd known.

After they left the club, by now squeezing past several journalists gathered outside, Bellamy remembered snatches of the further conversation the two men had back at the Bellamy home. By this time, Doug Lane was, not to put too fine a point on it, drunk.

'Well, it was Bill who started the band. Does he like where it's going?' said Richard.

'Bill and me, Rich. Let's get it right. Bill and I used to play duos, easy listening, weddings, parties, that kind of thing. But Bill in his younger days was a bit AC/DC, you know, like some lads tend to be. I think he and Tony had a thing together, back in the day. Bill grew up to be hetero. Tony didn't.'

'What does Manny think about it all, then?' said Richard.

'Oh, Manny's so laid back, he's almost falling apart,' said Doug Lane. 'Think of all the clichés you've ever heard about Latin guys, and then forget them. Excitable, spontaneous, all that stuff. Manny twangs away on his bass guitar, has a drink and a shower and goes home to the missus. I don't think he's taken an illegal substance in his life. He wouldn't recognise a joint if it got up and bit him in the bum.'

'So how did he join the band?' Richard asked.

'Tony saw him playing with some no-hope outfit in a pub, and he was impressed, mostly because Manny's a very good bass guitar, but also because Tony fancied his arse. Manny declined politely on the arse front, but he liked the idea of being in the band. Before then, we had session musicians doing the bass, and they're a bit hit and miss, to be honest.

'Manny's one of those guys who's very good at what he does, but not much good at pushing himself forward. Much like your good-looking young son and heir here, Rich.'

Bellamy remembered his twenty-year-old self smirking back at his father's old pal, while reflecting that women commenting on his good looks would be rather more satisfying.

He stopped the memory session abruptly and prepared to leave his office. Now he had more detail of both people and places. Eric Irwin, "Captain Storm", the Cougars' short-tempered manager. Cavelcombe House, where the band's members could let their hair down outside any public areas. And, of course, Josie

Massiter, maiden name as yet unknown, still Bill's wife, apparently, if estranged and separated some time ago.

He knew that the local police had already informed Josie Massiter of her husband's death, and he knew also that the news had been taken more casually than might have been expected, though it was understood that Josie and Bill had not lived as man and wife for some years. Now he could add the information that Josie and Eric Irwin may have been involved with each other at some point, and perhaps still were.

Checking in on Elaine as he arranged the car to take him to Josie's address, only some thirty-five miles from where Bill had been found dead, he heard that his assistant had been picking the brains of a few journalists, even as she was imposing hard and fast rules on them for what they could and couldn't do in the vicinity of Bill Massiter's big rambling home.

'The buzz I'm getting, sir, is that the Cougars broke up not because they'd shot their bolt and weren't having any more hits – although they had and weren't – but rather the growing tensions within the band, and most particularly between Bill and Tony Richards, which eventually caused the bust-up. Doug and Manny would have carried on, even just doing weddings and smaller gigs, but the other two had got to the point where they simply couldn't stand being in the same band.'

'OK, Elaine, keep your ear to the ground. When I get back from seeing Mrs Massiter, or whatever she now calls herself, we'll get together and decide where we go next.'

Bellamy never drove himself while on cases; he aimed to make use of the thinking and exploring time. He searched for Cavelcombe House on his phone, and found it was now a hotel. It was beautifully situated, right on the Cornish coast, and very isolated; the nearest human habitation looked to be a village some five miles away. As with other background issues accompanying previous cases, it could either be a significant clue to what caused the disintegration of the Cougars and the estrangement between their two leading members, or it could be a big, fat red herring, wasting a lot of police time and expense while leading precisely nowhere. But in the early stages of an investigation, and Bellamy was already largely convinced that this was a murder investigation, there was no alternative but to explore such avenues as seemed to be opening up.

He reflected on his father, as the sizeable market town where Josie lived loomed into view. His family and his professional life should always be separate had been the attitude he'd been used to adopting towards work; it seemed somehow an unacceptable use of his memories of Richard Bellamy to start using them in a case. He doubted his father would have approved, but he realised with a rueful acceptance of the kind of relationship they'd had, that if he'd only ever done things which his father approved of, the chances were that he would never have been either a crime journalist or a police officer. His father had left him a lot of money, including wealth he'd inherited from his own father, a successful businessman in the entertainment business, which Richard had continued to some extent, even when he became an academic. Max knew that one of the reasons his father knew the Cougars, apart from his old school friend Doug Lane, was because he had what he termed "a percentage" of them. Richard Bellamy's mixture of capitalism and idealism was perhaps one aspect of his character which his son had inherited. He knew his known wealth was something his police colleagues both envied and resented at the same time, and he knew it had already changed the kind of police career he was having. But Richard Bellamy was a free-thinking man because he could afford to be, and that was one aspect of his legacy to his son which Max rightly valued.

Josie Massiter lived in a comfortable detached house, which the agents would probably describe as of "executive" standard, set back from the road with a generous front garden and a double garage.

His background notes had told Bellamy that Josie was working as an assistant manager in a hotel where the Cougars stayed for a few nights after some local gigs when she and Bill met. He doubted whether that would ever have paid for a house like this.

Bellamy pressed the doorbell twice, and after several minutes, a young man, probably no older than his late twenties and naked apart from a towel around his waist, eventually arrived at the door.

'Yes? This isn't a good time, whoever you are.'

'No, so I see. However, I do need to talk to Josie, if she's available. I'm Detective Chief Inspector Max Bellamy, and I'm investigating the death of Josie's husband.'

The tone changed suddenly and dramatically as the man looked at Bellamy's identification card. This, Bellamy thought, was a guy who had had dealings with the police before.

'Yes, right. Come in, sir. I'll tell Josie you're here. She's just – resting.'

He showed Max into the front room, nicely appointed, almost as if it was a show house. As he waited, the murmur of voices came from upstairs. Not too many guesses needed, the police officer reflected, as to what Josie was resting from. But it was never wise to jump too readily to conclusions. That handsome, floppy-haired young male must be at least fifteen years younger than Josie, Max thought, even though he knew Josie was younger than her husband.

Josie herself appeared about five minutes later, casually dressed in a smock-like top and jeans, clothes which, Max reflected, were probably too young for her, though he had no pretensions to being an expert on female fashion.

'Sorry to keep you waiting,' she said, and the smile she then unleashed said volumes to Bellamy as to how Bill Massiter had noticed her when staying in the hotel where she worked. There was an appearance of warmth and empathy about it, as if she was genuinely pleased to have met the smile's recipient. The weary eyes and the developing bags under them were difficult to hide, however, as was the fuller figure which the smock and jeans were not hiding very successfully.

'You've just met that vision of manhood, have you?' She smiled again. 'That's my nephew Bryan. Such a sporty boy; always at the gym, or going off on his runs. I think he's been out for a few miles this morning. He was just taking a shower.'

She sat on the sofa, and Bellamy resumed the armchair he'd been sitting in. He tried not to give any visible signs of his awareness that what she had just told him was a blatant lie. The years had taught him all the most obvious signs that gave away liars, and she'd just been exhibiting two of them, failing to look at him when saying it and letting out a slight giggle after the word "runs", as if she didn't actually believe it herself.

Bellamy let the ensuing silence run for long enough to become uncomfortable for anyone listening at close quarters. He knew well enough that silence could be difficult to negotiate for someone who was, for whatever reason, attempting to hide something. He knew also the value of his own eyes in such circumstances. His wife, Louise, had once described them as "hypno" eyes – "for some reason, it's impossible to ignore them". His silent gaze settled on Josie Massiter, and they did what they frequently managed to do, making her speak.

'You want to know something about my relationship with Bill, I take it, Chief Inspector. I don't see why you'd come to see me otherwise. Rumour has it that you don't believe he killed himself.'

'Do you, Mrs Massiter?'

'Typical cop. Throwing questions back in my face. No, I don't see any particular reason why Bill would kill himself. He's ill, as you probably know, but people have lived for years with his kidney thing. He wasn't the depressive type. He carried on being Bill, good old Bill, even when the whole Cougar thing was collapsing around his ears. It's maybe mostly that which drove me a bit crazy about him, and not in a good way. That and the drugs; I suppose you know about the drugs now.'

'It's not difficult to work out, when he has cases marked as coming from Colombia.'

'Yes, well, he needed it. With everything that was happening.'

'What was happening, Mrs Massiter?'

'Oh, call me Josie, for God's sake.'

'OK, Josie. What was happening which made Bill need to take drugs?'

'Where do I start?'

At this point, so-called nephew Bryan, now fully dressed, came into the room looking expectantly at Josie. Bellamy had the impression that the boy – he wasn't much older than a boy – would prefer to be somewhere else, and quickly. The look he shot in Josie's direction was not, very obviously, the look of a nephew at his aunt.

'Do you want me to stay, Josie?' he said, his body already poised to leave.

'No, love, you trot along now. Go amuse yourself for an hour or two. I'll give you a call.'

Bryan turned and left, and Josie watched him carefully as he did so. Eventually, with an obvious effort, she turned back to Bellamy, and flinched at his steady gaze.

'Bloody hell,' she said. 'Those eyes. You're like a sort of silent Gestapo guy, aren't you?

What is it you're looking for, Mr Bellamy? What do you want to know? If you think someone killed Bill, am I a suspect or something?'

Bellamy leaned forward, and managed an enigmatic smile.

'Josie, all I'm seeking to do at the moment is find out about Bill, about his state of mind, about what was happening in his life. If he did kill himself, there must have been some reason why, some kind of pressure on him, something he just couldn't cope with. If he didn't kill himself, then obviously someone else killed him – for what? Money? Revenge? I'm not assuming anything, Josie, I'm investigating. I already have the impression that you cared for Bill, so I wonder why you and he are estranged, and if you couldn't live with each other, why are you still married and still using the name Massiter?'

Josie took a deep breath and wandered towards the window.

'I'm only Josie Massiter to people who know me through Bill. I'm Josie Wilding to my friends; Wilding is my maiden name and the name I'll probably use now Bill is – gone. I left Bill eventually because of a few reasons. I think he was half gay, to be honest; he used to have a thing with that Richards guy, so-called Rory Blaze, when they were boys, and he supposedly grew out of it, though I was not sure he really did. When we made love, I had a feeling sometimes it wasn't me he was thinking about.

'In any case, he wasn't married to me, he was married to the fucking Cougars; pardon my language, but they always rile me up. But they had tensions from the start. Richards seemed to think Bill had betrayed him, gone straight just to annoy him.

'Eventually I had to make him choose between me and the Cougars, and I thought he'd done that, I thought I'd won, but then he was still going to that bloody house; Cavelcombe, it's called, whatever Cougar name they tried to pin on it. He was still taking the stuff which mostly Eric got for him. He was still living in that rambling old farm or whatever it was where the Cougars made records, in between shooting up, getting pissed and shagging.'

She returned to her chair and made herself look into Bellamy's eyes.

'That wasn't my bloody nephew, as you knew well enough all along, didn't you? I'm a passionate woman. I might be fifty-three, but I'm still bloody alive. I still sometimes need a man to get me through the night. Bryan there is twenty-six years old, with a very handy taste for ladies older than him—'

'You don't have to tell me this, Josie,' Bellamy said quietly.

'I want you to understand what's happening, Mr Bellamy. For a long time, I wanted my Bill back, like he was when I first met him, when the Cougars were riding high, when he would leave the hotel where the band were staying, even after a gig, to come to me; even if he was tired, he liked to just spend time with me, have a drink, have a laugh. Bill. My Bill. Never mind all the band stuff, all the fan stuff. You should see the kind of mail I got from some of the so-called fans. Bill had been swallowed up by the Cougars, and still half under the influence of Richards, so-called Rory fucking Blaze.'

'Do you think Tony Richards killed him?'

'No.' Josie was immediately scornful. 'He wouldn't have the balls for that. He's mouth and trousers, really. You know, for all the rock god crap, he couldn't punch his way out of a paper bag. I could never carry on any kind of real marriage with Bill while the Cougars, especially Tony Richards, were always hovering in the background.'

Bellamy stood up.

'I think that's as far as we can go at the moment, Josie. But please give me your contact details, because I will keep in touch; I think you want to know what all this is about just as much as I do.'

'Yes, Chief Inspector, I do,' Josie said, and in spite of the emphasis with which she said it, or perhaps because of it, Bellamy concluded that she did know a good deal more about what had been going on than she was prepared to say as yet. Josie, he thought, was a lady who hedged her bets and played the percentages, and the whole range of what she knew about her husband's circumstances was only likely to emerge when she felt that she had no alternative.

Heading back to his office, Bellamy decided to turn his mind away from the case temporarily; having any case permanently on his mind could start it becoming obsessive. Minds, like bodies, needed a reasonable supply of rest and relaxation.

However, on this occasion, that wasn't scheduled to happen. A few minutes after he'd turned his car radio on, the hourly news bulletin arrived. Item three had him frantically telling his driver to find a lay-by and stop the car.

'A shooting incident has occurred at a speaking engagement of Louise Bellamy, MP,' said the modulated, unruffled news-announcer voice. 'Two people have been wounded, one of them severely. Mrs Bellamy herself is alarmed and upset, but remains unharmed. Police are searching for a lone gunman, who made a rapid escape after shooting at a small group of people, including Mrs Bellamy, as they entered a local hall to address a meeting. Police say no motive for the shooting has been established as yet.'

Fortunately, a lay-by appeared after only another two miles. Bellamy's driver pulled into it and stopped his car. Bellamy opened his window and began to take gasps of air. Only two minutes after he'd stopped, a call arrived on his phone, the caller's name obscured.

'Detective Chief Inspector Bellamy, we don't doubt that you are clever enough to take a warning, sir. On this occasion, your wife remained unharmed; next time, she will not be so fortunate. Mr Massiter's death is a great tragedy, but it was suicide and nothing but suicide, and your futile attempts to stir up trouble may prove to be very expensive for both you and your wife if you don't just accept the simple truth.'

Bellamy saw his hand shaking slightly as the message ended, but he knew the value of acting quickly when such things happened, and he immediately contacted a number he knew, available only to senior police personnel.

'Trace the call just made to this number, please, and send me the recorded call.'

His next move was to phone Louise.

'Max, thank God it's you.' The anguish in her voice stabbed Bellamy to the heart.

'Darling, darling Louise. Are you alright?'

'Yes. I'm shaken up to hell, but I didn't get hit. Harry Mallon was hit on the arm; he's lost a fair bit of blood, but the hospital says he'll be OK. But we had a local journalist with us, Steven Ryan, and he was shot in the back, or at least that's what it looked like. They're going to operate. He could be a cripple for life, Max. I can't live with this; no politics is worth this. They tell me I'll have police protection for a few days. Max, when will you be home…?'

Bellamy heard a single sob. He knew his wife very well, and even a single sob was uncharacteristic and exceptional.

'Where are you, Louise?'

Hesitantly but clearly enough, Louise mentioned the address of the constituency party office of the neighbouring constituency to her own, which Bellamy calculated was about twelve miles away.

'You have police people there with you now?'

'Yes, several, Max, both inside and outside. And as far as I know, they've got a car chasing the guy.'

'Right. I'll be there in a few minutes, darling. Stay right there with the police.'

Bellamy turned to his driver, an experienced sergeant, as unflappable as ever.

'Right, George, put this in your satnav' – he described the address – 'put that bloody siren on, and let's get there asap.'

On the way, Bellamy's phone sounded again.

'Somewhere in inner city Birmingham, sir,' a voice said. 'We should be able to track down the owner of the phone, though my guess would be it's almost certainly stolen.'

'Can you pinpoint the exact spot where he made the call?'

'We can get pretty close to it, sir, and when we do, we'll send people there to ask around.'

If they have the nerve and the organisation to carry out such a shooting and then the follow-up call, they will probably be able to cover their tracks, Bellamy thought, but it was circumstances like these which needed the bloodhound mentality. Some tiny detail could start a ball rolling down a mountain and collect a lot of material along the way.

Bellamy had never wanted to stand in the way of his wife's desire for a political career. After spending some time as an environmental journalist and remaining in touch with politicians on all sides, Louise had concluded that she wanted to be where things were actually being decided and acted upon rather than commenting on them from a distance. At the time, Bellamy had wondered what the consequences might be of his wife entering public life, but, seeing the support she was getting and her determination to succeed, he swallowed his doubts and determined not to rain on her parade. But he knew well enough that there would be those in the criminal world who would see the opportunities that having a wife exposed in such a way would give them.

With an experienced driver and a siren blaring, Bellamy covered the distance in a matter of minutes. Telling the driver to wait, he passed through the police cordon around the building and entered a room to the right of the entrance, half lounge and half office, where Louise was sitting with a cup of coffee on a small table beside her. On one side of her, talking on her phone, was the familiar form of Inspector Elaine Price.

Seeing him approach, Louise sprung to her feet and clasped her arms around him.

'Oh, Max, thank God you're here! Today has been a nightmare, a fucking nightmare!'

The language she used was a clear indicator of her state of mind. In spite of the colourful language often used in political circles, which Bellamy knew very well from previous events he had attended in support of his wife, Louise was usually reluctant to join in with the general expletives.

'How's Harry?' Bellamy asked. 'And the journalist guy – what was his name again?'

'Steven Ryan. He's in a bad way, Max. Not in immediate danger of losing his life, but he could be laid up for a long time. As for Harry, the bullet skimmed his arm, so he'll be OK soon, but they're keeping him in case there are any after-effects. Harry, of course, is pretty much unmoved. You know what a tough old bugger he is.'

Bellamy nodded. He'd got to know Harry Mallon quite well; he was an experienced political operator, and while his innate cynicism sometimes proved trying, Bellamy knew that he preferred someone like Harry to be with his wife on her political travels than a more idealistic or trusting individual.

The need for action was ramping up in Bellamy now, at the same time as he knew within himself that he couldn't possibly leave Louise, however much protection she had with her.

'Darling,' he murmured. He took both her hands into his. For the moment, he didn't want to tell her about the phone call he'd received; she was probably still in shock, and it would make more sense to tell her, as he knew he would have to, when she'd had the chance to recover from the initial shock of the shooting. A cold fear had settled in the region of Bellamy's heart at the reflection that he could well have been talking to her now at her bedside in the hospital; in fact, he might have been sitting next to her body.

'I'll arrange for you to go home right now if that's what you want, Louise, with a police detachment watching the house for at least the rest of the day, and when I get back, we'll talk about what we want to do. Do you want to go home?'

'Yes, Max, I think I do. Is there any chance I could have Elaine with me for a few hours, if you still have work to do?'

'Darling Louise, you can have both of us with you for the rest of the day, my love. Nothing I've got to do is more urgent than taking care of you. We'll head for home with an escort, and give you the chance to take it easy. Elaine and I will keep in touch with what's happening, and what progress is being made to catch the gunman.'

Ten minutes later, a small convoy moved away from the constituency office, and Bellamy for once found the attentions of the paparazzi deeply irritating. The car's back windows were shaded, and he knew he could safely V-sign emphatically at them to relieve some of his tension, but he didn't. There were too many other issues crowding in on his mind. The shooting incident had opened a Pandora's box of new anxieties and mysteries. Why was someone, or some organisation, desperately keen on making him accept that Massiter had hung himself, to such an extent that they were prepared to threaten his wife and effectively give themselves away, because someone being so keen to make him believe Cougar Bill's death was a suicide seemed to serve as an open admission that it wasn't?

But most of all, far and away most of all, they had physically threatened Louise. Once again, he felt his face going cold at the thought of what might have happened and realised that, experienced as he might be, he had some of the symptoms of shock. Why had he been so accommodating when Louise had first talked about entering public life? Was it just the married man's desire for a quiet life which had led him to not even mention the dangers of his wife living a public as well as a private life? From the moment she had told him of her acceptance as a parliamentary candidate, he had meekly acquiesced, and here, rapidly enough, was the price to be paid.

He and Louise were holding hands on the back seat of the car. He knew she was looking at him, and he realised soon enough the train of her thoughts. Deadpan and poker-faced as he had taught himself to be, for professional reasons, he was always an open book to her.

'I'm sorry, Max,' she whispered. 'I should have thought this through in more detail.'

'So should I, Lou. So should I.'

'Don't give me that. You knew, didn't you? You always know this stuff. You should have said something, Max. I wanted to be where all the big decisions were being taken; me, me, me. I couldn't see the wood for the trees. Now we will never have the peace we used to have. I must resign.'

Max sighed. He hesitated for a moment, but he knew what he had to say. He also knew that it probably wouldn't make anything any better, but he had to say it anyway.

'Louise, I'm a police officer. OK, I'm now a senior police officer and I don't do the front line as much as I used to, but I could still face some maniac with a knife or a gun any day of the week. I could still, today or tomorrow, face some murderer who's just killed and wouldn't think twice about killing again. It's my job. And if it's your job to stand up there and be a representative of the people for a political party which some people like and some most definitely don't, you carry the risk too. If it's inconsiderate and reckless for you to be an MP, it's no less inconsiderate and reckless for me to be a police officer. You could pack it in, I could pack it in, we could find ourselves a hidey-hole, a nice place in the country with roses around the door and forget it all, but would you be doing what you want to do, being in there where the power is? Could you live with yourself having thrown it all in? Could I live with myself having let all the bad guys I could have stopped from doing what they're doing carry on regardless? If we want to do what we do, love, it comes with the territory. And that applies at least as much to me as it does to you.'

Suddenly, silence, and no sound but the passing countryside. Their eyes met, and her arms were around his neck and her lips on his cheek.

'Darling Max. What did I do to deserve you?'

They stayed together in a long embrace. Eventually, he whispered to her. 'We have to think it through, Louise. We'll talk to Harry when he's recovered. There's lots we could do with his help. You could stay in London, with police protection arranged, for the time it takes to resolve the case. You could go on a fact-finding trip abroad; if it's a political trip with MPs, security protection could go with it. And I'll carry arms with me when I travel. And we already know where the phone call came from—'

'What phone call?'

Fool, fool, fool, Max called himself inwardly. He remained silent, trying to think.

'What phone call, Max? What bloody phone call?'

Caught with your trousers down, Maximilian. Face it.

'Someone phoned me on the way to you. Told me to accept that Cougar Bill killed himself and leave it at that... Or else – without specifying what the "else" might be.'

'Oh my god.'

'We're in the same place as we were, Louise. And at least we have a chance of tracking down who is behind this. As soon as they start making threats, they've emerged into the open and we have every chance of finding out who we're dealing with.'

Louise remained silent. Bellamy could see that she was not convinced and he concluded that she felt there was no point in them having an argument at this stage. The whole profile of their working lives had suddenly been thrown into different territory, and they were going to need time and space to work out where they went from here.

Bellamy couldn't help thinking about the risks he had taken in the past, most of which he hadn't told Louise about, and he reflected that, now he had portrayed so vividly the dangers that his job entailed, he may have fixed that particular poison in her mind permanently. But there was a limit to how much he was prepared to beat himself up; she really should have foreseen that moving into public life carried risks.

At that moment, his phone sounded. Bellamy cursed under his breath; whatever it might be, if it meant that he needed to make a decision, this probably wasn't a good time.

'Bellamy,' he growled into the phone.

'Max. Hell's bells. How's Louise?'

Mercifully, it was Tom Hollins. Bellamy relaxed. This was someone who might actually be able to help in a constructive manner.

'Shaken. Harry, her agent, did actually get hit; fortunately, only on the arm. But I've had a warning call, Tom, telling me to accept that Massiter killed himself and leave it at that.'

'Yes, I know, that's what I'm phoning you about. They've not only located where it came from, they've actually got footage of the guy. Like a fool, he made the call in the lobby of a hotel, presumably being too thick to understand that they have security cameras. The local lads even know who he is; Tyler Moss, small time con man, presumably recruited for his acting ability. Certainly not for his operational intelligence. They're already out looking to bring him in and frighten the shit out of him until he says who put him up to it. Where are you going now?'

'Home.'

'Right, fair enough. Now listen, Max. I'm putting a twenty-four-hour armed guard on your home until further notice. When you want to see Mary or Dean, tell them to come to you. We'll also put a check on your phone and see if anyone's intercepting your calls. We're not having people threatening a senior officer. And try and keep Louise at home with you if you can, Max, for the moment at least. I know she's a politician and she's not subject to us—'

'I don't think that will be a problem, Tom. We know we have a lot of talking to do.'

'OK, buddy, you go home and do it. I'll be in touch.'

'Thanks.'

Louise was still silent, and Max felt she probably shared his shock symptoms. They reached their home and saw that two police officers were already standing guard on the place, which was probably just as well as the journalists were gathering; about seven or eight of them so far, with photographers in tow.

Bellamy parked the car on his drive, and signalled the police officers to come to him. He wound down his window.

'Sergeant,' said Bellamy, noticing the stripes just in time, 'please will you and your colleague escort Mrs Bellamy into the house while I talk to that lot.' He turned to Louise. 'Just give me a minute with them, Lou, and I'll be with you.'

He moved towards the clutch of people, now seven men and two women, standing outside the wall of his front garden.

'Now then, ladies and gents, I'll tell you what I know and that's all you're going to get today, so you'll be wasting your time hanging around because nothing else will be forthcoming. I think you know the basic facts. My wife was leaving a speaking engagement when a man shot at her and the people she was with. A party agent, Harry Mallon, was hit on the arm and is being treated in hospital, though I understand his injury is not life-threatening. A journalist you may know, Steven Ryan, was hurt rather more seriously, though I understand his injuries are not life-threatening. My wife is badly shaken, as any of you who trespass on our property today will be. Now go and throw your sub-editors a morsel and get off our backs, there's good boys and girls.'

Bellamy hastened into his house and slammed the door behind him. On their sofa, Louise, still looking pale, had already poured them two large brandies and her eyes raised to him as he approached her. He saw a number of emotions there, but none of them, so far at least, looked like reproach.

PART TWO

The Hunters and the Hunted

Some people, defining Dean Matheson purely by what he did for a living, would probably describe him as a "nerd"; he did spend an inordinate amount of time in front of a screen of one kind or another. However, his appearance rather gave the lie to such a description. Dean was not only a good-looking lad; he also had a ruddy glow of health and well-being about him, which gave clear indications of the kind of thing he did when he wasn't at work, including playing midfield man for a leading amateur football side, being a member of the local swimming club and an occasional cross-country runner. He was also very keen – too keen, a few of his superior officers reckoned – on the company of young women.

'It's not surprising he's a whizz-kid on the computer stuff,' his immediate superior, Sergeant Matt Freeman, would say. 'The lad's got no energy left for anything else.'

Dean himself believed that working with computers wasn't so very different from the other things he did. If it didn't involve the same level of physical effort, it certainly demanded an equally intense level of mental effort, and as with football, swimming and running, it included judging what skills were appropriate and when, playing with hunches and instincts about the quality of the opposition, and putting up bluffs and feints when it seemed that they might be needed and might work.

His hacking and delving activities invariably started pointing things in certain directions, and as he examined what characterised the Cougars at the height of their fame, many of the signs kept pointing in the direction of Cavelcombe House and, in terms of the major personalities involved, Eric Irwin, manager of the group.

Much of the business concerning the Cougars' buying Cavelcombe happened before e-mail really began being widely used, and Dean found that the bulk of information available came from the archives of the local press. Isolated as Cavelcombe was, it became clear that the people who lived in the general area around it were unhappy about its new ownership and increasingly suspicious of the activities taking place there.

I am sure most inhabitants of this area would not be very keen on so-called "raves" happening in their vicinity, said one Mr Malcolm Pearson in the letters pages of a local paper. What now seems to be being proposed is to hand over one of the oldest and grandest houses in the area to people who want to turn the house and its grounds into a venue for a permanent rave.

This area lives and dies on its attraction to tourists, said someone signed "a local publican". If it now gets a reputation for being a headquarters for activities which make stag and hen nights look like tea parties, the kind of tourists we would all prefer will soon decamp to less decadent areas, and we will only have ourselves to blame.

This correspondence gave rise to an outspoken counterblast from Eric Irwin, and Dean considered that the language used did make clear enough certain characteristics of the man using it.

> *Those citizens of Cornwall still rooted in the days of Poldark and Jamaica Inn, who still want to see stage coaches rattling past on dreadful old roads and smugglers stashing their contraband away in caves near the sea, really do need to wake up and realise what modern tourists want, because if they don't, they might find their wish to be transported back to the old days might come all too terribly true, and all the many evils of the so-called "good old days" – poverty, squalor, disease, infanticide – will be coming back too.*

Eric seemed to have largely batted that one away, but a further burst of correspondence when Cavelcombe had been in the possession of the Cougars for a few years took a more specific and serious turn.

> *Cavelcombe House – Coastguard and Police Alerted,* said one headline. *After a Coastguard helicopter identified up to fifty or sixty people in the grounds of Cavelcombe House, most of them, both male and female, completely naked and some openly indulging in intercourse, the local police visited the house, suspecting, as many people in the area now do, that illegal drugs were being used. Tests conducted on some of the young people did suggest the use of various substances, legal and otherwise, and it is thought that closure of the premises is to be considered by the local council.*

This produced a burst of cold anger from Irwin, which moved beyond historical analogies to specific threats.

> *Cavelcombe House is a private establishment, and unless the law as I understand it has changed, people on private ground who are not exhibiting their bodies to the world in general (and it needed a helicopter to break into the house's privacy) are entitled to wear or not wear what they like, and if anyone, voyeuristic helicopter pilots or anyone else, chooses to challenge that in a court of law, I will happily entertain them. As for consuming illegal drugs, the management of Cavelcombe House, like most normal hosts, do not conduct strip searches on their guests, and if anyone was using illegal substances on our premises, they were not doing so with the sanction of the owners, and again, if people should decide to challenge that assertion, we will see them in court.*

Something about Eric Irwin, Dean felt, was disturbing. His defence, so fierce and potentially menacing, sounded as if he was protecting something or someone; that he knew he was sitting on a hornet's nest and couldn't get off, meaning he needed to severely warn off any unwanted curiosity.

Dean then took another look at the grounds of Cavelcombe House, this time without the nudity and the writhing bodies. Dean was young and thought of himself as generally open-minded, but he had been brought up with church-attending parents and naked orgies were rather too much for him to assimilate. He looked at a video prepared by the new owners of Cavelcombe, who had turned the place into a hotel and wanted to attract visitors.

This time, a drone had been used to fly over the present grounds of Cavelcombe, emphasising the comfortable garden and seating areas outside. However, the grounds were extensive, and much of it was simply grassland, though the grass was more carefully looked after than it had been in the former regime. Some bodies formerly exposed by the helicopter would not have been visible on the ground now because of the long grass.

Dean suddenly froze, almost as if his careful surveillance of a not particularly interesting area of grassland had just turned into something rather more sinister.

In his later years of schooling and his university days to follow, Dean had done various summer jobs to provide himself with holiday money. One of them had been in a cemetery, the job arranged for him by his councillor father, and mainly concerned with cutting grass and digging graves, and of course, some men he worked with found it amusing to tell him gruesome details of who was buried there and what the place was like at night, most of which were obviously fabricated and which he found more amusing than frightening.

However, on one occasion, when having a chat with one of the more friendly and intelligent guys whose name was Pete, though Dean couldn't remember his surname, the subject was treated more seriously. Dean wanted to know whether it was possible to tell if a body was buried under a patch of land, partly because he was a respectful youth and he didn't want to take liberties with ground which could be precious to some people, and partly because he thought it would be a useful thing to know if he was embarking on a career of fighting crime; his ambition to join the police had formed in his early teens.

Pete had a habit of being a bit of a "know-all", but on this occasion, what he said did sound generally plausible.

'It's quite likely that the grass might be longer than it is on normal ground, and the colour of it could also be a bit different, depending on what kind of soil it is, of course. On the other hand, if people have planted lots of flowers and whatnot in it and then all the people who knew the deceased have themselves died and the place is left untended, it will grow wild quickly. You can also find that gravediggers who are a bit too keen about filling the space will leave little mounds, or, more often, the ones who are lazy about it will leave slight recesses. In any case, you can reckon if land has been used to bury bodies, both the level of the ground and the colour of the grass will vary a bit anyway, perhaps quite a lot. It is likely that it won't be smooth or uniform. You don't get many bowling-green lawns in cemeteries, even in parts where bodies haven't usually been buried.'

The drone's leisurely survey of the grounds of Cavelcombe House Hotel included new flower beds, pretty and colourful enough, and scattered bits of woodland where the new owners had planted trees, but it also had a couple of areas further away from the house where the colour and level of the ground didn't seem to fit very well with the ground around it. Parts of the area were bumpier than others; parts had thicker grass, parts had odd mounds. Most people looking at it would just accept that the ground was variable, but to Dean, on the basis of his past experience, it was suspicious and disturbing.

Now he had to decide what to do. If he told DCI Bellamy of his suspicions and the decision was then taken to dig the ground up, even if the hotel owners could be persuaded to allow such a thing, and nothing was found, his career might not be ended but it would suffer a blow from which it might never recover. On the other hand, if he said nothing and bodies were subsequently discovered in the grounds of Cavelcombe House, fingers could well be pointed at him for having suspicions and not doing anything about them.

Dean was due for an after-work visit to his swimming club. He often found the rhythm of swimming conducive to thought, and at the moment, he needed quite a lot of it.

Dean Matheson's ambition to join the police had initially been triggered when he was thirteen after his father had been violently mugged and needed to spend four days in hospital. His two years of service so far sometimes seemed to him a process of draining away his innocence day by day. At the back of his mind, there was a suspicion that he was already seeing crime too easily. Did undulations in the ground and different coloured grass really mean that bodies might be buried in the grounds of a Cornwall country hotel? Would DCI Bellamy listen to him and dismiss his thoughts with a weary smile? Wouldn't it be a good deal less risky to just put his suspicions to one side until the case became clearer?

Twenty lengths of the pool, he calculated, would lead him to a decision.

Mary Stanhope, too, was finding herself with food for thought, if not thoughts quite so drastic as Dean's. With the use of journalistic articles on the Cougars and media interviews with them collectively and separately, she was piecing together the history of the band, and it didn't take long for her to discover that two relationships emerged as the most powerful and influential in their career. One was the difficult and occasionally very aggravated friendship between Tony Richards and Bill Massiter. They met at a gig in Leicester for another band – Richards grew up in Leicester – when Bill Massiter, a modest enough youth of nineteen at the time, was acting as a kind of "reserve member" of the group whose gig it was, in case their lead guitar was the worse for wear with drink, which he was quite often, apparently. Only after the Cougars broke up did Richards allege that his early relationship with Bill had a sexual element to it, which Massiter subsequently denied emphatically, saying he had just been strongly attracted to his eventual wife, Josie.

Their strained relationship expressed itself in the lyrics of some of their songs, including a few of the biggest – 'What Are You to Me?', 'Mask of Deception' and 'Love Pains'.

The second relationship was that between the band members and Eric Irwin. They didn't start with a manager. In the early days, Bill Massiter effectively ran their activities himself, but the other members got increasingly restive with some sloppy gig arrangements and mediocre venues, and the band initially asked Richard Bellamy, who had written supportive articles about them, to handle their affairs. For two years, they made considerable progress, though by that time, Richard was struggling to find time for them alongside his other press and media work and suggested to them that they would need to find someone else soon. When Eric Irwin, then a theatre impresario, came backstage to talk to them after a gig in Hammersmith and talked about what he could do for them, promising an ambitious approach involving foreign tours as well as in the UK, he sold his ideas to the band, even if selling them to Bill took rather longer than it did with the others.

Since then, Irwin had been the dominant figure in the whole operation. Doug Lane's drinking started to be a problem until Irwin told him in no uncertain terms to get his act together or leave the band – 'Drummers, Dougie boy, are ten a penny; boozed-up drummers are food for the dole queue.' Likewise, Manuel Orestes, generally indifferent to his personal appearance, had a tendency to turn up for gigs in old vests and torn jeans, and he was told to smarten himself up or leave the band; Irwin even arranged a "wardrobe fund" for him.

Tony Richards and his male fans were also put under strict

controls by Irwin, firstly by arranging a "reserve" dressing room where Richards could meet them without bothering the other members of the band, and eventually insisting on two dressing rooms for every gig. He also checked that any male fans allowed to see "Rory Blaze" after a gig were both over eighteen and aware that Rory was gay. He also weeded out the professional rent boys, which made Bill Massiter suspect that their manager had once been a pimp.

Irwin, older and more experienced than any of the Cougars, was the dominant personality in the whole set-up, but as far as Mary could see, his influence was generally positive and constructive for the band. It was only after Irwin had started managing them that the Cougars really made it to the big time, meaning the members of the group became very reluctant to question or defy Irwin's control of them, even allowing for occasional tensions between Irwin and Bill. Eric Irwin had two broken marriages behind him, which Mary, something of an expert on assertive and potentially dangerous men, suspected was because not many women would be prepared to tolerate the levels of control which Irwin wanted. The Cougars generally put up with it because Eric Irwin was making them rich; for his wives, it would have been a matter of being pushed around day after day, both in and out of bed.

People who knew something about Mary Stanhope's career might suspect her of being something of an agony aunt figure, very maternal and cosy, dispensing homespun advice and counsel. However, they would probably start to revise their opinions on meeting her. Mary was not stout and motherly; she was businesslike and sharp-eyed, with the ability to be everything from poker-faced to smiling and considerate. She had already been largely responsible for a number of convictions for both heterosexual and homosexual rape and sexual abuse. She knew something about the Irwins of the world and nothing struck her more forcibly about him than his similarity to the military non-commissioned officer type, the company sergeant major, determined to maintain strict discipline and perhaps even more importantly to keep the officers about him happy. Mary couldn't get away from the feeling that, much as Irwin was controlling the Cougars, some higher, unseen hand was controlling Irwin. All the members of the band referred, usually half-jokingly, to "Eric's maids", with the unspoken but clearly implied insinuation that Eric tended to favour brief liaisons with generally submissive women; they make his coffee and iron his shirts, Tony Richards commented in an article, and that's about as far as it goes.

Mary liked it when the cases she dealt with started to produce pointers in definite directions, and at the moment, the route sign was pointing quite unambiguously in the direction of Eric Irwin. Capable of murder? Probably not. Capable of serving someone who was capable of murder? Quite possibly. But, as far as talking to DCI Bellamy was concerned, she would suggest rather than define. On the basis of an admittedly brief acquaintance, she considered that this DCI was able to work things out for himself; she could point him in interesting directions without flashing big neon signs in front of him.

Max Bellamy, now in his own study with police guards at the front and back of his house, could at last take the time to think through the day as dispassionately as possible. He thought of himself as a man in charge of his emotions and if, as they had today, they threatened to dominate his thinking and planning, he needed to step back and look them over, as if placing an imaginary camera somewhere to look down on his wife and himself.

Louise had taken to her bed for the time being. Whether she was actually sleeping, Bellamy doubted, but he knew her well enough to know that she could think things through better when she was resting and not distracted by the demands of other people.

He was still conflicted within himself. On the one hand, he knew instinctively that he would be happier in his mind if she was working somewhere in a totally unthreatening environment. Her job as an environmental journalist had sometimes taken her to some potentially dangerous places, but they were circumstances of general risk rather than situations where people would be particularly focused on damaging or coercing her. Now she was in the public eye, up there in front of the cameras and on show to everyone who didn't like her for reasons which were bound to be malevolent or deranged because they couldn't possibly know her. She was no longer just herself; she was representing things, including her political party, women in power and authority generally, and Bellamy knew well enough there were people who could and would take violently against her for being a representative of any one of those things.

And however much he had seen of death and destruction, including most recently the ignominious end of a successful musician and friend of his father, he knew that everyone, including him, had their cliffside point, the edge-of-the-abyss experience when what had happened was more than they could assimilate or live with. For him, he suspected it would be the sudden loss of Louise, the sustenance of his life, and it dawned on him that, for once, he needed to extend to himself at least a consideration comparable to the one he generally extended to others.

His phone went again and he cursed under his breath for a few seconds, grabbing the receiver as if he wished to do damage to it.

'Bellamy,' he growled.

'DCI Bellamy, Jack Henshaw.'

Absurdly, Bellamy almost saluted.

'Hello, sir.'

'How are you?'

This was not a question a chief constable had ever asked him before. Bellamy made an effort to bring himself back to the here and now.

'I am well, thank you, sir.'

'And Mrs Bellamy?'

'She is relaxing, sir. I think the guard we acquired so quickly has enabled her to rest and recover.'

'Good. I think I probably know the answer to this question, Bellamy, but you are a much-valued member of this force and I think it's only fair that I should ask it. We all know we are ourselves at risk, more or less every time we set out on a case, but when it comes to our loved ones being put in danger, that, I think, can be above and beyond what might reasonably be expected. The Massiter case was obviously going to be high profile because of the Cougars' media standing, but this shooting today has put it into a different league, and I am perfectly willing to hand it over to Scotland Yard if need be, which will remove the future risk from you and your wife. I'm not asking you to tell me here and now what you want to do; you will want to consult Louise, of course, but no one, I repeat no one, is going to think any the worse of you if you decide to hand it over. There are things which are even more important than police work, sacrilegious as that might sound to some people, and I think you must have options available.'

With a sudden sense of alarm, Bellamy thought he had been struck dumb, but he demanded of himself that he started talking, right now. Playing the coy wallflower on a murder case was not how he worked. He forced his words out.

'Thank you, sir. I think I can speak for both Louise and myself in this matter at least; we are grateful for such consideration. My own inclination is to stay with the case, having got this far and having some personal interest in it; my father was, for a time, agent for the Cougars and he was at school with their drummer. But in this instance, I must confer with my wife and if she is adamant that she wants us to disassociate ourselves from it, I will accept her point of view. May we have a couple of days of consultation?'

'Of course. In the meantime, Inspector Price is well able to keep an eye on things. Write this number down, Bellamy' – he read the number – 'and when we've finished the call, phone me back on it when you're ready to. Then we'll take it from there.'

'Yes, sir. Thank you, sir.'

And three bags full, sir, thought Bellamy. But then, he had no great problem with "sir-ing" people when they sounded and behaved like Jack Henshaw had just done.

He went into the main bedroom. Louise looked to be asleep, but he had no sooner walked into the room when she spoke to him, without opening her eyes.

'Who were you talking to, darling?' she said.

'No less a being than Chief Constable Jack Henshaw. He's offered to hand the whole thing over to the hard cases in Scotland Yard.'

Louise sat up. 'And what did you say?'

'I said I would talk to you, which is what he was suggesting I should do. I think he thinks I might be too likely to get shot if I'm not careful.'

Bellamy saw the gleam in his wife's eye and subsided into silence. He knew that gleam; it meant that she had something to say and she was going to say it.

'If you'd asked me about that just after it happened and I was deeply worried about Harry – Harry can be and is a pain in the neck sometimes, but he's my pain in the neck and he's good at what he does – I would have said yes to that; get the London boys on it and get you off the hook. But I didn't just marry you because I fancied the look of you, Max, though I did; I'll not deny that lust entered into it. I married you because you're good at whatever you do, and I hoped that some of that would rub off on me, and it has; I'm an MP, for God's sake. All these London spooks cavorting around us day and night, I think it would drive me crazy quite soon. We'd be better off with you doing what you do. I'm sure now that Henshaw will give you any backup you ask for. And in any case, as you said before, it's part of what we do; it comes with the territory. I'm not giving up what I want to do for the sake of some crazies waving their dicks around. Now gird up your loins, Bellamy, and come over here, because I need consoling, and you can spend an hour or two consoling the hell out of me.'

Bellamy, now with a grin fixed immovably on his face, went across to her, with the mounting sense of anticipation these moments always aroused in him.

Dean was taking a shower at his local pool. His twenty lengths had done what he wanted them to do, more or less; he had decided that he did need to talk to DCI Bellamy about what the grounds of Cavelcombe House were suggesting to him. Arriving at the decision didn't mean that he was yet entirely happy about it. DCI Bellamy was sometimes referred to behind his back as "Daddy Cool", and yes, he had a relaxed, easy-going air about him, fair enough, but it was also well known that he didn't suffer fools gladly and he was quite capable of cutting up rough when the mood took him, or when someone was talking what he considered to be nonsense. Dean could see in his mind's eye Bellamy's cold blue-eyed stare resting on him, followed by some devastating put-down, all the more cutting because of the dispassionate way it was expressed: "You've been watching too much crime drama, Matheson; what have you been doing, bingeing on Silent Witness? I never knew you were such an expert on grass, Dean; do you do gardening in your spare time?"

Well, the answer to that would be a kind of yes, Dean thought, stepping into the drying area in front of the showers. His suspicion of the ground around Cavelcombe House wasn't based on nothing; it arose from this temporary job in the cemetery.

Dean felt, without seeing, a man's eyes resting on him as he towelled himself. He had been a good-looking boy and now he was a good-looking young man, and his fitness activities, including the swimming, had built him a lean and athletic physique. His current girlfriend, a trainee teacher called Rachel, liked to watch him showering sometimes; they also showered together on occasions.

Dean had no problem with men looking at him. Rachel, a strikingly attractive girl, had told him of the unwanted attentions she had to deal with sometimes, and Dean was aware that there wasn't as much difference between the sexes in that respect as some people made out; young guys could be seen as sex objects by some, just as much as girls could. He knew the way he felt about Rachel at times; yes, she was a clever and accomplished young woman, but on occasions, he desired her with a depth and intensity which quite frightened him.

Cavelcombe House, he knew, had been used for overtly sexual purposes on a number of occasions, including the nude parties, verging on orgies, which the local coastguard had seen. It wasn't so difficult to believe that such events, involving very young people who were reputedly using drugs as well as drink, could sometimes get out of hand, with consequences which could be very serious indeed.

By the time he was dressed and ready to go, Dean had resolved that he needed to take his suspicions to DCI Bellamy. Yes, he might be shot down in flames, and his knowledge of Bellamy was still quite limited, but somehow he doubted it, and even so, if it had to be, it had to be. Duty was a word Dean had heard a lot in his training, and the way some people defined it didn't always agree with the way he defined it, but duty was what it amounted to, as far as DC Matheson was concerned.

Louise and Max had made love, not frantically or wildly, but in the considering, deliberate way which was typical of them. On this occasion, it was Louise who had fallen asleep afterwards and Max was glad of it; he knew how shaken she had been by the shooting and the fact that she had recovered sufficiently to be able to sleep was a positive development.

He had turned his phone off before they started and inevitably, when he picked it up, there were already three calls waiting. He put the phone back down on the bedside table and sighed. Working himself into the ground had never been Bellamy's philosophy and he knew well enough the mistakes and miscalculations which could be made by exhausted police officers, particularly senior exhausted police officers whose mistakes could snowball until they involved a lot of people both inside and outside the police force.

The Englishman in Bellamy forbade him from wandering about stark naked, even in his own home, and he put his underpants back on before taking the phone with him into what he and Louise treated as the guest bedroom, with its own en suite.

Sitting on the bed, he returned the first call, which was from Inspector Elaine Price.

'Max. Are you OK? God,' she said, before he had the chance to say anything. Her breathless tone and her very rare use of his first name showed just how unsettled she was, a rare occurrence for Elaine.

Bellamy was immediately touched. His new seniority didn't stop him from appreciating people who genuinely cared for him.

'I'm OK, Elaine, thanks. Louise was shaken up, of course, but she's asleep now. Have we made any progress yet?'

'Some. We've got the guy who made the call. His name's Tyler Moss, a pretty small-time con man, and not, I think, the gunman at the constituency office. Moss probably isn't the sort of guy you'd trust to do such a thing. He is both known to the police and not the smartest operator. He phoned from a hotel lobby meaning he was seen on their CCTV. It seems to me that they, whoever they are, grabbed the first known crim they could get their hands on and told him what to do. The stupid sod is still denying it even though they've got him on camera doing it. He's small fry, anyway, and I doubt whether he'll ever tell us who put him up to it, I suspect because what we could do to him doesn't match up to what they could do to him. A night in a cold cell is one thing; having the shit beaten out of him in some disused warehouse somewhere is quite another.

'He will say nothing but "it was an important man", so we don't know, at this stage, whether it was politics or terrorism, or some kind of private vendetta. They're examining his calls in case they can trace the one where they told him what to do, because I very much doubt whether they would have let him see them face to face.'

'No, probably not.'

A silence; Bellamy's mind still half on the case and half on his wife's situation. Elaine realised this was as much as she was going to get at the moment.

'Are you coming in tomorrow, sir?' she said eventually.

Bellamy roused himself to concentrate on the matter in hand and try to get the repeating spectacle of his wife's face as that gunman suddenly appeared to rest for a while.

'It depends, Elaine. We've got a police guard on the house, front and back, at the moment, but I don't know how Louise is going to feel about me leaving the house. If she wants me here, I'm going to stay here and do what I can to run the case over the phone. I'm due to talk to Mary and Dean shortly, anyway.'

Another silence. In her mind's eye, Elaine saw him there, with that slightly cast-down look on his face, the nearest she'd ever seen him get to emotionalism. She could tell from a certain quality in his voice, perhaps an uncharacteristic element of weariness or resignation, that he was still knocked off course himself. She had known this guy since he joined the force from journalism; he'd made his way up through the ranks and taken her with him. Notions of his indestructability had formed in her mind, but of course, as she knew very well, no one was. Something inside her had always said that this guy was different, this guy was more than the average macho chancer who stayed just about inside the law without bothering himself too much about bunny-hugging human rights stuff. Bellamy was, in some ways, a one-off, and losing him to some less dangerous and challenging occupation would be a severe and damaging loss, both to the force and to her personally.

'Sir?' she said, even as she was trying to form the words.

Something in her tone, even contained in the single word, alerted Bellamy. He forced his mind to concentrate on the person, not the police inspector.

'I dare say you immediately get suspicious if people from lower ranks start paying you compliments, and it's not something I would usually do, but I've worked with a few and you are the best. I know you have a lot to think about, but please don't allow yourself to conclude that you are anything but a hell of a good police officer, and you would be a serious loss to the force. And to me. Sir.'

Bellamy had made himself, over time, control his own emotions having realised that they were usually more of a hindrance than a help, whatever he was doing, and that had made him instinctively suspicious of emotions in others, but he could spot the genuine clearly enough when he heard it. In spite of himself, he was touched.

'Thank you, Elaine. That means a lot to me. Yes, I need to think but in some ways this business has made me more determined than ever to take down whoever is behind all this, because doing what they've done has made it personal. Louise and I have already, I think, decided that we can't stop doing what we're doing because of this; it would mean that criminals would be forever afterwards handed a perfect way of stopping people from investigating their activities. I want you to arrange a meeting of the team in my office tomorrow at ten thirty, the team to include you, me, DS Stanhope and DC Matheson, and we'll then thrash out where we go from here. In the meantime, Louise and I will work out what we do about the politics of the situation.'

'Yes, sir. Thank you.'

Over a long evening, Max and Louise Bellamy discussed the situation. After a meal, the weather was temperate enough for them to spend some time on their covered patio, and Louise had already worked out that, by this time, Max would have had some thoughts about who the culprits were and what they should now do.

She glanced across at him, sitting in his characteristic pose of one leg over the other and taking occasional brief sips at his wine. She knew him very well and it seemed obvious to her that he was already over the worst of his anxiety and shock, and he had been giving the whole business some thought. Time, she thought, to wind him up and let him go.

'So, Max,' she said. 'Any thoughts about what or who we might be dealing with?'

'A few. In the first place, this strikes me as an individual, or at most a couple, rather than a large criminal organisation. An organisation would not have relied on some small-time chancer who didn't have the sense not to make a call in an area likely to have CCTV. They would also know that getting me off the case is not going to stop the investigation from going ahead; a practised criminal organisation would know well enough that if one senior police officer is not available, for whatever reason, another one will take their place. They would also know that nothing is quite so likely to encourage the police to go after people as physical threats to their personnel. So we're talking about a single person, or at most a couple, who have, for whatever reason, been panicked into doing something highly inadvisable which they might already be regretting.

'Secondly, it is almost certainly someone closely connected with the Cougars, and someone who had something to do with the death of Cougar Bill. And I'm afraid, Louise my love, that there may well be other deaths involved here somewhere along the way. They have already almost confessed that, because they know as well as we do that if Bill had simply killed himself, whatever investigations we might undertake would come to nothing anyway. This suggests powerfully to me that this is not an isolated incident; it is the culmination of something which has been going on for some time.

'Thirdly, of the people we know so far, I would rule out Manny Orestes and Doug Lane being knowingly involved in this, Manny because he's too laid back, and I think that isn't an act – he really is like that. And Doug because he just isn't bright enough to be a conspirator. I would think that Tony Richards knows more than he is yet letting on; Richards, to me, uses his very upfront persona as a gay man as a kind of camouflage so that people will think that, because he is open about that, he is therefore open about everything else, but I don't think he is. I also think Josie Massiter knows more than she's letting on; she gave me the impression that she was covering for someone, and I don't mean her young fancy man.

'Fourth, I think illegal drugs are mixed up in this somewhere, and we have to consider the possibility that the death of poor Bill is largely a red herring, an accidental offshoot of something much bigger, for Bill to have been using drugs as liberally and casually as he was – his storeroom was full of the stuff and while I don't doubt he could produce receipts and sales documents to prove that it was all coffee or something and none of the boxes contained drugs, I wouldn't attach much weight to that. It's still very difficult for the authorities to catch drug traffickers and dealers, especially when they're able to surround their activities with effective cloaks which they've developed after years of experience.

'Finally, before I shut up and let you have your say, much as it grieves me to say it but I do think they are likely to have another go. They have acted impulsively and made a mistake which they are probably now realising, but once you start this kind of stuff, stopping it becomes more and more difficult. As soon as you stop, you are seen to be retreating, and then you have lost control; you are the chased, not the chaser. It's this last bit that's got me worried the most, and I thought about doing what I suppose a lot of husbands would do, the line of least resistance, saying "it's all a flash in the pan, darling, they've already burnt themselves out" but I don't think it is. So far, the only person to get really hurt is the journalist, poor Steven Ryan, more or less an innocent bystander, but once they realise that the frightener hasn't worked and their bluff has been called, next time they are likely to go for a bigger hit. And in spite of what I just said about the police getting more keen if their personnel are threatened, we have to bear in mind, as with the Manningham case again, that police work isn't just about the police any more. It's also about the politicians, and if someone in your whips' office, or even the whips' office on the other side, starts telling the guys up top that the death of some clapped-out old pop star – that's not me being cynical, it's the kind of cynicism I would expect from them – is not worth all this hassle, you and me could find ourselves put out to grass for a while so some tame coroner can pronounce that Bill has "committed suicide while the balance of his mind was disturbed" and we'll see no more gunmen because whoever it is has got what they wanted.'

He sipped at his wine again and looked at Louise to see how she was taking it.

'Oh, Max,' she said eventually, 'how dearly I wish I could find something in that summary of yours I could disagree with, because if you're right, we are going to see more bloodletting. But, as usual, you are making a lot of sense and as much as I would want to shoot holes in your reasoning, I can't. So what we are going to have to do now is work out what precautions we will need to take for the foreseeable future. I've never let bully boys run my life, and I'm not starting now.'

Bellamy looked across at his wife, and not for the first time, a flood of gratitude that this courageous and constant woman was his wife overcame him. He walked across to her and kissed her.

They then got down to the business of making arrangements to cover the next three months of Louise's political and Max's police career. The planning included phone calls to Tom Hollins and to Louise's agent, Harry Mallon. They established that Steven Ryan, the journalist who had been shot outside the neighbouring constituency office to Louise's, was comfortable in hospital and his injuries, as it was turning out, were neither life-threatening nor life-changing. The gunman had been captured on CCTV, though the pictures were not particularly helpful as he was well disguised and obviously knew that, this time at least, his brief was to injure, not to kill, and to make sure whoever was injured would be someone peripheral rather than the main characters who were the real target. It was the fear of what could happen to them next which was the main weapon, and if and when it did happen, the threat would expire.

Louise's engagements were examined in detail. Her weekly MP surgery would be given a security guard, for the time being at least, and any visits she made would involve a careful survey of the access issues, with a view to as little public exposure as possible. She would be also accompanied by an armed security guard. Bellamy would himself be armed whenever he left the confines of his office. Neither of them was very happy with arms being involved, but as Louise announced at one point in the proceedings, 'The good guys have to be able to fight dirty as well.'

The next day, Bellamy left for his office while Louise stayed where she was, still with a police guard on the house, for Harry Mallon to pay her a visit. Bellamy was all too aware of the gun in a concealed pocket just above his waist on his left side, making it an easy matter to reach into the pocket with his right hand. He also wore a bulletproof jacket under his uniform shirt at Louise's insistence.

He chose to see Dean and Mary separately, meaning he could concentrate entirely on what each one of them was saying, rather than have to juggle the importance of their contributions between them. He started with Dean, on the rather thin basis that this one would probably not take as long as Mary's investigations of the relationships between the Cougars.

Dean arrived, looking oddly awkward, as if unsure of himself. Bellamy was surprised at this; Dean Matheson was very young, of course, but he was known to be a bright boy, and in Bellamy's experience, youth and intelligence rarely resulted in a lack of confidence.

However, if gentle handling would be needed to produce his best, so be it. In DCI Bellamy's book, rank did not go with mindless authoritarianism.

'So what have you got for me, Dean?'

'Suspicions, sir. That's mostly what it is. Whether you're going to see it as any kind of evidence, I'm not sure.'

'Well, try me.'

Dean swallowed and took a deep breath. He turned the screen he had with him towards Bellamy, and all Bellamy could see was grass, trees and bushes.

'This is drone footage of the grounds of Cavelcombe House, sir. It's obvious from the local reports and correspondence between the Cougars and their manager, Eric Irwin, so-called "Captain Storm", that the house was used by the Cougars for some time for partying, more often than not with some of their invited fans, and we know the locals were suspicious about what was going on, not least from the letters to the paper which Irwin sometimes answered himself.

'I worked for a while in a cemetery, sir, sort of a summer job, because my father worked for the council. I got to know a fair bit about how human remains can alter the appearance of the ground. Some of the guys who worked in the place had been there for years, and when it came to finding new plots, they could usually tell which ground hadn't yet been used, partly by the disturbance of the soil, partly by the different kinds of growth on the ground. If you look at the grounds of Cavelcombe House carefully, there seem to me to be reasonable grounds for supposing that there might be bodies buried in there, and I don't mean in the archaeological sense, sir, I mean from the last ten to thirty years.'

'You mean, from the times when the Cougars were having their parties?'

'That's what it looks like to me, sir. But I was still a bit unsure about bringing this to you, because there are other things which might be responsible for this; there could have been attempts at different kinds of gardening made during those years, though there doesn't seem to be much record of that. And it's interesting that Mr Irwin in particular was really fierce about defending the Cougars' parties from the locals, and adamant that the house and grounds belonged to them and no one else.

'It's also known that the kids who went to these parties came from all over the country, sometimes without telling their parents or friends they were going. If there were cases of missing kids, it might not have occurred to anyone to look to Cavelcombe House as a place where they might have gone, because they probably wouldn't have told their parents they were going there. And even if anyone did suspect Cavelcombe House, it would be easy enough for Irwin to deny any particular individual had been there.'

Bellamy was watching DC Matheson carefully. He saw Matheson as a bright young man, but still with elements and echoes of the boy, with a boy's romantic and sometimes adventurous imagination. This case was beginning to appear to him like a snowball rolling down a hill, doubling its size every ten minutes. What had started was a suspicious, though to most people quite straightforward, suicide of a man whose best days could fairly be said to be behind him and who might have legal and financial problems associated with importing drugs. Only Bellamy's previous knowledge of the subject concerned had thrown them off the suicide trail. Almost immediately afterwards, someone had reacted angrily and violently to the denial of the suicide allegation and had been prepared to mount a shooting to try and prevent further investigation. Now the suggestion was that the place where the Cougars used to let their hair down could also be a graveyard of as yet unidentified victims – of what? Illicit drug taking? Murder? And as Bellamy examined the countenance of his bright young constable, a powerful instinct was telling him that taking the easy option, that of telling Matheson that he was letting his imagination run away with him, would not do.

DC Matheson let the drone footage go on for several minutes longer, and it could not be denied that, viewed from the air, the grounds of Cavelcombe House were odd. But, of course, there could be many explanations, depending on the previous uses of the house.

Dean stopped, and a heavy silence descended over the two men. Bellamy, lost in thought, looked up and saw the younger man was looking very uncomfortable.

'You are right, Dean,' Bellamy said, and it was gratifying to see the boy's eyes relax. 'It is odd, and it's odd enough to warrant further investigation. But we have to go about this carefully. That place is now a hotel and we will probably need a search warrant to get anywhere near digging up their ground. Then, if we failed to find anything at all, we could find ourselves on the end of a lawsuit. Do we know much about the house before the Cougars got hold of it?'

'It spent some time as a school, sir, in the mid-nineteenth century, after the previous owner died – it was built in 1847 – and when the school closed down after some scandals about the boys running an alcoholic still and betting books, a local squire, Sir Wesley something or other, took it over and he was quite a bad lad, by all accounts, in terms of smuggling in various stuff and hiding it in the basement below the house. He was eventually done by the excise men, and the house became a hotel for a while. During World War I, it was used as a hospital for wounded troops, mainly navy men, and then it was owned by the Prendergast family for a good while until they could no longer afford to keep it going and they sold out to Eric Irwin, buying it on behalf of the Cougars.'

'So it wouldn't be too difficult, would it, to invent a cover story, either based on some episode in the house's history or some suspicions of what might have been there back in Roman times, perhaps, before the house was built? If we could camouflage our investigations with an archaeological dig, the owners might be more keen on the idea; it will put their hotel on the map, make a tourist attraction out of it. If nothing is found, no one's any the worse off; if something is, then we can take the investigation on.'

'Do you know any archaeologists, sir?'

'Only vaguely. But I know my wife does. Before she was elected as an MP, she worked as an environmental journalist and she's covered a few digs and explorations in her time. And given the history of Cavelcombe House, I would guess that a few archaeologists would be only too happy to have a go at it.'

'Thank you, sir.'

Bellamy saw that DC Matheson was beaming at him. Like so many people of his age, his smile performed a remarkable transformation of his already good-looking features, and Bellamy was touched in spite of himself; he sensed himself grinning in return.

'What for, Dean?'

'Taking it seriously, sir. I was afraid you'd tell me to dream on, or something.'

'This case has already caused my wife to be subjected to a terrifying experience by a gunman. Any leads we turn up are worth pursuing, Dean, because the sooner we crack this, the happier I'll be. Thanks for your thought and your observation, and I'll take it from here. Anything else you find out about the Cougars' past, or the past of the increasingly interesting Mr Irwin, please let me know.'

Bellamy allowed himself ten minutes before talking to Mary Stanhope. He was considering an archaeological professor friend of Louise's whose main job was concentrated on various digs in the general vicinity of the Midlands university where he worked, but he also wrote on environmental issues and had presented occasional programmes on those themes. Brian Duffield was bearded and fierce on occasions and Bellamy suspected that any favours he might be prepared to do for the police would come with a price which the police powers-that-be may or may not be prepared to pay, but he was certainly convincing and he knew his stuff. Cavelcombe House was outside his usual territory but it was the kind of place which did lend itself to archaeological excavation. Bellamy understood that some kind of building had been there long before the present house had been built, and knew of the tendency archaeologists talked about of new buildings being constantly built from the remains of older ones.

It was, undoubtedly, deceitful in some ways, but unlikely to do anyone any harm. If it did prove to be an interesting archaeological site, which it might well do, it would be a feather in Duffield's cap without too seriously ruffling the feathers of the present owners of the place, and if there were more recent bodies buried in the place then it immediately became police business and the owners by then would just have to like it or lump it.

However, it was time to turn to Mary Stanhope. As soon as she came in, Bellamy knew she had something to tell him. Unruffled and unhurried as she was, a sense of urgency still surrounded the brisk way she came in and settled herself down.

'OK, Mary, what have you got for me?'

She took a few pieces of paper from the folder she was carrying and laid them in front of him. People who actually wrote things down, Bellamy thought; they were a dying species, but they gave him a feeling of permanence.

'Mr Eric Irwin,' she said. 'I've done a summary of everything we know about him so far; I will transfer it to your computer, sir, but I thought you might want a quick look at this.'

Bellamy saw a few convictions in the man's younger years and time spent in a young offenders' centre, followed by football hooliganism charges in his late teens. And then, fairly suddenly it seemed, a change of direction. He took on one of the heavy metal bands whose members had a reputation as "bad boys" and became known for his sometimes highly outspoken defence of them. He started being treated as a kind of spokesman for "youth culture". He worked for one of the major record labels and then, still only in his late twenties, the Cougars, taking them from being a backing band for more famous acts, doing the colleges and universities, to a big noise in their own right.

'As you can see, sir,' Mary said, 'something happened to Mr Irwin along the way.'

She displayed a picture of the present day Eric Irwin. Immaculately suited, he looked like an ex-soldier who had made it in Civvy Street. Tall and now almost bald, Irwin had dark, prominent eyes which carried a certain menace about them which, combined with his muscular build, made him a figure few people would care to cross.

'He's dropped most of the East End from his voice,' Mary continued. 'You can almost hear him straining to remember to put his aitches in sometimes.'

She pressed her phone and Irwin could be heard being interviewed on some business programme, by the sound of it.

'All that pop froth, it's all old hat these days. Nice lads, in the main, and a few nice lasses, too, though not as many as there were, these days. I enjoyed managing the Cougars; special, they were. Didn't realise their own talent in the beginning. Modest lads. But those times are gone. Property is what it's all about these days; that's where the big business is. Ain't so much of a laugh.' Irwin could be heard trying to dilute "laugh" into something at least a bit distant from "larf", until he finished up almost putting an "e" on the end of it.

'There are two things which particularly strike me, sir, about Eric Irwin. One is the transition, which seems so complete and so relatively fast, from "down with the kids" pop group manager to big time, suited entrepreneur, that it's almost as if someone did a kind of conversion job on him, a sort of male Pygmalion/My Fair Lady thing, turning the cockney street boy into establishment man. Two, is the constant suggestion with him, to me at least, that someone is still pulling his strings, that underneath the now very smooth exterior he's still basically a gangster with a boss somewhere in the background. It was known that one of the reasons why the

Cougars made it to the big time was not just his ability to get them in line, like telling Rory to be careful with his boyfriends and Manny to dress himself properly, but also his big, wide elbows, shoving other bands off the line-up to get the Cougars in, even threatening people who wouldn't include the Cougars in their plans for the year.'

'Threatening them with what?'

'Reprisals. Putting the word around that the venue was awkward, or their security was lax, or they were too fond of letting the drug dealers in, that kind of thing. There are more venues competing for them than there are top bands ready to do live shows, which are very expensive. Irwin's methods of business, then and I think probably now, were intimidating and heavy.'

'Yes, I can remember my father referring to Eric Irwin a few times, come to think of it. He didn't like him. Irwin always refused interviews in those days and he wasn't too polite about it.'

'I didn't know your father was in that business, sir,' said Mary.

'Yes, he was a kind of poacher turned gamekeeper, I suppose. He started as a music journalist, and then started doing publicity for some of the bands. He was briefly an agent for the Cougars and he knew them well enough, though he tended to avoid them when Irwin was around.'

Bellamy found himself wondering why he had never included Irwin in his memories of the Cougars and he suspected his father's dislike was probably the main reason; if his dad didn't care for someone, the chances are his young self wouldn't either.

Mary ventured on the personal.

'Did your father like the idea of you becoming a police officer, then, sir?'

A "mind your own business" snappy retaliation came into Bellamy's mind, but he tended these days to think before he spoke, and it was not unreasonable for the people who worked as his subordinates to want to know more about their boss.

'No, he didn't, as you would probably expect. But I'm going to put to you, in the strictest confidence, Mary, what Dean suspects, and then you can give me your opinion as to whether Eric Irwin, as you know him so far, would be capable of such deeply dark stuff as Dean's suspicions suggest.'

Bellamy summarised in a few sentences the kind of secrets which Dean Matheson thought the grounds of Cavelcombe House might be hiding.

'Cut to the chase, Mary,' Bellamy said. 'Do you think Eric Irwin could be a murderer?'

'Not him personally, sir, not now, anyway. In his younger days, possibly, but now, he would get someone else to do it for him. I think he would be capable of that. There seem to me to be elements of the psychopath in Eric Irwin. He's also, to me, more of a number two than a number one, more likely to arrange things on behalf of a big boss man than do them under his own steam.'

When Mary had gone, Bellamy spent some time pondering over what Dean and Mary had offered. Not only food for thought, but a five-course meal of thinking, it seemed. And, as usual, it was the guy at the top who had to make the decisions about how, why and where such thoughts should be acted on, decisions which could cause him potentially career-threatening, even life-threatening problems if he got them wrong.

A man in late-middle age, whose best days are clearly behind him and who is probably an addict, takes his own life. Sad, deplorable, but it happens, too often. A simple little nettle in the great undergrowth of the world, but it seems as soon as this particular nettle is grasped, a whole spreading mass of poisonous weeds is slowly uncovered.

He had already asked Mary Stanhope to broaden her investigations so as to take in the full panoply of Eric Irwin's relationships, not only with the Cougars but with other manifestations of Irwin's business empire. A picture was forming in his mind as the huge jigsaw of the case began to fall into some kind of place, but it was a picture whose darkness was still widespread and very full of people who didn't want to be involved in anyone's investigation, people who could quite possibly be prepared to kill to save themselves.

Not for the first time, Bellamy felt a twinge of nostalgia for his journalist days, reporting the workings of others' minds rather than puzzling through the mazes himself. And always, with this case in particular, Louise was there in the back of his mind, Louise who he did not think he could live without and who could be seriously threatened by this case.

The thinking-fest grounded on.

PART THREE

The Spreading Poison

Four Weeks Later

Standing in a windy field in Cornwall, looking over grassland, sand dunes and eventually, the sea, Max Bellamy was having a rare moment of merciless self-criticism, mingled with a growing and frightening sense of being in over his head.

He already knew that, were it not for Louise and her political allies, the case would probably already have been taken out of his hands and landed on the desk of someone at Scotland Yard, or quite possibly even the murky corridors of MI5. Louise had insisted, with the backing of some senior people in her party, that because Max and his father had known Bill Massiter and the rest of the Cougars personally, he was more qualified to deal with the situation than any anonymous Londoner.

Max himself had also continued to repeat that it was his case and should remain so, but he admitted privately, if to no one else, that there had been moments when the idea of some metropolitan hotshot taking the thing over had been tempting.

It was all getting very messy indeed. Only about fifty yards away from where he was standing, protective white tents were covering parts of the Cavelcombe House grounds, where five bodies had been found so far. A week ago, the archaeological fiction had been finally abandoned in the teeth of local and media scepticism, and the police had finally admitted that bodies had been found and still were being found, and they were bodies of people who had died not longer than twenty years ago.

Bellamy had won the co-operation of archaeologist Brian Duffield on the basis that, if the site did prove of archaeological interest, it would be given over to him and his company; if it didn't, the police would take over. The management of Cavelcombe House Hotel had co-operated on the basis of it being an archaeological dig which would "put Cavelcombe on the map", as Duffield had argued. With Bellamy's connivance, Duffield had also said, as no more than a passing thought, that if there were bodies buried on the site, the police would need to be informed. The bodies had been duly found, the hotel management were appalled and suspicious now of the origins of the whole project, saying that they should have been told the full story in the first place and arguing that they would need compensation for the "ruination of our business", as the manager Eileen Soames put it.

The situation was exactly what DC Dean Matheson's theories had implied, but Bellamy was still finding it difficult to adjust to the discoveries, not least because the forensic work done so far had intensified rather than clarified the general sense of perplexity and bewilderment the case was causing. Initial theories, that the bodies were young people who had died as a result of drug-taking or excessive alcohol consumption, or both, at the riotous Cavelcombe House parties conducted when the Cougars owned the house, had been largely confounded by the DNA evidence. Trying to match any of the bodies, all of them male, to young people who were known to have gone missing had proved impossible. It had been established that none of the bodies was actually British, and while they were all relatively young, none of them looked younger than their mid twenties. The racial origins of two of them still remained mysterious, but of the other three, two were almost certainly Iraqi and another was very likely to be. They had all been buried naked, but their clothes appeared to have been removed so carelessly and probably violently that small threads remained attached to them. No documentation of any kind had been found.

Already, Bellamy was having to face the reality that this had moved way beyond the apparent suicide of a single fading rock star, or even some manifestation of wild youth culture at the Cavelcombe House parties.

So far, the police had remained very tight-lipped about the whole business in an attempt to prevent a media feeding fest making life even more difficult for Bellamy than it already was. Several days ago, when the archaeological fiction had finally been abandoned and an increasingly frustrated print and broadcasting media were ensuring they had correspondents getting as close to Cavelcombe as they would be allowed, Bellamy had had a meeting with the three surviving members of the Cougars. Eric Irwin was also asked to attend but he declined, adding to Bellamy's difficulties. He said the Cougars were ancient history to him now and he was not going to be dragged into any pointless complications of the straightforward matter of Bill Massiter's suicide, sad and deplorable as it was.

Orestes and Lane were so shocked and upset that they seemed incapable of fully taking in the information they were given, and Bellamy had assumed neither of them was that good at acting and more or less discounted them being involved in whatever had resulted in these bodies. Tony Richards, shaken as he was, took his usual belligerent line, demanding to know what any of this had to do with the Cougars.

'I went to most of the Cavelcombe parties,' he said. 'Yes, there was a lot of sex going on, both in and out of the house, but mostly it was just bunches of kids having a lot of fun. As for drugs, Eric threatened anyone who came to the raves with the intention of selling drugs to the kids with all sorts of things up to and including castration. Some people who come out with that stuff might be regarded as blustering and trying to sound tough, but when Eric said it, people knew it was real. He did catch a few toerags who were trying to peddle coke or something, and though he didn't actually castrate them, he did beat the shit out of them before booting them out. But he never killed anyone, and when he had given some guy a working-over, he would phone an ambulance and say the guy had been fighting and was in a bad way, and none of them was going to say anything different in hospital in case when they got out, Eric did castrate them.'

Bellamy noted from this that not only had Dean Matheson's suspicions proved well founded, but Mary Stanhope's assessment of Eric Irwin's character was also proving to be accurate enough.

As he was watching events unfold, Bellamy noticed Elaine detach herself from behind one of the tents and start to move towards him. He knew Elaine as a tough and resilient character, but even she was walking a little unsteadily and he could see long before she was close to him that her face was paler than he could ever remember seeing it.

'Body number six found, sir, I'm afraid. Identification so far probably Iraqi again. Also buried naked. No identifying clothes or papers. I hate to say it, sir, but I think we're going to have to call in more people and expand the search area. And those guys over there' – she looked at the now large group of cameramen and journalists gathered on the boundaries of the Cavelcombe estate, about 200 yards from where Bellamy was standing – 'are starting to push their luck. With the best will in the world, we might have to start making arrests if any more of them sneak over that fence. I found one standing not more than fifty yards away from a tent; he scarpered pretty quickly, but I can remember his face and his shape, and if I see him again, I'll nick him.'

'OK, Elaine, I'll go over there and read them the riot act. Send me a couple of constables who are not doing anything in particular at the moment and I'll tell them to stand behind me, looking fierce. Preferably a couple of big lads.'

'We've got enough of them, sir.'

Bellamy headed for the journalist pack, now including, it seemed, three camera crews, feeling that he was in the right mood to deal with them today. Having been one of them himself, he was generally more inclined to see things from their point of view than many senior police officers might be, but this case seemed to have touched on something inside him which frightened him because he was uncertain about what it amounted to. He was aware that it felt like a kind of fear, with the mass discovery of bodies coming on top of a pointed threat to his wife, and indicating that whoever they were dealing with here would literally stop at nothing. How these discoveries were connected with the shooting incident had yet to be established, but identifications of when the men had died were so far clearly during the time of the Cougars' ownership of Cavelcombe House. Bellamy was always more ready to assert himself when something was threatening to trap him in a corner.

Two constables, both of them well over six feet tall and with muscular bodies to match, were duly detailed to accompany him, and the media chatter subsided gratifyingly as his triangular cohort approached the fence.

'Right. I mentioned before that I used to be of your profession. I didn't tell you that to suggest to you that we're all pals together and you therefore have carte blanche to do what the hell you like on a crime scene, but I think the more experienced of you will readily understand that there are rules governing behaviour on a crime scene, and if you and the police are going to work together, you have to be prepared to observe them, as we have to. I recognise that a mass burial of people who appear to have died quite recently is in the public interest and you have your jobs to do, but this is a very delicate situation and things could very easily turn nasty here if we're not careful. I don't think any of you needs to have much of an imagination to understand what the police officers on duty here are going through. We have found six bodies here so far; we know they are all male, that most of them are probably not older than about twenty-five, and none of them, as far as we can tell, is British. That, people, is all we know at the moment, and no amount of trespassing or other illicit activities are going to provide you with any more information, because we haven't got any more information. The officers on duty here are tired and stressed – they are human beings, like you – and if you lot contrive to make their jobs more difficult than they already are, there are going to be consequences, and that's no idle threat.'

Bellamy started to walk away, but stopped when a female voice called after him.

'Fair enough, Max, but when do we get a press conference?'

He turned in the direction of the voice, and saw the young woman briskly telling the photographer with her to "get a picture of him, now!".

'You get a press conference when we've got something to tell you,' he said. 'All we can do at the moment is conjecture, and you're not going to get much of a story out of that.'

As soon as he finished speaking, Bellamy realised the decision he had been thinking about was made, and he called Elaine to him.

'You said we know where Eric Irwin is, Elaine?'

'Yes, sir. He lives in Plymouth. He said he's working from home. He's happy to talk to you, but he doesn't want to come here – he "can't afford the time", sir.'

Her use of the quotation marks was very pronounced.

'Shall I bring him in, sir? Or fix up a phone face to face?'

'Arrange a face to face, Elaine, will you, and tell him straight out that if he can't find the time to talk to me, we'll find the time to send a car and bring him to us. And get the guys over there to fix me up one of their tents, so I can talk to him – and you – without that lot over there rubbernecking at us.'

Bellamy realised his moment of uncertainty and doubt had gone, and when he was in the tent appointed for the purpose, he looked at the face on the screen before him. Eric Irwin was now, like the Cougars, in his sixties, but he had worn better. He was handsome in a sharp, angular way, with a jaw which was only just beginning to turn into jowls, and dark, angry eyes. Bellamy suspected he was the kind of man he'd had dealings with before, who had not been as successful in life as he'd wanted to be and lived in a permanent state of barely suppressed anger and indignation.

'What can I do for you, DCI Bellamy? I'm not sure why or how this is any business of mine, and I'm a busy man. Time is money.'

In his present mood, this was more than Bellamy was prepared to take.

'Listen to me, Mr Irwin. So far, we have found six bodies in the grounds of Cavelcombe House, and they can be dated to the time when you and the Cougars owned the place, so there are questions to answer and I don't care how busy you are or how much time it takes. I'm investigating the deaths of six – so far – young men, and if you don't co-operate, I will send a car to bring you here, as of now. Is that clear?'

'Bloody hell. You are a bigshot, aren't you? OK, tell me what you want to know and I'll do my best to accommodate you. But don't treat me as if I'm a criminal; I have lawyers, Mr Bellamy. I also have a boss, like you have a boss, so just bear that in mind.'

'Are you threatening me, Mr Irwin?'

'I'm threatening no one, Mr Bellamy. But if you're intent on coming on the big man to me, bear in mind I have a few big men of my own. Just tell me what you want to know.'

'I want to know everything about your tenure of Cavelcombe House. Let me explain the seriousness of this situation. You – specifically, you – were the registered owner of this place for some years. Bodies have been found and their deaths can be traced back to your tenure, therefore, obviously, I must talk to you. So you can talk to me fully now or we can talk with lawyers present in the more formal circumstances of a police station.'

A brief pause followed, but the silence served to accentuate the tension rather than relieve it. Bellamy suspected that Irwin, however irate and dominant a personality, was not a stupid man. If it had to be a shouting match, so be it – Bellamy had been there before – but reasoned conversation was usually much more revealing. And quicker.

'OK, Chief Inspector, we seem to have got off on the wrong foot here. I am a bit shocked by what you're telling me – to be honest, I had a feeling to start with that this was some kind of grotesque prank. When I bought Cavelcombe House on behalf of the Cougars, they were desperate for somewhere to be left alone. They were well fed up with touring and hotels; they wanted a place where they could do as they wished, which wasn't anything complicated, just relaxing with their girlfriends or boyfriends as the case might be, in a place isolated enough to be sure that if any hacks or paparazzi appeared, their presence would be very obvious and they'd be easy to get rid of. Yes, we had parties there, and they got a bit raunchy sometimes, but that's just young people enjoying themselves. Now you tell me it's some kind of graveyard. And what makes you so sure that these bodies date from the relatively short time that the Cougars owned the place? That house has been there for a long time—'

'Dating techniques on bodies are very sophisticated these days, Mr Irwin and that's how we know. I'm perfectly prepared to show you the evidence if you wish. And at this stage, I'm not directly accusing anyone of anything. Who else, apart from you and the members of the Cougars, had access to the house, either by day or by night? We know that at least one member of the band had a drug habit – presumably he didn't bring that stuff in during broad daylight? There must have been visitors to the house occasionally – relatives or friends of the Cougars, and of course, all the people who went to the parties. Caterers would have delivered, cleaners would have come and gone, occasional media people would have attended for interviews, taxi drivers would have picked up and brought back members of the group and their friends. Quite a number of people would have known the layout of the place and how to get in and out, if necessary without being seen.'

'I think you're answering the questions for me, Mr Bellamy. All of that is true. Countless people could have worked out how to sneak something into the grounds of the place. It's a substantial estate, acres of it. To mount twenty-four-hour security around the entire place would have been ludicrously expensive. We concentrated on making sure the house and the area immediately around it were protected by CCTV, but to do that to the entire perimeter just wasn't on. We weren't going to have a panic on every time some stray cat or badger or something – it's in a rural area – wandered about.'

'We're not talking about occasional small wildlife, Mr Irwin. We're talking about bringing in human bodies, probably by night. To haul a human body over a perimeter fence in the dark is a serious undertaking, and that's to assume that they died elsewhere and were buried at Cavelcombe; it's possible that they died at Cavelcombe and were buried there. We're talking about serial killing here, Mr Irwin. We're talking about mass murder.'

With her usual immaculate timing, Elaine Price shoved her head around the flap of Bellamy's tent and raised seven fingers up to him. She looks even paler, Bellamy thought.

Irwin still hadn't replied.

'Inspector Price informs me that the body count is now seven,' Bellamy said quietly.

Irwin's voice was now more subdued, if still containing a distinct note of scepticism.

'OK – I will make enquiries of my own, Chief Inspector. I know the people who handled the security for the house at the time. However, there is a possibility you seem to be overlooking. Those men could have died elsewhere and were then, for whatever reason, brought to the house during the time we owned it, with the deliberate intention of shifting the blame from whoever actually did the killings to us.'

As I thought, Bellamy reflected, the man is no fool.

'Yes, sir, that is possible, and I will not discount it. I am simply aiming to get at the truth.'

The conversation ended in better spirits than it started, with Irwin agreeing to do what enquiries he could and then meet with Bellamy face to face in a couple of days. Bellamy still remained with the uncomfortable feeling that he had been fobbed off, and he also took note of the fact that the subject of the Cougars' drug suppliers had been carefully evaded.

Bellamy could not rid himself of the suspicion that, assertive as Irwin always was, he was the puppet rather than the puppet master, and his main concern was to cover for someone more powerful than himself. In fact, bearing in mind the shooting incident, the spontaneous hiring of someone who was hardly up to the job to make a threatening phone call, and the peculiar circumstances surrounding Bill Massiter's actual death scene, the growing implication was towards an authority higher than any of the individuals encountered so far. And that someone, whoever he or she might be, was feeling threatened, meaning that their actions might become increasingly desperate, and even reckless.

Bellamy resolved on further communications with his team. Something else was going to happen, probably quite soon, and if he and they could anticipate it, they might begin to be able to unravel the maze facing them.

In the Bellamy home, Louise was consulting with her agent Harry Mallon. She had known Harry for some time now. She knew his negative side well enough. Harry had already had quite a long career in the company of politicians without being a politician himself, and his constant underlying cynicism was not surprising in view of that, but he was also a competent and occasionally inspired administrator, and his legendary unflappability served him well in circumstances like the present one.

Aware that there were police officers to both the front and the back of the house, Louise and Harry were in the large front room, overlooking a substantial stretch of well-tended grass between them and the nearest road. It seemed a less than threatening environment.

'So how's Steven Ryan?' Louise said, half to herself, as she walked up and down the room consulting some papers she was holding, a habit she had in her normal office surroundings.

Harry was following a couple of streams of thought at the same time, as he not infrequently did. He rapidly adjusted to the question put to him.

'The bullet skimmed him rather than buried itself in him. He'll have a scar on his side, probably for life, and he'll be walking with a limp for a while. The girls in that office will be going nuts over him, no doubt, stuffing him with fucking cake and what have you.'

'Charmingly put, Harry. You missed your vocation, you know that? You should have been a counsellor, with such empathy and fellow feeling.'

'Very droll. Most politicians I've known don't need counsellors, they need shrinks.'

'Oh, really? Is that me, then, Harry? Do I need a shrink? Many more people taking pot shots at me, I probably will.'

'No, Louise, you're one of the sane ones. There are still a few, thank God. And that's the nearest you'll get to a compliment from me, if that's what you were fishing for.'

'If you're going to start being nice to me, Harry, then I really will need help…'

She stopped, as the faint buzzing noise she had noticed started to increase. Harry got up and moved towards the window. The distant dot expanded within a few seconds and they suddenly found themselves looking at a drone, hovering about fifty yards from the window.

'Kitchen, Louise, quickly. Right now – right now!'

He grabbed her arm and she started to turn, though not before seeing something long and black emerging from the body of the drone.

They had almost reached the kitchen when a massive bang resounded from outside the house, causing parts of the window to break. They both flattened themselves against the wall and saw the tall figure of Sergeant Phil Rhodes emerge in front of the window, carrying a large tubular gun under his arm.

After one booming shot, the drone had disintegrated and, small as it was, bits of it were spread in a wide area from the Bellamys' front garden to halfway down the road outside it.

Rhodes moved up to the window.

'Sorry about the glass,' he said. 'But that drone had a gun and it was about to riddle the house.'

Louise was still partly in shock, but she could already recognise the importance of what the police officer had just done.

'The glass can be repaired, Sergeant,' she said. 'We can't. You did your job, and we're grateful for it. Do you know any glaziers, Harry? You know everyone else round here.'

Louise saw that her hand, still carrying the papers she had been looking at, was shaking. Harry, a few feet in front of her, stared open-mouthed at the window. She seemed to hear him muttering something, but she could only identify the words "fucking glaziers".

'I told them it should have been a safe house,' Harry said. 'I told them. So bloody obvious that they'd have a go, whoever the bastards are, at Bellamy's own house. Fucking hell.'

Sergeant Rhodes handed the big gun to a constable and came into the house.

'I think the gentleman is right, Mrs Bellamy, even allowing for the colourful language. We will get in touch with Mr Bellamy and Mr Henshaw. I think they will be in agreement that we now need to find a safe house for you and Mr Bellamy.'

Three hours later, after quick approval and arrangements by the chief constable, Louise Bellamy and her police protection were travelling to the safe house, with no better information than it was in a largely rural spot some fifty miles from where they lived.

Max Bellamy, now trying to fight off a sinking feeling within him that the case was running out of control, was on his way to the safe house, but he was also listening to Elaine Price updating him on the latest developments. Elaine still didn't know about what had happened at the Bellamy house, and Bellamy had decided not to tell her until he and Louise were reunited. Whoever or whatever this was that they were now fighting against, Bellamy was determined to take one thing at a time and not be panicked by the pace of events into doing something stupid.

Elaine, on Bellamy's phone, looked, by her standards, red and flustered.

'The hacks have actually contributed something useful, sir,' she said. 'One of them had managed to break away from the group gathered in front of Bill Massiter's house and was checking out all the other one-storey buildings on the site. He saw someone rooting around inside one of the buildings, the one that looks like Bill used to use as an office. Filing cabinets, shelves, drawers all over the place. Our enterprising hack managed to get a few photos of this guy. As soon as he saw he was having his photo taken, the intruder scarpered very quickly. I'll bring the pictures to your office, sir. In the meantime, we've decided to turn over that building ourselves to see if we can work out what the guy was looking for.'

'Not to the office, Elaine. Not for a while, anyway,' Bellamy said. He then explained what had happened.

'O… M… G,' she said. 'We're going to have to start turning up some answers on this one pretty quickly, sir. I'll come to you as soon as they tell me where the safe house is, sir, though I'll take care not to pass that information on to anyone.'

For a moment, Bellamy was silent. Still the nagging insistence in his head continued. These people are setting the pace, he thought, and all we can do is chase our tails. We need to seize the initiative back from them.

'Elaine, get as many constables there as you can – phone in for a few more if you need to. After what's happened, I think Jack Henshaw will authorise just about anything. Turn Bill Massiter's place over, and get everything together that looks even the least bit interesting: any receipts for stuff bought from Colombia, even if it only looks like coffee; anything remotely connected with Cavelcombe House. When you've got a collection, move it all out of there and securely onto police territory somewhere. Then it's probably best if you head back to Cavelcombe House and see nothing gets out of control there. I'll get back to you as soon as I've sorted out where this safe house is and made arrangements to protect it.'

Twenty minutes later, Bellamy had arrived at the safe house, and he could already appreciate why it had been chosen for the purpose even as his car was drawing up outside. It was on the outskirts of a nearby market town, a building on its own in the middle of a field, with only one access road to it and the surrounding flat field enabling whoever was inside the place to see anyone approaching from several hundred yards away.

Louise came to the front door as soon as she saw Bellamy get out of the car, and ran to him. As they embraced, he could feel that she was still slightly shaking.

'We've got two private lines fixed up, Max, one direct to Jack Henshaw, and one to the National Crime Squad. They're analysing the bits of that drone to see if there might be any clues as to where it came from and whose it is.'

He held her hand as they walked together into the house.

'Whoever is doing this is incredibly anxious that we're getting close to finding something,' he said. 'They must be getting pretty desperate to be prepared to do what they're doing, now more or less taking on the entire police force. Something big is going down here, and I'm convinced it's to do with those bodies at Cavelcombe House. What we have to establish is what did Bill Massiter know about it?'

'Their willingness to do just about anything suggests that you're probably getting closer to them,' said Louise, 'and if Bill Massiter did know something about it, whoever is behind this wouldn't hesitate too long about arranging a convenient death for him.'

Bellamy felt the immediate effect of the safe house as he walked into the main living room. He knew the elaborate precautions which were taken when it was deemed necessary to move people to a safe house, and he was able to reassure himself that, for the time being, Louise would be safe here. It was only now, when he could accept the truth of this, that he realised how much it had been worrying him.

He went into the kitchen and made a couple of coffees which gave him the chance to find out where things were, and then he took them into the living room, a generous space with light coming in from big windows front and back, and comfortably furnished. This was the kind of place where important people were sent when they needed to be protected. With a vaguely startling understanding, he realised that an important person was what he had probably become.

Looking at Louise, it dawned on him that he hadn't yet shown her any physical affection beyond a brief embrace. His mind was still buzzing with questions and surmises, but he could and did put them to one side when proper attention needed to be given to the emotional demands of a relationship. Louise was a tough and resilient woman, but she needed support, as everyone did. He joined her on the sofa, and for some minutes, they hugged and kissed, ignoring the sounds of the police personnel to the front and rear of the property.

Eventually, Louise broke the silence.

'I can't help thinking, as Harry was saying before he left our place, that whoever is behind this is pretty emotionally unstable, and beyond the stage where they're thinking straight. Do they really think they can frighten off the entire police force?'

'Yes… Harry. Where is he now?'

'He left when the decision was taken to move me to a safe house. He was deeply indignant and, once again, very angry, because he thinks it's about time the party started lending us as much support as the police force are doing. When Harry gets a bee in his bonnet, he's just as likely to storm into Downing Street and beard the PM in his den.'

'What does he think the party should be doing?'

'Backing up the security, to start with. The police won't be able to keep this cover up indefinitely, and having police round the place does kind of send a signal to the locals that something's going on here. He thinks the party, since they are now in government, should be "bringing in the spooks", as he calls it, both to guarantee the security of you and me and to help with the investigation of the case.'

'And what do you think?'

It wasn't in any way unusual for Bellamy to ask his wife's opinion, even on intricate police matters, but this time, he thought he might have caught her off guard. She was looking at him somehow uncertainly.

'Well, I'll tell you,' she said eventually. 'But if you start coming out with any even vaguely sarky remarks about "female intuition", I might just untell you again.'

'Do I have a habit of making sarky remarks about female intuition?'

'No, to be fair, you don't. Well, anyway, here goes. It seems to me that whoever is behind this is kind of showboating – that's probably the best way to put it. They want it to be a big deal. They want the police force and the party and the powers that be to be scattering around trying to work out how to react. I haven't been in journalism and politics for this length of time without finding out certain truths about different kinds of people, and the single character behind this – because that's what it looks like to me, some strong if not very stable personality is pulling the strings here – has an exaggerated sense of his own importance. The person is almost certainly male, I think, and I'll go into why I think that if you want me to, and he is deriving satisfaction from getting people running around, some of whom are people in high places. It's almost like a naughty-boy-pushing-his-luck scenario, testing the limits of what he can get away with, daring anyone to catch him and punish him.'

'I don't see how he could have known that the police protecting our house would have a big gun, almost the equivalent of an anti-tank gun, with them. If they hadn't had a gun capable of blowing a drone into little pieces, that drone could have—' Bellamy was about to say "killed both you and Harry", but he couldn't get the words out.

Louise was silent for a moment.

'Well, here's where I'm probably going to stretch your credulity too far. I think whoever is behind this has someone inside the police. I think he knew they had that gun.'

Max Bellamy gazed at his wife for some moments. He didn't want to say what had now come into his mind, but he knew he had to.

'If that's true, Louise, whoever it is will soon get to know, if he doesn't already, where this safe house is.'

'Yes, Max.'

'Good God, Louise, if you thought that, why did you agree to come here?'

'Because I hadn't thought it through then, and because I was so terrified after the incident at the house that I just wanted to get away from there. And because it fits in with this guy, whoever he is, and his showboating. He stages a shooting incident, but the only person who gets shot is a journalist who has nothing to do with anything. He gets some incompetent idiot to make a threatening call, knowing full well we'll find out who did it, while realising that he could do it again with someone more competent. That guy outside the constituency office was only a few feet away from us; unless he was the most incompetent marksman in the world, he could have shot me or Harry if he'd wanted to. He could have killed Steven Ryan if he'd wanted to.

'Then he fixes up the attack on our house, having found out where it is from his tame policeman, and attacks the house in a way which he knows perfectly well the guarding police will almost certainly be able to defeat. Each time he's ratcheting up the pressure, tightening the screw a bit more, so he can enjoy us running around thinking of what to do. Next thing, he'll probably mount some obvious attack on this place; there will be a shoot-out, and his men will at least wound one of the police here, but probably not fatally, so once again, he's setting the agenda, he's asking the questions and he's got the inside man telling him what we're doing next before we do it.'

Bellamy found himself staring open-mouthed at his wife.

'Bloody hell. If you get sick of politics, Louise, I'll get you into the police force by the fastest track imaginable.'

Louise grinned, but said nothing more. She knew when Bellamy had more to say.

'I'm pretty sure you've got this right, but even if you haven't, I'm not going to take the risk. We have to find somewhere you can go, somewhere that only you and I know about. That way we're not only giving you proper protection but we're also letting this guy know we're onto his game and we're not playing any more.'

'I have a Scottish cousin, Max. She's been to a few family dos, including our wedding. She lives on her own in the Highlands. Moira, the name is.'

Bellamy searched his memory banks and, as usual, something stirred. A neatly dressed, pugnacious-looking woman, economical with her words and radiating an air of Gaelic independence and mystery.

'If I went up to spend some time with Moira, she wouldn't tell anyone where I was if they put her on a rack.'

'Is it feasible to carry on your constituency duties from the Scottish Highlands?'

'It's Scotland, Max, not Outer Mongolia. I can do as much as is necessary by e-mail. And judging by my postbag, the general public think it would be best for me to find a suitable hiding place until all this, whatever it is, blows over. The British are a pragmatic race.'

'I'm going to struggle without you.'

Louise smiled and kissed her husband lightly on his cheek.

'You say sweet things, Max, but you're not going to struggle much. You've always been one of the great self-contained. But what I can believe is that you would find it easier to work this one out without the constant background anxiety of what's happening to me. I know a few people in the north I could visit on my way to Scotland, just to throw a zigzag trail behind me, and Moira knows a few men in the local community up there who would be prepared to do just about anything to protect her. She never married, but she's had a few dour Caledonian affairs along the way.'

'OK, my love, but I'm telling no one, as in not a living soul, about it whether they're in or out of the force, up to and including your mother. She can cover me with cake mix and put me in the oven, but still not a word will pass my lips.'

Louise giggled. 'Are you trying to say my mother is some kind of insane cake-maker?'

'I'm not saying. Get the cake mix out yourself, I'm still not saying.'

And so to the nitty-gritty of the plan, Bellamy being content with it. He'd already realised that Louise was right about his constant background of anxiety about her, which continually gave the case an extra identity outside police work, misting the usual barriers between his personal and professional lives and making it difficult for him to achieve the kind of detachment he usually needed to be able to look at cases objectively.

He had also benefited from a moment of revelation as soon as Louise advanced the notion of an insider, a police officer reporting developments on the case to outsiders. He already had a theory as to who that police officer might be.

The name that came to mind was Inspector Frank Mellors, Mary Stanhope's immediate superior. It was well known that Mary and Mellors didn't get on. Mary herself generally kept quiet about it, though Max suspected she had made it clear to Mellors that she wouldn't keep quiet about it if he deliberately made her life difficult. It was also fairly common knowledge that Tom Hollins had accepted that Mary would be made inspector before much longer and would then be moved out of the orbit of Mellors, who was in any case only about five or six years away from retirement.

Max could remember the conversation he'd had with Mellors after Mary's secondment to the Massiter case.

'I know there's not much I can do to reverse the decision, sir, since it comes down from Mr Henshaw himself, but it's typical of what's going on, as far as I'm concerned. Boosting up females to be so special when they really shouldn't be in police work at all. I've had to send her off to be a kind of agony aunt to all these girls who go out and have too much to drink and then complain they've been raped when they were too pissed to remember what happened; that's the only bloody use I've ever been able to make of her. Maybe I'll get a proper sergeant now. I keep my lines open to my informers; keep in touch with the crims, particularly the higher up ones. You know what's going to happen before it actually does; we scratch their backs, they scratch ours, that's how it works. As in men's business…'

Bellamy felt bound to interrupt at this stage.

'As I've fundamentally disagreed with everything you've said so far, Inspector Mellors, I would advise you to shut up before you do yourself any more damage. Mary will be working on the Massiter case for the foreseeable future and that's all you need to know.'

'Sir.' The single little word was almost spat out at the other end of the phone.

Now Max wondered just how many "crims" Mellors was talking to. Even if none of them was directly behind recent developments in the Massiter case, they might well know who was. And be talking to them.

Bellamy could foresee a difficult conversation with Jack Henshaw. Getting a bright young constable to hack the e-mails and phone calls of an inspector was a big ask, but if his wife's life might depend on it, he was willing to give it a go.

As usual when he was in the process of deciding on a course of action, his phone sounded.

'Hello, Elaine,' he said, and a note of alarm sounded in his mind as he looked at his assistant. Inspector Elaine Price was widely seen as a tough character, quite remorselessly unsentimental and focused entirely on what she saw as her duty, but Bellamy knew well enough that everyone had their limits, and the face on the screen before him seemed to signify that Elaine was very near to hers. Bellamy found himself facing a real spasm of guilt at having left her at the scene of the carnage at Cavelcombe House, to cope not only with the surrounding media, now no doubt very numerous and growing all the time, but also the impact of a succession of rotting bodies, looking at one time as though the number would just go on going up and up relentlessly. He was well enough aware that his duty as a husband, never mind as a police officer, made it inevitable that he should be with his wife when people were shooting at her and potentially threatening her life, but Elaine had a partner too, the phlegmatic and laid-back lawyer Bryn Price. From what Bellamy knew of Bryn, he was generally even less inclined to panic than his wife, but now he was entitled to feel that a lot, perhaps even too much, was being asked of Elaine.

'I sent a team to go and do the job on the Massiter place, sir, because I thought I should get back to Cavelcombe; I had a message saying things were getting out of hand. The count eventually seems to have stopped at ten, sir,' she said, and the faint crack in her voice on the last two words served to tell Bellamy all he needed to know. 'We have a media frenzy going on now; national TV is on the scene, and I can detect a few general American and European accents now appearing amongst them. What's happening with you, sir?'

Bellamy told her, briefly, about the drone attack on the house and the armed police officer's rapid response; if anything, she seemed to grow even paler.

'Listen, Elaine. I'm going to send reinforcements to where you are now, with at least a sergeant in charge to hold the fort. As soon as they turn up, I want you to leave there and go to my office, where I'll meet you; phone me when you're on your way. Louise is shortly going to be on her way to a friend's place some distance away; I'll explain when I see you.'

Now Bellamy allowed himself some more thinking time, and his responsibility both to himself and his colleagues thrust itself into his mind. What the TV and the movies never show: police officers in the throes of a nervous breakdown; police officers weeping in the privacy of their homes; police officers finding something more than they can live with and taking their own lives. He'd known it happen; once would be more than he'd be capable of forgetting, but it had been rather more than once.

For some criminals, it was nothing personal; they chose to make a living out of crime, for whatever reasons, and it was the job of the police to stop them – so be it, fair enough. But there were those, like the man – or men, though Bellamy suspected everything in this case centred on one particular man – who didn't just want to evade the forces of the law, they wanted to destroy them, including the individuals specifically there to uphold the law. Anarchy was not something they were afraid of, presumably because they thought they would be clever enough to survive in it.

The police saw human beings at their worst, and it was sometimes enough to destroy their faith in humanity altogether, meaning they found themselves reduced to the same level. The result was police rapists, police corrupted, police who'd effectively crossed over to the other side. Which is why some police personnel didn't like to stop and think too much, in case thoughts turned into their enemy rather than their friend.

Bellamy knew this case was shaking him, and he also knew that if he was a family man, and his children were also being threatened, the pressure could get to be more than he would be able to bear. Elaine, he knew, had kids, who she had to go home to and behave like the typical mum, a typical mum who'd just come from dragging out body after body from the grounds of a hotel; naked, rotting bodies, of men too young to have had their lives so cruelly abbreviated. She might dream about them; they might suddenly invade her mind when she was on a summer trip with the kids, or when she and her husband were making love. She needed enough leisure to know the difference between her life and the criminal life, so she could hold on to the values which took her into the police in the first place.

With his usual slightly weary detachment, Bellamy turned to himself, now handling the case while his wife moved hundreds of miles away and having to face the fact that whoever he was dealing with had already used firearms twice and could have done more damage than he did on both occasions.

Attack wasn't always the best form of defence. Like most truisms, it didn't necessarily work some of the time, even occasionally most of the time. But for this one, it was necessary now, he thought, to make whoever this guy was less complacent about his opposition and start giving him a few questions that needed answers rather than let him go on creating questions for others, fancying himself as some master criminal puppet master.

Perhaps now that Louise was safe – because even a mole couldn't know of Louise's network of friends – her own political "minder" Harry didn't – some of the mist of anxiety surrounding the case would dissipate. Bellamy knew that he was due a one-to-one with both Mary and Dean the next day, which might well give him both the backup information he needed and an idea of what should happen next if they were to go on the attack rather than responding to events all the time.

The following day, before his meeting with his team in the afternoon, Bellamy was installed in a serviced apartment only a few hundred yards from the main police HQ, treated as a "maximum security venue". Elaine had gone on three days' leave, part of the mountain of leave due to her from recent years.

Sitting in a pleasant alcove in his sitting room, overlooking the outskirts of the city with generous amounts of greenery on offer, Bellamy summarised in his mind all that he knew about this case. There was the death, supposedly by suicide, of Bill Massiter; the fairly obvious connections between him and deliveries of cocaine from Colombia; the assumption of control of the Cougars by Eric Irwin; the riotous Cougars' parties at Cavelcombe House and the burial of ten naked male foreigners in the grounds of Cavelcombe during the Cougars' tenure of the place. He had to acknowledge the possibility that they might not be connected, that Irwin and whoever his big-man controller boss was, suggested by Mary Stanhope, had gone off on adventures of their own that the Cougars knew nothing about, but even then, Bellamy couldn't rid himself of the idea that Bill, the oldest of the Cougars and their generally acknowledged leader, in spite of all the swagger of Rory so-called Blaze, must have at least suspected what Irwin was up to.

In spite of his new surroundings, Bellamy slept soundly, all the more so after a phone call from Louise, to a number only she and Bellamy knew about, to say that she was in Scotland and everything was fine.

Tomorrow, he decided, the tables would start to turn.

PART FOUR

Patriot Man

Ten Years Earlier

Lord Hugh Railton was in one of his favourite places, which he called his "operations room". On the south coast of Cornwall, it provided an excellent panoramic view of the English Channel, and not just the kind of view to be obtained from simply looking out of a window. Railton's sophisticated scanners could cover the Channel for up to ten miles out; the bank of screens in front of him could detect crafts of whatever size either moving from east to west, or west to east, or heading towards the English shore, or away from it.

Hugh Railton had inherited his money from his banker and stockbroker father, though he personally found both banking and stockbroking tedious and left it to what he called his "underlings" to at least maintain the family fortune, if not increase it. Any "underling" who managed to lose money didn't stay in his employ for very long. Judicious political donations had eventually won him a life peerage.

However, steady as he and his underlings generally were in the investment area, Railton had an occasional habit of "walking on the wild side", when some venture appealed to something inside him and caused him to invest in it, regardless of the underlings' opinions. Recently, the Cougars, now a fading presence on the pop scene, had become one of his wild-side walks, despite the grumblings of their so-called leader, Bill Massiter. Eric Irwin, the Cougars' manager, had been recruited by Railton some time ago.

Eric Irwin, at some point in his turbulent career before meeting the Cougars, had found himself facing bankruptcy. Irwin's hectoring, bullying kind of leadership didn't generally work very well, and was no more effective in relation to showbusiness than it had been in his previous efforts. Railton had also acquired a cocaine habit, partly as a result of finding a relatively cheap supplier to enable Irwin to keep Bill Massiter happy, and in the process of celebrating the fact that they at last had some effective "leverage" over the stubborn and opinionated Massiter, Railton had tried some of the stuff himself and found it to his taste.

In most respects, Railton saw himself as a conscientious patriot, and his expensive apparatus for examining the Channel was mostly about defending the shores of England from those drug dealers and people traffickers who might think the southwest coast was a soft touch for getting their cargoes, whether drugs or people, into his England.

On occasions, he would point to his "war experience" and describe himself as a "Falklands veteran". He still walked with a slight limp, which he called a "war wound". The reality, which only he knew and no one ever asked him about because he only ever spoke to people who worked for him, was that he arrived on the Falklands as a young "diplomatic escort" to an army reserve unit about twelve hours after the Argentinians had surrendered, and his "wound" was picked up when he was standing next to several other novices learning about guns when one of their guns accidentally went off and shot him in the foot.

Lord Railton had helped Eric Irwin, another of his underlings but for whom he had a sort of affection – "Eric is a game trier, if nothing else" – out of debt, and then helped him again to buy Cavelcombe House, in which Railton had a controlling share, although none of the Cougars knew that. Giving the Cougars an isolated playground of their own enhanced Irwin's hold over them, which had been becoming more tenuous in recent years. Rory Blaze could enjoy his boys without the ever-present paparazzi threat; Bill Massiter could have his coke delivered to him without it having to approach through the massive housing estate which had been built right next to his once isolated home. The other two nonentities, as Railton saw them, could at least be nonentities out of the public gaze.

At the moment, Railton was looking particularly at a large dinghy with about a dozen people on it – all of them, as far as he could see, young men. His Lordship had, by now, acquired a good deal of knowledge about boats crossing the Channel, and his state-of-the-art long-range cameras could pick up as much detail as he needed to know. The prevailing wind had blown this boat off course; its engine had stopped, and instead of a short crossing, the boat had been slowly drifting westwards. However, the wind had started to drop, the tide was coming in, and the boat was now heading directly for the Cornish coast.

Railton's face hardened. All this stuff, he thought, about fleeing war and persecution; these people were invaders, these people were illegally entering British waters with a view to becoming immigrants the country didn't want. All young males, too, no doubt intent on having their wicked way with British womanhood and infecting the home gene pool with God only knew what plagues and diseases brought from their own countries.

But, as he was fond of saying, "even in this day and age, not all of us are negligent of our duty", a phrase which always acted like a clarion call to Eric Irwin, who was currently waiting patiently outside the "operations room" until His Lordship determined on the actions he had decided to take. Irwin knew enough about Railton by now to be able to interpret the odd mutterings and miscellaneous noises which emerged from the room. Railton would shortly pronounce on what actions he deemed immediately necessary. Irwin stood waiting, quietly and obediently, to be told what to do.

Those people who knew Eric Irwin, or thought they did, would be puzzled at this relative meekness on his part, and surprised to see him obeying orders rather than giving them.

But Eric Irwin's father had been an army officer, and he had seen it as part of his duty as a father to teach his son to take a proper attitude towards his superiors, by thrashing it into him if necessary, and for Eric, being the kind of boy he was, the necessity soon became obvious.

'If you turn out the way I hope you will, Son, you won't have many superiors, but the ones you do have need to be respected and obeyed, without question. I got to the rank of major, which is pretty good going by any standards, but still with colonels and generals above me, some of them, quite frankly, degenerates and no-hopers of various shapes and sizes. However, rank is rank. Just as I am your father and you my son and heir, it is my bound duty to tan your arse when I consider it necessary and yours to take your medicine without whingeing or blubbing about it, and if you think your father is wrong, you can do it your way when you have boys of your own; as it is, you do what you're told and you learn the lessons your father teaches you.'

So Eric Irwin, whatever grief he chose to give to those below him, which didn't include sons as he hadn't yet been able to find a woman to have them with, obeyed His Lordship as a dutiful employee. Waiting to be summoned by His Lordship always gave him a sense of waiting outside the headmaster's office, even though he had spent more occasions waiting to be commended by his headmaster at the "traditional" private school paid for by his father than waiting to be punished.

Suddenly, so suddenly that even the generally stoic Irwin jumped in his seat, a cacophony of music sounded from the operations room, and Irwin sighed. In spite of being in his sixties and of an age when most men disliked loud noise of any kind, his employer had a regrettable passion for "heavy metal". Which particular groups he liked Eric neither knew nor cared, as to his ears all of them sounded much the same; a discordant, blaring row. The Cougars' music was as heavy as Eric tolerated, though he had got into such a habit of only judging how much money an individual record was likely to make the group – and him – that the intrinsic merits or otherwise of the music were beyond his critical judgement.

What was more significant for him was the indication the music gave of Railton's mood. A blast like this usually represented a prelude to some decisive action, which may or may not be legal; Irwin was well aware that he had already crossed the border of legality for His Lordship on so many occasions that one more wouldn't make much difference. Railton now owned him body and soul. Everything illegal Railton decided on was passed on down the line, and at each level the passing continued, with the deliberate intention of creating so many levels that the origin of the action became so smothered in obscurity as to be virtually undetectable. Eric knew various "functionaries" who would do what they were told and, if they knew what was good for them, also carry the can if they were caught. If they hadn't realised what was good for them, Railton and Irwin between them would take the appropriate action, because if the functionaries didn't have vulnerable points which could be used against them, they wouldn't have become functionaries in the first place.

Four of Railton and Irwin's functionaries were currently in prison with reprisals against them that even behind bars were possible to arrange if they were indiscreet about who they chose to talk to. Two of them had recently died, indirectly at the hands of Railton and Irwin, but so indirectly as to maintain the impregnable walls surrounding them.

Railton fascinated Eric Irwin. He was, in some ways, like a child, given his tantrums, his wild enthusiasms and his apparently unlimited energy; Irwin had no illusions about the "work experience" girls who regularly appeared amongst Railton's staff. But he was also clever, sometimes very clever indeed, knowing with great precision and calculation exactly what he could and couldn't get away with and then carefully placing impenetrable protective layers around himself. Bill Massiter, the original member and effective leader of the Cougars, who got what he needed from the arrangements ultimately attributable to Lord Railton's South American contacts, and so-called Rory Blaze, who thought all his pretty boys were fans, were both in the pocket of Lord Railton, and all they knew of him was as an "associate" of their manager.

If he'd had to choose someone to mortgage his life to, Irwin considered, on the rare occasions he bothered to think much about it, he couldn't have done much better than Lord Hugh Railton.

The rock faded, and a voice sounded loud and clear on the speaker above Irwin's head.

'Mr Irwin, a moment of your time, if I may,' the immaculate, upper-class tone announced.

That, Eric thought, was another thing about Railton; cultured manners. No abrupt "get your arse in here, Irwin" about him. As smooth and as deadly as a rapier's edge.

Railton was wearing a blue dressing gown – Irwin suspected, from past experience, that it was all that he was wearing, probably meaning he had just had or was about to have an interview with one of his "work experience" girls. Railton was tall, six feet five to Irwin's six feet two, and he had a long, flawless body – Irwin had seen it naked more times than he cared to remember; bereft of any tattoos or other such vulgarities, smooth skinned and almost hairless, as if he was a big grown boy who'd omitted to acquire some of the normal accompaniments of manhood. Railton's rumoured schooldays had included the relentless exploitation of a number of boys, and occasionally teachers, who had been foolish enough to fall in love with him.

'Eric, my right-hand man, as ever. Come in, come in. Drinkie?'

Without waiting for an answer, Railton splashed generous quantities of good malt whisky into a couple of glasses, handed one to Irwin, and then led him through to the bank of screens on the wall of the room.

'See that boat, Eric, drifting ever closer to good old Blighty?'

'Yes, My Lord.'

'Oh, don't start that crap again, Eric, old lad. "Sir" is as good as anything. See it?'

'Yes, sir. A big dinghy.'

'Yes, isn't it? And that's what makes it interesting. There's only about a dozen on that boat; it's luxury class, by Channel boat standards. It's even got an engine, though it's obviously not working now, if it ever did; they're drifting about. Now that suggests two things, Eric, to my agile mind. Either they've chucked out all the women and children, which is a bit rich even by trafficking standards, or they're – what shall we call them – elite payers?'

'I'd guess the latter, sir. Leaving trails of dead women and kids scattered about the Channel isn't good for anyone's business, and certainly not traffickers. Even the most desperate asylum seekers are not going to try if it's odds on they'll finish up drowned, and the greater the number of casualties, the more unlikely it is that new people are going to have a go.'

'Yes, you're probably right. Sound old Eric. But what we haven't touched on yet, Eric old chum, is what the hell do they think they are doing coming to our shores?'

'I don't know, sir.'

'Yes. Exactly. I don't fucking know either. It's no use expecting the Royal Navy to resist this big dinghy invasion, seeing as they've now only got about two boats and only one of them is seaworthy. So we must step into the breach, Captain Irwin, mustn't we?'

'Captain Irwin, sir?'

'Absolutely. How many decent sized boats have we in our boathouse, Eric?'

'Two, sir. Your yacht and your larger power boat. The smaller power boat is being maintained.'

'Rock the fuck on, Eric. The bigger power boat will do. It's got arms on it, hasn't it?'

Irwin's eyes opened wide.

'Arms, sir?'

'Arms, Eric. Big pop gun, like an anti-tank thing. A couple of machine guns.'

Panic rose in Eric's insides.

'I wouldn't shoot them, sir. The shells or bullets will be traceable; for that matter, sir, so will the boat, if it's one from Your Lordship's boathouse.'

'Yes, good point; good points, in fact.'

A pause for thought followed. Irwin tried to calm his guts down.

'Well, I tell you what, old soldier Eric. I suppose, when it comes to it, shooting the fuckers is going to cause a bit of a stink. Something more subtle is called for; keep a distance, as with our usual tactics. Do you know any boat owners along our coast who are up for a bit of adventure?'

'I know a few, sir. Since the fishing business has become so difficult, some of them will hire their boat out for just about anything – tourist jaunts, a bit of up-to-date smuggling, whatever.'

'OK, rustle one of them up. Not you, of course, get someone you know to do it. Nothing attributable. Don't tell them anything too specific, for God's sake. When it's coming on to dark – tell them to wait until at least dusk – and the dinghy is two or three miles out, we could perhaps look at an unfortunate accident. In the growing gloom, with an unlit dinghy.'

'Over two miles out, sir, they might drown.'

A curious expression passed over Railton's face, one which Eric had seen before but still wasn't quite sure how to read, as if His Lordship knew he should care about what had just been said, but knew just as emphatically that he didn't.

'They're taking the risk, Eric. They are the invaders; they're the ones who are doing what they shouldn't be doing. And in any case, if they're all fit young guys, they should be capable of getting themselves to shore, or at least splashing about until some boat sees them. That's the Channel, the busiest sea passage in the world, and if it's an elite boat, they should at least have availed themselves of life jackets of some kind.'

Eric Irwin took a few deep breaths and fixed an unwavering eye on his employer. Ever since Eric had found himself, against his better judgement and wishes, firmly in the pocket of the very rich Lord Railton, he had been through a constant sequence of anxious nights and mounting doubts, and his instinct was that a dinghy, even if it was a clearly larger and superior craft to most of the leaky and wretched things the migrants drifted in on, would still disintegrate quickly enough in a collision with a much larger boat.

'Firstly, sir, the water temperature at this time of year would create problems for anyone, regardless of age and gender. Secondly, it's possible that a coastguard vessel has already picked up on them, and they will be quite professional enough to know if another boat bumping into them was an accident or quite deliberate. If any of the men on that dinghy drown, we could find ourselves having to answer some awkward questions.'

Lord Railton's eyes were closing and lips pursing long before the end of this speech. He sat himself down on the chair where he observed his screens, and looked up into Eric's eyes.

'We? Who's we? Do you know, Irwin, people are supposed to learn from their experiences, but you seem to take an eternity to get your head round yours. We, as in you and me, are not going to have anything to do with it. Wagons round, Eric, remember? When the Indians are attacking, the cowboys gather their wagons in a circle and shoot out from defensive positions. If you can contrive, like they did in the old English castles, to have at least three or four lines of defence around you, like ring after ring of wagons round, there won't be many of them left by the time they get to you, if they ever do, and by then you might have found a way of scarpering anyway.

'How many times do I have to tell you, Eric? You get someone you know to find some broke chancer in a pub or somewhere who is ready to do just about anything for a bit of cash, tell him what you want doing and how much you'll give him to do it, while pointing out to him very clearly that if he ever mentions your name to anyone at any point, he will have to spend the rest of his life minus his balls, and we have contacts in most of HM's prisons who will do it if we want them to do it. Then we sit back in my private little cinema of life here and watch the fun. My name, of course, does not feature in this at any point either, or it might be you being deprived of your testicles, which would be a great shame for a gentleman in his prime.'

Inside Eric Irwin's brain, his usual defensive mechanisms for justifying what he was doing with his life were working overtime. Like many others who had a sense of self-entitlement for one reason or another, finding himself being the agent for someone else's violent or destructive instincts was a kind of humiliation which excited a deep sense of indignation in him, because he considered he was better than this, that he deserved more. But his life was moving in an inexorable downward spiral, and something seemed to be telling him that it was now beyond his ability to reverse it.

'OK, My – I mean sir. I'll make the necessary arrangements. There are plenty of no-hopers trying to find something to do with their boats which might make money—'

Railton had turned back to his screens.

'I don't want to know, Eric. Just do it, don't tell me about it.'

At this point, Lord Railton turned his heavy metal soundtrack back on to send himself into his own kind of oblivion, his customary way of declaring the interview to be at an end.

Solid gone on his old guy music, Eric thought, with a strange mixture of admiration and head-shaking contempt. The kind of stuff rich guys do when they want to persuade themselves they're young again. But, as Major Irwin would say, powerful and successful men frequently have eccentricities, Son, and do you know why? Because they can afford to have eccentricities; it's one of the things that makes them powerful men. You can accept it, is what they're saying, or you can go fuck yourself.

Planning his operations carefully was another trait Eric had inherited from his father. He knew well enough by now that Railton was only interested in two aspects of any operation: one, making what he wanted to happen a reality, and two, that there would be no comeback and no "collateral", meaning inconvenient events happening on the side of the main event. And what that meant in this case, as far as Irwin read it, was that Railton didn't care whether the men on that dinghy lived or died, as long as he wasn't implicated in the whole business.

That same evening, Railton was in front of his screens again, and he was looking at the dinghy in great detail while the heavy metal screeched in the background, and even scanning some of the men more closely. Middle Eastern, he thought, without a doubt, and it wasn't difficult to work out who the leader man was; a large figure, probably something like six feet five, he guessed, sitting in separate splendour at the head of the boat, swathed in several layers of clothing and keeping a careful eye on everyone. Railton saw him suddenly rise and shout something at one of the men lower down the boat; the man's shamefaced reaction and raised hand in acknowledgment of his fault, whatever it was, made clear who was in charge of the boat. Huh, thought Railton, what an empire for a big man to control, one sad, wet little boat drifting towards someone else's country.

The light was fading, and the boat, monitored on a smaller screen next to the main one, looked to be about three miles from the shore.

'Come on, come on,' Railton muttered to himself. This, he thought, was no way for anyone to treat his motherland, especially not this group of whatever they were – terrorists, rapists, rampaging young bucks coming to ensure an easy life living on the soft underbelly of Britain.

Suddenly, so suddenly that His Lordship jumped and shut off the blare of his music, two piercing lights loomed out of the dim light, and a boat, looking about ten times the size of the dinghy, was so close to the dinghy that there was no chance of the impending collision being avoided. Railton prided himself on having a strong stomach when it came to warlike incidents, but this was a desperate and terrifying business, with several of the men clearly dispatched unconscious into the sea after being knocked about ten feet into the air. The big boat had ploughed into the middle of the dinghy, and most of the men had no chance of any kind of avoidance.

But Railton saw the big man at the end of the boat rise himself as the boat veered up, and calmly take off the heavy outdoor coat he was wearing, before plunging into the sea and starting to swim with great strength, his long arms plunging in and out of the water, which was calm, even if cold.

No operation is ever that straightforward, Railton thought, as he tried to count the figures moving away from the dinghy. The bigger boat, having ploughed through some of the men who'd fallen from the dinghy, carried rapidly on its way in the direction of the shore, making no attempt, as yet, to pick up casualties.

Getting cold feet was just not what happened to the likes of Railton, Eric Irwin would say to his various associates, legal and otherwise. However, now and then it did, at least a little, though His Lordship would never acknowledge such a thing.

As Railton remained glued to his "adventure screens", a few sobering reflections on reality went through his mind. He didn't like to see himself as timid when it came to having the nerve and the balls to push through a difficult operation, and he found himself having to acknowledge to his secret inner self, the one who kept telling him there was nothing he couldn't do, regardless of rules and regulations, that this business could have some very difficult repercussions.

There was no sign of any coastguard boats, and none of them would suspect trouble like this along such a quiet part of the coast. Men who were knocked unconscious would be dead within minutes of being immersed in the water, young and strong as they may be. By the look of the collision, a few men would have died instantly. The swimming men, and he could only make out two of them now, would be lucky to make it to the shore; it would be some time before they even saw it. With the prevailing wind, it could be only a matter of hours before bodies started washing up on the shore, and bodies on the shore would mean investigations, police investigations, perhaps even the spooks getting involved. And if any of those men did get to the shore alive, they would then be living witnesses of what had happened to their dinghy.

'Fuck,' said Railton quietly to himself. Too much impulse, not enough planning. Too much righteous crap that this can't be happening to dear old Britain and not enough thinking the thing through. Maybe all this blaring rock had addled his brain.

He picked up his phone and pressed the right button for Eric. The screen suggested that Eric was still wandering around somewhere on the coast, which wasn't too good an idea but might suit for present purposes.

'Eric, listen to me. Listen to me carefully. No, don't say anything; you can say what you want to say in a minute. You need to have people on the coast – not you, not on any account you, but people – and they need to be there, all night – the next twenty-four hours, in fact. If any unwanted cargo is washed up on the coast, it needs to be moved somewhere else before anyone realises it's there, and that applies whatever state the cargo may be in – do you get my meaning, Eric?'

'Yes, sir. I told the crew of the boat their job would not end with the collision; they know what's involved. Whatever state they arrive in, dead or alive, they'll deal with it. It's going to run to money, sir; this kind of operation doesn't come cheap.'

'Good man, Eric. No problem; I didn't expect that it would be cheap. I don't want the economy package. You pay peanuts, you get monkeys. Keep me in touch with exactly what's happening, Eric, on this line.'

'Yes, sir.'

A large, bedraggled figure stepped slowly out of the waves like a saturated phoenix. He could hear vague, slight noises – English voices – further down the coast; trained to operations, he tiredly noted the fact for future reference.

Ex-muqaddam, or lieutenant colonel, of the Iraqi Republican Guard Haidar Alwan, once, to his pride and joy, described by a general as "a mountain of a man, and just as solid", had lost a few of his clothes in the long, exhausting swim to shore, but the eagle and star insignia of his army days still nestled next to his chest in a protective and warming inner garment which he had decided to wear as a precaution against what he had heard was the wretched English weather. He had reluctantly conceded that he was not as young as he used to be. He allowed himself a moment to sit and try to regain some breath and warmth. There had been moments during the swim when even he had begun to doubt his immense strength and stamina, until at last the lights of the coast came clearly into view, and gave his heart such an immense boost that the final stretch was the easiest.

For a while he breathed heavily and tried to expunge from his mind the feelings of hopelessness and despair which were threatening to engulf him. Two of his sons and one of his brothers had been on their dinghy when the huge figure of the invading boat suddenly crashed its way into them. One of the men hit full on by the boat and knocked, severely injured, into the sea was his youngest son, Baravan, aged just twenty-one, a dreamy, abstracted boy who his mother sometimes felt was somehow of a different world than the one he lived on, with his mystical love poems to girls he'd never spoken to and his long, lonely walks around his home village and sometimes much further afield. Whatever Baravan was or wasn't, he didn't deserve to die in freezing cold English waters, and in Haidar's opinion, his death had to be murder. Yes, the light was poor at the time of collision, but even small boats these days carried warning systems; that boat's action was deliberate. Haidar knew there were many people in Britain who were protective of their wealth and privilege and resented sharing it with refugees from poorer countries, and there were aspects of that which Haidar could well understand. But the Americans and British had crashed their way into his own country, invited by no one. American weapons, enormously powerful and fired from places the defenders of his country couldn't even see, had humiliated even the bravest Iraqi soldiers, some of whom were already on their way to joining other young men in planned fatwahs, and if the present incident was anything to go by, perhaps there was no alternative but to fight, if the only alternative seemed to be submission or starvation.

For some minutes after he emerged from the waves, Haidar stood motionlessly, hoping fervently to see another figure in the water whom he recognised. After all they had been through – the tortured negotiations with the ruthless traffickers, indifferent to anyone but themselves, the freezing and very wet crossing, the refusal on behalf of everyone to lend any kind of help at all, the inadequacy of even the thick English clothes to keep out the cold; surely, by even the vaguest notions of divine justice, his family was entitled to at least a modicum of good fortune.

High-ranking officers of the Republican Guard were not expected to weep, under any circumstances, but it took all of Haidar's iron self-control to prevent the disgrace of tears running down his weathered face. Much as he tried, he could not clear his mind enough to work out the next move.

Then, two sights became clear to him simultaneously, one in front of him and one behind him, in spite of the now almost totally dark night, as if providing an answer to his mood.

Sudden flashes of white waves in the gloom of the water showed that someone was moving in the sea, and on the moonlit skyline at the top of the nearby cliff on his right, a figure was silhouetted against the sky, and it was waving, not in a threatening or abusive way, but friendly, welcoming.

Haidar had been trained to rapid action. He waved back to the figure on top of the cliffs, beckoning whoever it was to come down; even if it was the English police, it would mean shelter, warmth, a way to get inside away from the cold. If they were hostile, Haidar was trained to fight, and his hand revolver was still locked in its pocket below his trousers.

Then he moved towards the edge of the water in time to see an exhausted and half-naked man emerging slowly and painfully from the waves. Of course, Haidar thought, it was Kassim. Reprobate as he was, a potential menace to any young women in his vicinity and, while physically a big man now, still not knowing his own strength, his mental growth behind his physical, Kassim constantly seemed to have all the luck in the world at his disposal. Occupying the precious position of his father's son and heir, Kassim bluffed and blundered his way through life.

Even as tears did now sully his cheeks, Haidar helped his son onto dry land. Kassim, at least, was still with him, relentlessly tough and amazingly lucky as ever, and Haidar could reflect that the now obvious loss of the beautiful and ethereal Baravan had not, as he had feared, wiped out all of his heirs. Kassim was in undershorts and a saturated T-shirt; he was almost shaking with cold. Notoriously unemotional as he usually was, he threw both arms round his father and Haidar could hear him murmuring a prayer to himself.

Breaking free, Kassim sank to his knees, another highly uncharacteristic movement.

'My father, I did everything I could do to get to Baravan,' Kassim said in his native tongue. 'I couldn't see him, but I saw that boat hit him head on.'

'I'm sure you did, my son,' said Haidar, reverting to the English he had been insisting on the people in the boat using as much as they possibly could – 'Our chances of making any kind of a life in this country, away from bloodshed and banditry, will never be good unless we can speak their language,' he had said at the beginning of the boat's journey.

Haidar's own English was mostly faultless. He had spent some time in his teens and early twenties in a British college studying vehicle engineering, trying to ensure that his knowledge of cars and other vehicles would always enable him to earn a living in any country. He had joined the guard as a specialist, not a common soldier. When the Americans and British obliterated the Iraqi forces with hardly a blow being struck and then marched their men into the country, Haidar saw unfortunate things happening because of the language problems involved, and to protect his people from the sometimes harsh treatment they could receive from Allied soldiers, Haidar took to working as a translator, not least in helping wounded men under his command to get the treatment they needed. The British in particular seemed to appreciate his services, perhaps because he had learned his English in Britain and he found much of the American way of speaking difficult to understand. After some time, Haidar realised that he had incurred the enmity, even the hatred, of some of his countrymen for what he was doing, which astonished him, because all he was doing, as far as he was concerned, was helping to prevent dangerous misunderstandings between Allied servicemen and Iraqi civilians.

He spoke to a British officer called Captain Norwood about the possibility of him being admitted to Britain as a reward for his translating services, as it became painfully clear to him that he and his family could well be in great danger when the Allied forces left Iraq and the growing fury of the defeated soldiers needed to find suitable victims wherever they could. Haidar also felt that many Iraqi citizens would try to flee to the West as a result of the chaos following the war, so that even if his car maintenance skills couldn't provide him with work, his translating skills would.

Approaches made through official channels produced nothing but the certainty that, even if Haidar was admitted to Britain, it would take a long time for this to happen, and by that time, Iraq could well be in civil war and more of Haidar's family would have fallen victims to the so-called jihadis.

After the brutal murder of three more family members, he and a number of his ex-army comrades banded together to live in a protected neighbourhood, benefiting from his good relations with the occupying forces and able to protect themselves from the increasingly threatening atmosphere. Haidar used his contacts to get his Jordanian wife, Lateefah, and his daughters, Derifa and Sadiya, to their relations in Jordan, the general idea being that the menfolk of his family would seek to find well-paid work in the West and send money to Jordan. Four of the men on the boat had been directly related to him, two more distantly related, and the remaining five were ex-army comrades or their sons.

Now, it seemed, only he and Kassim were left. Haidar felt his fists clenching. Even his eldest son, widely seen as one of the toughest men of his generation, looked deathly pale, soaking and cold, and here they were in a foreign country, not knowing what part of it they had landed in and with no idea of the reception which would await them when they climbed the cliff behind them, assuming they would be able to climb it at all in their weakened state.

Those traffickers, those silver-tongued devils, were to answer for this. Haidar had thought the generous sum his family had got together would be enough for a decent boat, perhaps even an escort, and if they were picked up by the British coastguard, Haidar would convince them that he was a veteran of the war and an official army translator. But it was only enough, said the traffickers, for a "superior dinghy – with an engine, and more than large enough for your party, my friend, big, strong men as you are." Even the "superior dinghy" was no match for a pleasure boat, or whatever it was, crashing into them out of the gloom.

But, as he held Kassim close to him to try and inject more warmth into him, Haidar was thinking the situation through. He had seen much worse – men burnt to death in their tanks and troop carriers before they could fire a shot, men literally blown apart, leaving a scene of nothing but pools of blood and scattered body parts, men screaming to be mercifully shot before they died from the pain of their wounds, and he had done that a few times himself.

They would manage, somehow. He had contact details of potential helpers based in London, and his English by now was good enough to deal with most situations.

He looked again towards the cliffs to try and work out if there was a path of some kind which would make the climb easier, and he froze as he saw a torchlight, obviously held by someone slowly descending to the beach.

He glanced around him. If they were coming towards him with evil intent, there was very little he could do. The little pistol was still in its tight pocket, but even a waterproof pocket might not have protected it enough for it to be used. But he and Kassim were soldiers, and they turned to face whoever was approaching, ready to fight if they had to.

Eventually, only a few yards away, the faces of two men became visible, and one of them spoke. To Haidar's deep relief, he spoke in Iraqi Mesopotamian Arabic.

'You are Haidar Alwan?' he said.

Haidar nodded and smiled.

'Welcome, Muqaddam Alwan. My name is Ahmed, sir. We had a message from our London friends that your boat might be drifting towards this part of the coast; even traffickers can sometimes have their uses. They have weather charts and mysterious information sources. But—' He stopped in bewilderment. 'There are twelve of you, Muqaddam, are there not?'

'Only me and my son Kassim here have reached the coast so far. Our dinghy – a good one, yes, and large, yes, but still only a dinghy – was rammed and overturned by some big pleasure boat, or whatever it was.'

The man suddenly looked rather shamefaced.

'My apologies and condolences, sir, but it is not safe to wait now. If the accident was seen from the coast, the police or coastguard will be examining all of it soon. We have dry clothes – nobody ever travels in those dinghy things without getting saturated – and two cars near the shore. We can get you and your son to a safe house in Plymouth, not far from here.' He turned to the younger man beside him who was opening the bag he had on his back. 'Fadel – for the gentlemen…'

Two blankets were handed over to Haidar and Kassim to throw around themselves. Haidar almost gasped at the sudden access of warmth. He paused to gaze out to sea, hoping that there might be some sign, however slight, of at least one more swimmer.

'Forgive me, sir; we must go. We may get more information from our friends. Your arrival is widely talked about; we do not often have such distinguished visitors in these parts of the country. We will return to investigate further when you are settled and comfortable, sir.'

Kassim, clutching tightly to his blanket, coughed and vomited slightly. The young man Fadel wrapped an arm around him, and the group began their trip up the long path to the top of the cliffs.

Haidar, bringing up the rear of the group, paused halfway up the cliff to once again scour the beach and the expanse of the sea – the full moon was now illuminating more of it than could be seen from the shore. He had fought a totally one-sided war when the pride of his country's military had been dragged in the desert dust, and he thought he had experienced more heartache than any man should have to suffer in a single lifetime. An image of the boy Baravan, aged perhaps seven or eight, a strikingly beautiful child, gazing wistfully out of his bedroom window as his father entered his room to say goodnight and talk a little about the events of the day, suddenly came powerfully to his mind.

Moonlight played on the boy's big eyes and faultless complexion and his father, standing at the door momentarily transfixed, saw an inexpressible sadness in his son and wondered, then, how someone so young could be so unhappy, and why. Could it be that the boy had some kind of instinct that he would never live beyond the age of twenty-one?

As Baravan turned to greet his father, his face broke into that electric smile which could melt the hardest heart. Haidar told himself to hang on as well as he could to the smile.

Reaching the top of the cliff, Haidar saw a boat on the horizon, one which could well be the same one that had hit his dinghy. He stopped, not knowing what to do.

Ahmed, split between impatience and respect, was once again beside him.

'Forgive me, Muqaddam. We must move quickly, sir.'

At the same moment as Haidar and Kassim and their rescuers were driving away from the shore, Eric Irwin and His Lordship Railton were in tense and agitated conference.

'The prevailing tide is inwards, sir. There will be a number of bodies washed up on the shore, and perhaps even a few men might make it to the shore alive, should they be strong swimmers. If the coastguard picks up any bodies, there is bound to be an investigation.'

'So?' Railton was gazing almost hypnotically at a now empty sea. 'I know you to be an efficient operator, Eric, otherwise I would never have agreed to work with you. I assume you have made the properly water-tight, if you'll forgive the expression, arrangements to ensure that whichever toerags you may have used as channels of communication, none of them will be stupid enough to implicate you, let alone me.'

'Of course, sir. And even if they did, we would say we commissioned a boat to go out to the dinghy's rescue and it collided with it by accident in the dark. But if we can pick up any bodies washed up on the shore before daylight, there may not be an investigation at all. There were no coastguard boats in the vicinity. And if any men do make it to the shore, they will seek to make contact with their friends. If any of them are hospitalised, they are unlikely to tell anyone that they were trying to enter Britain illegally. A simple boating accident, they will claim. Nevertheless, we still have a chance to forestall any possibility of an investigation if we can get to the bodies before anyone else does.'

Railton bestowed a rare smile on his lieutenant.

'Such immaculate logic. I don't wonder that you managed to take that bunch of misfits and perverts to the top of the pop music tree, Eric. One point, however, does rather spring to mind. If your boat does collect the bodies, what is it going to do with them? We can hardly just fetch up at someone's funeral parlour, can we, and then organise a funeral which will have all the hacks in the south-west, and maybe even the nationals, sniffing all over it?'

Irwin was, as usual, ready with an answer.

'We will bury them, under cover of darkness, in the grounds of Cavelcombe House, sir,' he said. 'Only Massiter and his wife are staying there at the moment, and in the small hours of the morning, they are both most likely to be stoned out of their mind on drink or drugs or probably both.'

Railton laughed delightedly.

'Wonderful! Our very own private cemetery! Eric, at times you are pure genius. We could even reserve a space or two for any of Rory-fucking-Blaze's pretty boys, if they get uppity and start thinking of talking to the press. If push comes to shove, maybe even Rory-fucking-Blaze himself, come to think of it!'

He paused, his face becoming suddenly serious.

'But strip them, Eric. Totally. We don't want any giveaway clothes, rings, bracelets and what have you. You know what these foreigners are like. Let them end their lives in the same costume as they entered it.'

'Absolutely, sir. I'll see to it.'

As Irwin descended the stairs, one of Railton's favourite bands was booming out behind him. Eric smiled. His employer was satisfied.

Bill was awake. Josie was asleep. This, he thought, is getting to be the norm. He had things on his mind, one of them being Josie. If Josie had him on her mind, she was either a very good actor or she just didn't.

Bill had earlier made another attempt to make love to Josie, and he had been rebuffed – again. Not with hostility or contemptuous dismissal; more a matter of weary indifference. It seemed that the sexual side of their relationship was more or less moribund, and Bill was struggling to work out why.

When Josie had suggested they sleep in different beds, Bill had reluctantly agreed, though he had always loved the feel and scent of her body beside him. He could recognise that his own feel and scent these days were probably not of the freshest; he seemed to sweat a lot now – partly, of course, because of what he had on his mind, and perhaps also because of the "substances", as he called them, a euphemism for different strands of cocaine. Bill knew that mood swings and ultimate impotence could be the longer term consequences of taking cocaine, but he saw it as a fine judgement now; if he gave it up altogether, the effects of stopping might be the final nail in the coffin of the Cougars.

Perhaps that was it. Perhaps that was the simple choice he was facing, Josie or the Cougars. The band were increasingly on their last legs. Both Manuel and Doug were exasperated with the behaviour of Tony Richards, and they knew, as Bill did, that the media could well now have enough on Tony to launch a major blitz, which could include interviews with his ex-boyfriends and people who'd been involved in the Cavelcombe House parties. Yes, Tony was generally pretty careful with the age limits, but if he had crossed the line a few times, when he'd had too much of whatever form of booze he fancied at the time, it could mean prosecutions and a kind of stink attaching to the whole band.

Bill got out of bed, as he did so often now in the middle of the night, either to visit the toilet or just to try and walk or read himself to sleep. He moved into the living room adjoining the bedroom; the wall clock said twenty to three. He sat just inside the balcony looking over the Cornwall countryside.

He remembered the sex he had had with Tony when they were still at school; dares, getting bolder and bolder, which he saw as games, just dirty games, but Tony probably saw them as more than that. Dares to run naked along the street, dares to moon at passing cars, and then, suddenly, a new level; 'Do you dare wank me off, Bill? I mean, all the way, so you get to see me cum? If you manage it, I'll give you a prize – I'll do it to you – see how much you can get out.' And then Bill had found another lad to "join in the fun"; so it accelerated, like a big, fat snowball rolling downhill, until, a good year after leaving school, Tony wanted Bill to get in his bed, and made it clear enough what he was going to do to Bill when he did.

That was the end. 'No, Tony, not that. Fun's fun, but not that. I'm not gay…'

He remembered the hilarity which greeted that statement. But, by then, the Cougars were starting to do gigs, if you could call them that; school halls, small colleges, birthday parties. Bill had met girls – he'd never heard the word groupies then, but he got used to it later. Very willing girls, interested girls. He'd grown out of Tony and all that, and Tony accepted it, or seemed to, eventually.

Then along came Josie, appointed by Eric to smarten the band up, getting Doug and Manny out of their torn jeans and beer-stained T-shirts, and fitting Tony up with the Rory Blaze gear; ludicrously tight bright trousers and leather jackets.

So all was well; Bill had Josie, Rory had his smart lads, leathered up to catch his attention, and even Doug and Manny were doing alright. The Cougars were set to conquer the world.

Richard Bellamy, the music journalist who'd noticed the band from the start, described them as "a real breath of fresh air in the tired old miasma of British pop", and everyone thought that really summed it up, or they did when they'd worked out what a miasma was. For a while, the band were so pleased with Richard Bellamy that they asked him to act as their agent, though it became clear soon enough that he was a better journalist than he was an agent. The kind of bullying ruthlessness which agents need to push their bands along was not in Richard Bellamy's nature.

But he did fix them an American tour, which could have made the Cougars' name on both sides of the Atlantic. However, what actually happened was the Cougars' attempt to conquer the world came to an abrupt halt. They gave their all to America, and America threw it right back in their faces. The tour only just broke even; the Cougars had to accept that they'd played most of the gigs for next to nothing.

Since then, it had been pretty relentlessly downhill; minor hits to follow the major ones, negative press, stand-up rows in changing rooms, and increasingly nasty lectures from the new manager – a manager seeming a much better idea than an agent – the manager being Eric Irwin, so-called "Captain Storm", and the mysterious, very-big-deal sponsor he said was backing the group behind the scenes.

Even Cavelcombe House, intended to be the Cougars' getaway, like Bill's house had once been before they built a huge housing estate right next to it, started getting hostile write-ups in the local press and local councillors getting their faces on the TV to denounce "this den of iniquity" amongst them.

Josie was fed up with the Cougars, frightened by Eric and increasingly indifferent to her partner. Bill shook his head, trying to resist the temptation to reach for a phial of powder.

Then he heard a noise, like a scuffle or someone tripping, below the balcony. It wasn't too unusual when a party was going on at Cavelcombe to hear some of the fans still prowling about the place in the night, but there was no party tonight. By decree from Eric, almost all of that stuff had been knocked on the head.

Taking care not to put any lights on, Bill moved quietly onto the balcony and looked down. He almost shouted out. Men – too big to be women – were passing below, carrying long oblong boxes as quietly as they possibly could. They were still outside the boundaries of the house, but Bill knew there was a gate, further along to his left, which entered the grounds of Cavelcombe.

What on earth is this about? he thought. Yes, Eric was still buying in stuff to equip the house; parties, and even just the maintenance of the place, needed resources of many kinds, usually including Bill's supplies of what he needed, all the way from Colombia.

Yes, of course, he thought. Eric was bringing in the necessary supplies, knowing that all the band now indulged from time to time, if not as often as Bill. Bringing them in during the deep, dark night, so no nosey individuals could see them and wonder what was happening.

But, still, the whole business was strange, like some low-grade horror movie, box after coffin-size box going past in the night. Eric really needed to find some more subtle and less spooky method of bringing in the necessaries.

It didn't make sense, somehow. But the mystery had served as a final knockout blow to Bill's restless wakefulness. He walked, or rather staggered, back into the bedroom and for once he appreciated the separate beds arrangement, as he could climb back into his own bed, neither disturbing Josie nor being disturbed by her, and simply sink slowly into sleep.

In the morning, it took a while for him to remember what had happened in the night, and when he did, he wasn't sure if it hadn't all been a bad dream. Only in the following days did the realisation dawn on him that it hadn't actually been a dream and it had really happened. Those passing figures and their coffin-shaped burdens were indelibly fixed in his mind. It soon became an immovable, perpetual clamour in his mind, by day and by night.

Five Years Later

Bill Massiter was sitting on an armchair in a dressing room which could probably most kindly be described as "compact"; no more the copious, hotel leisure club-like open spaces the Cougars had enjoyed at the height of their fame.

He was stark naked, and intended to stay that way for some time, until his normal breathing pattern had returned and he had managed to stop sweating, or at least seen the sweating subside a little. Doug and Manny were close by him in various stages of undress, but the Cougars had long since ceased to care, or even notice, each other's nakedness.

Tony Richards was in the other dressing room that the terms of the band now always insisted on, though the exercise was pretty pointless these days, as Tony's supply of handsome young bucks had all but dried up. During the Cougars' lacklustre set, someone had shouted "sad old poofter" in Tony's direction, and a few other members of the crowd, if about 150 mostly middle-aged looking people half filling a place which resembled a village hall could really be honestly described as a "crowd", seemed to be registering amusement at Tony's "Rory Blaze" antics. The crutch grabbing and pelvic thrusting of Rory's "cock rock" antics worked reasonably well when the guy doing them was young, lean and good-looking, as Tony had once been, but not so well when he was a paunchy looking guy with at least two chins.

The Cougars had been persuaded, or more accurately intimidated, into a "reunion tour" after their supposedly final break-up two years previously, most spectacularly marked by a stand-up, shouting row between Richards and the rest of the band, when even the normally placid Manny had been so moved as to be screaming obscure Spanish curses in Tony's direction. Tony had ignored the usual musical and vocal arrangements the band normally observed; he kept leaving the stage and going walkabout, playing hell with the microphones and making approaches to young male spectators which were usually emphatically and noisily rejected.

As their audience drifted away, not without shouting a few ribald comments behind them, the shouting row stormed on, until Eric Irwin did a bit of storming himself, stamping onto the stage and demanding an end to it.

When everyone had calmed down, Eric moved into his customary pep-up speech.

'Now. This is when we see what a class outfit you are, boys. We can and we will put this behind us and push on – the Cougars' story will go on and on…'

But, for once, even Eric's sergeant-major-like authority didn't work. For once, the leader of the group was to speak his mind. He had started it; he was going to end it.

'No, Eric, no. Enough is enough. Let's be realistic for once. We've lost it. We haven't had even a minor hit for three years, we're all playing like we're doing solos and half the crowd don't know who the hell we are. Enough is enough, Eric. Finito.'

And with that, the entire band left the stage to go to their separate dressing rooms, Richards now in splendid isolation in his.

Eric had started to speak, but no one was listening. That, as far as they were all concerned, was the end of the Cougars.

But they were to discover that bringing down the curtain on the career of a clapped-out pop rock band was not as easy as that. The taxmen were still asking awkward questions. Leaving Eric to handle that side of things had not turned out to be a good move – some concert venues which had made a loss on the Cougars' gigs were demanding compensation, and Bill, Manny and Tony all had health issues outstanding and needing treatment, sometimes costly treatment in the private hospitals the band used. And, of course, there were the suppliers of what Bill in particular now found it impossible to live without, and the band's growing suspicions that Irwin had been siphoning money off from their profits for some time, even if they were wary of spending money they didn't have going to court about it.

So, here they were, just two years later, going for a big and hopefully very lucrative reunion tour, everyone swallowing their differences as best they could so as to provide some ready money to deal with the circling financial sharks. Eric seemed to be the only one immune to the problems, with his big sugar daddy in the background, who they all knew now was Lord heavy-rock Railton, although Eric never allowed any discussion relating to His Lordship.

The big reunion tour turned out to include a number of small venues along the south coast, with a few within commuting reach of London without actually being in it. The bigger venues had decided the Cougars would not fill them up, and demanded vast insurance payments to even think about putting them on.

There were no more rows now. The band were simply too tired and dispirited to bother.

Bill sat on, waiting until he cooled down and the tightness in his chest had eased. This time, he'd decided, the end really was the end, and he would have already told Eric so, but Eric had disappeared before the end of the gig, so perhaps he'd already realised it.

Doug Lane emerged from the shower. He, alone among the band, still retained the slim, young man's body, more or less, that he'd had from the start, remarkably so as he now tended to drink like a fish. He seemed to have a metabolism which allowed him to sweat all the booze out when he was hammering seven bells out of his drums.

Doug looked across at Bill and exchanged glances with Manny.

'You don't look too good, Bill. In fact, you look like shit.'

'Oh, cheers, Doug. I love you, too.'

Doug sat down in the nearest chair to Bill's.

'Sorry, Bill, I'm not trying to slag you off. But, let's face it, we're done, aren't we? I can't do this, Bill. After the great gigs we've had in the past, even with Tony leaping around like a maniac, this is just too much of a downer. I think we need to call it a day; I mean, permanently this time. We should have told Eric to stuff his reunion tour. In any case, he's bloody Railton's bagman these days.'

'I think he's been that for a while, Doug. But you're right. It's all played out. If the money stuff is still difficult, we'll have to declare bankruptcy or something.'

'And you, Bill, will have to stop going on about Cavelcombe House.'

Manny Orestes didn't say much, but what he did was very much to the point. Bill reacted by finding himself on the point of saying something equally direct in Manny's direction, but his instinct with all the rest of the Cougars, even including Tony, was to try and avoid confrontation as much as possible. Manny, for all his laid-back persona, could be very obstinate when an idea was fixed in his head, and he remained convinced that Bill's problems had started to make him rather paranoid in various directions.

Bill played for time by resuming his underpants and trousers, though the sudden movements started him sweating again.

'I'll say two things about that, Manny, and for the moment,

perhaps we can leave it at that. If we are to go our separate ways, I'd rather we did it as friends, and I wish everything about Cavelcombe could be nicely put to bed, but we all know it can't. We bought that place on a percentage basis, fifty per cent from Eric, or more accurately, I think, in relation to where the money came from, His bloody Lordship, and fifty per cent from us, split into four. That still isn't the way the money has been split. We all know it sold for a good £100,000 more than we paid for it, meaning we should be entitled to half of that additional profit, not just what we paid for the place with a pathetic little bit of interest. Eric can talk as much as he likes about extra funds needed for keeping the Cougars afloat, and the losses made on this tour, but if he's the Cougars' manager, and he and His Lordship have got their skin in the game just like we have, then they have to cop the losses as well as reap the profits, as we all do. Secondly—'

Orestes turned round from combing his hair in a dressing-room mirror, his face registering a kind of amused exasperation.

'Hell, Bill, listen to you. What are you, an accountant, a lawyer, now? This whole outfit would have fallen apart a long time ago without Eric's drive and willpower. He never much wanted to sell Cavelcombe, but you've had a bee in your bonnet about it for years. Doug and I both know what your second thing is going to be. All that "bodies in the night crap"—'

'I saw what I saw, and earlier that same day, some people have said there was a dinghy with people on it drifting in to the coast—'

'Change the fucking record, Bill,' said Doug Lane, as he started getting dressed. 'I don't want to be unkind, buddy, but you've been coked up to buggery for years now, and if you stood up in a court of law and talked about bodies being carried past you in the night, the other side would have a whole bunch of tame doctors to say what a cokehead you are. They'd also take one look at Josie and wonder why you weren't giving her one rather than wandering around in the dark…'

This was too much. Bill shot up out of his chair. For a moment, the three men stood eyeing each other, everyone wondering whether the end of the band was going to have to be marred by violence. Bill normally assumed the peacemaker role, which had been his most characteristic contribution to the Cougars over the years. This time, it took him a two-minute effort of slow breathing and yet more sweating, but the Cougars had always been, first and foremost, his baby, in his mind at least, and as this now obviously was the end of it, he wanted to try and do it as agreeably as possible. At the back of his mind, he knew that another confrontation with Tony might soon come along when he told him that the band was winding up. If he couldn't take Manny and Doug with him on that decision, the hoped-for amicable parting of the ways could turn into something much, much worse.

'OK, boys, OK. We all know enough about this business to know what happens to some bands when they break up. We've been doing this for a long time, and we all know each other very well; how many times have we been in dressing rooms like this over the years, sometimes after really great gigs when everybody loved us, sometimes after playing to about twenty kids who were all more interested in fucking each other as soon as possible? Every band has leftovers when the break-up comes. But, most of the time, I've had a ball, and I hope you have, too.'

'Sure,' said Manny. 'Don't get us wrong, Bill, we still love you, you old fucker.'

'Right enough,' said Doug. 'This band would never have existed without you, Brother.'

An awkward embrace between three half-dressed middle-aged men followed.

'Now all we've got to do is tell Tony,' Bill said.

'Well, he's spent plenty of time telling us how good he'd do if he went solo. Now he's going to have the chance to demonstrate it,' said Manny.

'He could turn into a gay icon,' said Doug.

'Or a geriatric one,' said Bill, and the mood melted into general hilarity.

Manny's prediction of Tony Richards' reaction proved to be very accurate.

'Yeah, OK,' he said, as the band's hired car pulled out of the town which would forever be the scene of the final Cougars' gig. 'It's probably about time, and I don't want any bad feelings about it, guys, but I have been thinking for a while that I would probably be better off on my own. I would like to include Cougars' stuff in my solo repertoire, if none of you guys has a problem with that. You'll still get payments for performances of them.'

The other three members couldn't help grins breaking out.

'Sure, Tony,' Bill said. 'Good luck getting the backing musicians. I'm sure it's only a matter of time before we see Rory Blaze records making it to – what – the top 150? 200?'

'Bollocks,' said Richards sullenly, and the car purred on its way.

Fifteen Months Later

In a house neatly positioned behind the restaurant which made the host family most of their money, Haidar was talking to a group of his close confidants, all Iraqi exiles, including his son Kassim. They were waiting for a visit from Ahmed, the universal Mr Fixit for so many of their countrymen and women in England. Haidar had not initially been particularly impressed by Ahmed, a man of indeterminate age, perhaps anywhere between thirty-five and fifty, soft spoken and almost apologetic in his very presence. But he soon discovered, partly through talking to others about Ahmed's status in their lives, that this man was the ultimate diplomat, with contacts all over the country, and an apparent ability to go wherever he chose and get to the people who mattered. He was the kind of man Haidar would gladly appoint as his aide-de-camp, whether in a peace or war situation.

For Haidar himself, things had moved on quite profitably. With the help of consulting a few informed sources in his home country, he had been able to place the names and regiments of British officers, including Captain Norwood, whom he had worked with during the war when his main intention was to prevent misunderstanding and unnecessary bloodshed, whatever the wilder accusations of collaboration made against him by some malign people trying to pretend that the actions of people like him mainly contributed to the defeat of Iraq. Haidar regarded such accusations as nonsensical; it was clearly the technological superiority of the Allied forces which caused the Iraqi defeat.

He had faith in the integrity of the British officers, and it looked at the moment that his faith might well be justified; the lawyer working in the interests of him and his remaining son believed the chances of asylum being granted were reasonably good.

But one big issue remained unsettled. Not only were members of his family, including his youngest son, still unburied, there was still a lack of clear information as to what had happened to their bodies.

Haidar was not naturally a particularly suspicious man, and he knew well enough that, given the weather conditions on the night concerned and the collision in the near-dark with a much larger boat, most of the ten missing men might well have died almost instantly. But his combat experience had included an awareness of the importance of prevailing tides, and he knew well enough that the tide was inward when he had swum to shore. Strong swimmer as he was, it would have been almost impossible for him to have made it to the shore before his strength gave way if the tide had been going out.

Somewhere along the way, Haidar now strongly suspected foul play. He no longer believed, having gone over the whole incident in detail with Kassim, that the much larger boat had collided with their dinghy by accident. Yes, the light was fading, but boats now invariably carried equipment to reveal nearby craft, however small, to them, and in any case, the dinghy would certainly have been visible to the people on that boat in time for them to avoid the collision, if they had seriously intended to avoid the collision.

Haidar's connections in Plymouth, established after the generous hospitality offered to him and Kassim immediately after their traumatic arrival in Britain, had looked at the possibilities of those local powerful people who were on record as being implacably opposed to the "little boats" taking such action as deliberately sabotaging a dinghy, and though Lord Railton and his bagman, a man called Irwin, had been high on their list after a few of Railton's public pronouncements on the subject, they had completely failed to establish even the slightest link to them. And it had become obvious that the area where Haidar had swum to the shore was populated by a large number of boats and their owners.

Kassim, perhaps because he had not seen as much of life as his father had, seemed to be prepared to regard the collision with the boat as an accident.

'Perhaps, my father, some of the men who control these boats here are idiots and don't have the proper equipment needed to see other craft. In any case, if they really wanted to kill us, a single machine gun would have done the trick.'

'Kassim, this is not a country where people keep guns in their houses like part of the furniture. If they wanted to kill us without any blame attaching to them, they would arrange such a collision, and then there is nothing they can be accused of. Use your brain, boy.'

Haidar had mixed feelings about his eldest son. He was tough and fit enough, a source of pride to his family, and the only other man who had made it alive to the shore. But he seemed almost indifferent to the loss of his younger brother, Baravan, and Haidar had long suspected Kassim harboured a certain amount of jealousy of his brother, who may not have been as physically tough, but was certainly a good deal cleverer. Haidar's plan for Baravan had been for him to train in law, meaning the family would have a qualified legal voice to argue their case in future. Baravan was also beautiful, and much as many men were scornful of beautiful young men, women were not, and Baravan had always represented the family's best hope of marriage into a successful and influential family, whether Iraqi or British.

Ahmed arrived, but as usual when this happened, it was a moment or two before the company realised he was amongst them; Ahmed's talents included an ability to remain almost invisible, when he needed to.

'Ahmed, my friend, you are very welcome among us. You look quite tired; do you have news for us? We are always grateful for your efforts on our behalf.'

'It is my joy and privilege, Muqaddam, and yes I do. I cannot tell you in detail how the information I am about to give you came to me. It is necessary at times to use some of the more attractive ladies of our nation to gather information from our British friends, knowing how fond some of them are of young ladies and alcohol, always a potent combination for anyone seeking accuracy in their knowledge-gathering. I shall not name the lady in question because it is important that our sources for this kind of thing remain anonymous, if they are to be effective.'

'Of course.' Haidar's face was not, he hoped, registering approval. He did not care for such methods, but he remembered them being used to good effect with British and American servicemen, and not always with girls. Someone had once made a suggestion to him that his son Baravan might be useful in this regard. Haidar had frozen the man with his stare.

'A young fisherman – well, a fisherman when the weather and circumstances allow, although he is one of those who will at other times use his boat for other purposes, including tourism and even moving drugs and stolen goods – wanted to impress his beautiful partner with his prowess as a man making "good money", as he called it, and told her that he knew the owner of the boat which collided with the dinghy. "Maybe I can make it up to you, darling," he said to our girl at one point, "since I know the guys who sent some of your men to Dave Jones's locker" – meaning, sir, killing them.'

Haidar's fists clenched and his face paled. Kassim was studiously looking at his feet.

'The man had heard a rumour that the boat had been directed to do what they did by someone who was a known contact of Mr Eric Irwin. "I've seen that guy with that military-type Irwin before," he said. He was slurring his words quite a lot by this time, but the "military-type Irwin" was quite distinct. "And bloody Irwin, everyone knows, is a bagman of His fucking Lordship up the hill there" – forgive my use of the language, sir, but it does convey the emotion the man seemed to feel.'

A long pause followed. The other men were looking at Haidar with some anxiety. He had paled still further, and as iron as they knew his self-control to be, the anger inside him seemed to be becoming so strong as to be uncontrollable.

'So,' Haidar said slowly, his voice thick with emotion, 'it seems the architect of our family's slaughter was an English "milord".'

'I do urge you, Muqaddam, not to act too rashly. A violent attack on a "peer of the realm", as they call them, would have disastrous consequences for your family—'

'How disastrous, exactly, Ahmed?' Haidar said, the anger now only too audible. 'Disastrous enough to kill another ten of us? Disastrous enough to let further members of my family die without proper burial, without us even knowing what was done with their bodies?'

He stopped and looked around him. All eyes were now firmly fixed on the floor. Haidar sighed, and then got to his feet. He held out his hand to Ahmed.

'Once again, Ahmed, my family is in your debt. And you are, of course, right. We will consider this important information, and revenge, when it comes, as it will do, will be carefully planned and executed so as not to do further harm to the family.'

Ahmed made a slight bow. He felt once again that he had done his duty and passed on the information the Muqaddam needed. It was now, he reflected gratefully, out of his hands.

One Year Later

In his younger years, Bill had a habit of running his fingers through his hair in emotional or troubled moments, and even though he didn't now have much hair left, the gesture remained, now concentrating on the side of his head, where just about enough hair remained to avoid the gesture looking strange.

Josie, sitting to the right of him, knew the gesture well enough, and at one time, she would have immediately reacted by trying to get to exactly what was bothering him. However, on this occasion, she knew exactly what was bothering him and her reaction was more impatient than sympathetic.

'Bill, for God's sake! Ever since the band broke up, you haven't had enough to do, and you're making up for it by concocting these ridiculous conspiracy theories, just to put a little excitement back into your life.'

He glanced across at her. Yes, she was a few years younger than him to start with, but she had undoubtedly worn better, even allowing for all the warpaint and adornments which women were allowed to use to disguise their age, which men weren't. He hadn't forgotten when they'd been sitting together in the hotel lounge which was next to the swimming pool – it was all he could do to keep her concentration on what they were talking about as her eyes kept straying to the young Adonis figures, which this hotel seemed to have in abundance, powering their way up and down the pool or sitting chatting poolside, as near naked as it was possible to be and still remain decent. Bill could only thank his lucky stars that he wasn't sitting with Tony Richards, whose eyes would be bulging out of their sockets.

Matters had not been going well between him and his wife for a while now. She had never liked his cocaine habit, which he knew well enough had affected various aspects of his life, including his sexual performance. But that wasn't the main reason why it irritated Josie; the expense and danger of it were the main bones of contention.

'When all's said and done, Bill, you are breaking the fucking law, you know. Not to mention buggering up the finances. You're not making loads of money from the Cougars any more, though most of that was finishing up with Eric Irwin anyway.'

The digs and jibes were coming at him thick and fast these days. It never seemed to occur to her that the break-up of the Cougars was still hurting, and he had to somehow make his way through that before anything else could happen. As for the bodies passing under his window that night, however long ago that had been, it was just not something he could "forget and move on from", as she constantly put it.

'Josie, it's not a matter of excitement in my life. I was the founder and lead member of a pop band which recorded phenomenal success for years; I've had enough excitement to last two lifetimes. But I know what I saw that night, and I know well enough the rumours that have been going round the area around Cavelcombe House. Whenever you think they've finally gone away, they come back again. Yes, I know no one saw anything and no one could prove anything, but locals still talk about an accident that night, bodies collected from the sea; the stories still persist, even after all this time.'

Alright, Josie thought. Enough is enough. Affection lingered in her heart for this man who had been mainly responsible for catapulting her into a more exotic and pulsating existence than she had ever believed possible. When he started talking to her after that gig in Nottingham, she could hardly believe her good fortune. He was so, so different then; handsome, bright-eyed, with a smile that could pierce you right through to the heart. Their first love-making was epic; five times, they managed, one autumn night in Paris, when at last she had him to herself, without a Cougar in sight. Even then, Eric was giving her the eye, but her eyes were entirely for Bill. Now he'd turned into this drug-crazed, paranoid junkie, balding rapidly, struggling to raise a cheer, even if she could be convinced that he still fancied her. She knew the stories about him and Tony Richards. Maybe now he was just reverting to what he'd always been. Maybe that's why they'd never had children.

She was still young enough to find someone. Eric might take her on, though, she suspected, most women would see Eric as too much like hard work, and in this case, most women included her. It was a big bullet to bite, but she had to bite it.

'Bill, darling. Let's stop this. It's over, my love. There's no point in either of us bashing our brains out over it. Maybe you're right. Maybe something did happen that night. And I know breaking up the Cougars has hit you hard. But they're all symptoms, Bill, aren't they? We know what the disease is. When you try the romantic weekend in a nice hotel bit, Bill, I know you're aware yourself that we're in trouble and we need somewhere to sort it out. But do we really need to drive ourselves crazy? We've both still got enough about us to find someone else, rather than spend the rest of our lives battering against each other. Face facts, Bill. It's over.'

Bill looked at her long and hard. OK, he thought. I know well enough what this is about.

'What's the matter, Josie? Not enough glamour for you any more? Do you remember the words? "In sickness and in health, to have and to hold, till death do us part." Except, when it gets a bit sticky, when you can't flirt around in nice hotels while I'm working my balls off in front of thousands of people, that's it, is it? Fuck you, Bill, I'm off. You're not a star any more, and I only lay down for stars, old man. Or Eric Irwin. Does he count as a star, Josie?'

Bill looked down at his drink as soon as he'd finished speaking. Yes, she was right, it was over, but he'd never meant to hurt her like this. He didn't look at her face because he couldn't. And when he finally turned to her, she was gone.

PART FIVE

Back to the Present: Resolution 1

Max Bellamy had registered a number of unforgettable days during his career, but he had little expectation that this was going to be one of them. Whatever invisible hand was behind the tortuous situation he faced, it was clear enough that they still had the initiative, and he and his team were running to catch up. His wife was still in Scotland, though she had now rented an apartment of her own as a certain amount of tension had arisen with her cousin, who usually lived on her own. The local police knew who she was and where she was, and as far as anyone knew, there were no moles in that area of the Scottish force, but that only partly eased Bellamy's perpetual anxiety.

In every case, and in particular, complicated ones like this, a period would occur somewhere along the way when the whole business started resembling walking through treacle, with every step very difficult and no step actually managing to cover much ground.

Bellamy's instinct was telling him that there was a connection somewhere between the ten bodies discovered in the grounds of Cavelcombe House and the death of Bill Massiter, but instinct wouldn't do in a court of law. Some of the reasons for his instinct were logical in anyone's language; the evidence suggested that the bodies were buried during the period when Cavelcombe House was owned by Eric Irwin and the Cougars, and nobody had to spend much time looking at the communications between Irwin and Massiter to tell that their relationship was regularly tense, to say the least. But Bellamy had met Eric Irwin and knew quite a lot about Bill Massiter, not least from Richard Bellamy's occasional writings, sparse as they were, and neither of them struck him as men capable of killing, including killing themselves.

Richard Bellamy's notes hadn't proved very revealing; his prose style in his notebooks was sparse, rather different from the discursive and analytic tone of his articles. In any case, Richard had known nothing about most of the events of this case. He also tended to avoid saying too clearly what he thought about people in his notes; journalists always had to be aware of the laws of libel, even in relation to private journals, knowing they could one day be published. But there was enough about Bill Massiter, who Richard clearly liked, to suggest that he being the kind of man who would kill himself was certainly not how Richard Bellamy saw him.

Mid-morning was going to include one of his regular sessions with Mary and Dean, though Bellamy was not anticipating much emerging from it. Dean's achievement in noting the lie of the land at Cavelcombe House had not, as yet, been followed up by any equally trenchant insights, and Mary seemed to find herself marching up various blind alleys as a matter of course. They were both able and resourceful officers, and Bellamy was not in much of a position to criticise since his preoccupation with his wife's situation was not helping him to see what, in both police and journalistic work, tended to be referred to as "the bigger picture". No further threatening phone calls or bizarre shooting incidents had occurred. It seemed that whoever was pulling the strings in this case was content enough now to see the forces of law and order chasing their own tails.

But, as Mary and Dean made themselves comfortable in the DCI's office, palatial compared with most of the working environments they were used to, they both seemed to have an air of optimism and energy about them, and the routine meeting already seemed to be taking on the nature of something else.

'OK,' Bellamy started. 'We can discuss tactics and new avenues of investigation in a little while, but first of all, you both look as though you might have something interesting to tell me, so let's do that before anything else. Ladies first.'

'Sir, I've been contacted by an Iraqi man, who speaks good English since it appears that he worked in this country for some time and he also says that he served as a translator during the Iraq war, helping both the British and American forces. He has admitted to me that he is in this country illegally at the moment, but he is willing to accept whatever fate the authorities decide for him in order to correct what he calls a "monstrous injustice". He has hesitated for some time to come forward, knowing the difficult situation it would put him in, but he says there are more important things at stake. When he saw on the news the bodies being discovered in the grounds of Cavelcombe House, he says he knew it would be dishonourable for him to remain silent any longer.'

Mary went on to tell the tale in her inimitable way, adding her own impressions of the man who had told it to her, and the two men with her were enthralled with her account as the many implications of it occurred to their police officer's minds.

'Finally, he tells me that he was in a position where his need to get out of Iraq was becoming extremely urgent, and much as he would have preferred to attempt to get into Britain by legitimate means, the situation was becoming highly dangerous because of the way some of the more extreme Iraqi organisations were seeing his efforts to act as an interpreter for the American and British forces, "to avoid misunderstandings", as he puts it. He names an officer, a captain at the time, called Edward Norwood, who expressed the army's appreciation of Haidar's services – his name is Haidar Alwan – and said that when he was in Iraq he was prepared to support an application by Haidar and some members of his family for political asylum, but Norwood was recalled before the application could go ahead. Haidar's wife, Lateefah, is originally from Jordan and has Jordanian citizenship, meaning she has been able to go to relatives in Jordan, taking their daughters Derifa and Sadiya with her.

'Of the twelve men on the dinghy, Haidar and his eldest son, Kassim, managed to swim to shore on an incoming tide. Haidar says that he believes the remaining ten, several of whom were directly related to him, died either as a result of the collision with the larger boat or by drowning, or a bit of both. He is particularly devastated by the loss of his younger son, Baravan; this was the only time in our conversation that I saw tears in his eyes. Haidar is prepared to give us chapter and verse on the traffickers who arranged the trip, because he believed the considerable amount of money he paid should have entitled him to a proper boat, not a dinghy, and should have resulted in a safer landing point.

'I haven't, as yet, checked on the officer, Captain Norwood, to see if he is still in the army and still prepared to support Haidar's application; I thought it better to await your orders on that one, sir, in case the powers-that-be in the army and the police accuse me of exceeding my authority.'

'I will look into that myself, Mary. Even if he is no longer in the army, it shouldn't be that difficult to track him down,' said Bellamy, whose sense that this particular mystery was at last beginning to unravel was already starting to put new heart into him. 'Just to be clear in my mind, Mary, about exactly what we're looking at here, I take it that Haidar is convinced that the ten bodies found at Cavelcombe House are those of the men with him on the dinghy.'

'Absolutely, sir, and while we will need to check the forensic reports carefully, as I understand it the estimates that have been given about the age of those bodies would gel neatly with the time when this incident supposedly occurred, according to Haidar and also with reference to a few vague newspaper comments at the time. It would also explain why the bodies were all naked, presumably an attempt to remove all traces of identity, though DNA checks have still been possible and have already suggested their likely racial identity, which would bear out the drowning story.'

'I see. Well, the evidence is already suggesting several kinds of crime may well have been committed with references to the men on that dinghy, and my instinct is now shouting at me that there is something which links the dinghy incident to the death of Bill Massiter. Did Massiter see something? Did whoever caused the deaths know Massiter had seen something? In the absence, as yet, of evidence concrete enough to stand up in court, I am going to have to start talking to people, and Haidar might be a suitable place to start.'

'Haidar is very willing to talk to you, sir, but he has made a request that the conversation does not take place in a police station. It appears that the immigrant community in general, and the Iraqis in particular, tend to regard one of their number talking in a police station as tantamount to an admission that they are informing. His language is very respectful and formal.' Mary took an individual piece of paper from her notes and read from it. 'If the senior police officer is prepared to talk to me person to person, regardless for the moment of the asylum issue, I submit that I will be able to supply the gentleman concerned with valuable information regarding the death of ten of my countrymen, including relatives and friends, in their attempt to enter Britain. I fully admit that this attempt was illegal, and will supply information which could well lead to the conviction of a number of traffickers, but my family and I had been so threatened and intimidated that I was forced to arrange for my main female relatives, my wife and two daughters, to flee to Jordan, where my wife fortunately has Jordanian citizenship. My work in helping the occupying British and American forces to avoid misunderstandings, intended only to save bloodshed arising from simple misinterpretations, has been seen by some as collaboration and my relatives and I are under a very real threat of severe violence. I suspect Haidar must have an English adviser, perhaps an ethnic Iraqi born and bred in Britain, to help him put this letter together.'

'I'm grateful to you, Mary; we may well, as a result of this, gather a number of good leads to solve ten unjustified deaths, and I will certainly talk to Haidar for as long as is necessary. But it would help with the politics of the business if you could track down the English officer who Haidar says will support what he says about his help with the Allied forces. I don't want the Home Office breathing down my neck, or at least, if and when they do, I want to have a clear case to put to them.'

'Yes, sir. I will get on to that today.'

Bellamy paused for thought again.

'Clearly, we must pursue the whole business of the ten bodies and exactly how those men died; it sounds to me like we could be looking at a case of mass murder. But we do have to bear in mind that this investigation started with the death of Bill Massiter, and even though that is one death compared to ten, we do have to remember our original aims.'

'I might have a lead there, sir.' Dean Matheson, still looking the picture of health and fitness compared with his older colleagues, referred to his notes.

'It's almost impossible to track down exactly who was in residence at Cavelcombe House, sir, at any one time, but the security company who are now in charge of looking after it before the impending sale, when the interested parties have finally made their minds up, maintain that it is clear enough that Bill and Josie, for whatever reasons, did continue to use Cavelcombe House after the break-up of the Cougars. Bill seemed to feel, from remarks we have attributed to Tony Richards, that now the Cougars were over, he was at last entitled to his own leisure time, and staying at Cavelcombe was as comfortable as being in a hotel but a good deal cheaper, now that Cougars' gigs and record sales were not keeping so much money flooding in. So, on the basis of what we know about the timings of these bodies being taken to Cavelcombe House, it is at least possible that Bill and Josie were there at the time, even if we can't name any dates.'

'Absolutely, yes, thank you, Dean. And, unless I mistake my Bill Massiter, including my father's opinion of him, he would not have liked that one little bit. For once, we've got the big fat arrow pointing in a big fat direction. I'm going to have to have another go at Josie, who I've always suspected wasn't telling me the whole truth, and at Irwin, who I'm now just about certain isn't telling me the whole truth. What about that authority figure in Irwin's background, Mary, that you've always suspected?'

'Oh, yes, sir, I was going to come to that. Eric Irwin has for some time, including during the time when he was effectively managing the Cougars, worked with Lord Railton, an eccentric gentleman with, let's, say, some far-right views. I think Railton might be the sort of father-figure type, even if the relationship is not likely to have much family affection about it, which is necessary to Eric Irwin's character.'

Time to think. Now he spent most of his time with people he outranked, it became that much easier; explanations did not have to be offered, explanations which he'd always thought were essentially redundant anyway. He had actually physically turned away from the two other people with him in the room, and now he got to his feet – thinking also needed movement at times – and went to the window as if the view of the car park and the spreading countryside beyond would somehow help the thought processes.

'It all stinks, doesn't it?' he said, half to himself.

'Sir?' Dean was leaning forward in his chair. He knew Bellamy well enough by now to know that this sort of thing almost always led to direct action of some kind.

'Ten deaths. Well, eleven if you count poor Bill Massiter. And Bill is the only one of the eleven we can actually name, and even then, we can't say with certainty how he died. It's bizarre. And it's deeply disturbing. A whole bunch of unexplained and ambiguous deaths, and people going to great efforts to stop us finding out about them.'

He walked back to his seat, and looked up at the two expectant faces before him.

'Either someone in this case – well, at least one person, though it could be more – is too afraid to tell us the truth, or this person or persons are so confident of themselves that they think we are too afraid to go looking for the truth. If it's the latter, then we must now show them, not only that we're not afraid, but that we are coming after them with all guns blazing. I want you, Mary, to look closely at the past record of His Lordship Railton, including public speeches he has made and the business deals he's been involved in over recent years; I also want to know how many of them also involved Eric Irwin, and in what capacity, either proved or suspected.

'Dean, I want you to look in detail at the movements of Bill Massiter and his wife, Josie, including who they regularly see apart from each other, and please try to get me some detail of what was happening in Cavelcombe during the period when it's assumed that those bodies were buried in the grounds of Cavelcombe.

'What I'm going to do, assuming you're wondering about that – if you weren't, you should have been – is start getting heavy with a few people I'm now sure have been holding out on me from the start, such as Josie Massiter and, of course, Eric Irwin, and I'm going to impress upon their tight little minds that the longer they don't tell me what I need to know, the more I'm going to make life difficult for them. We've had long enough pussyfooting around. And after I've spoken to Haidar, I'm also going to put the wind up this Railton character, peer of the realm or not. I suspect he might know that some of the asylum seekers, including Haidar, suspect him of monstrous crimes.'

Bellamy unleashed a rare grin in the direction of his assistants.

'Let's go to it, boys and girls. Call me a hopeless optimist if you will, but I am seeing some light at the end of this particular tunnel, and there are times when throwing your weight around has the potential to pay dividends, something both of you might bear in mind if and when you reach senior ranking, which wouldn't surprise me with either of you. To put it more basically, it's kick-ass time. Off you go. I'm going to go on my travels; Haidar first, if you can fix the time and place for that, Mary. It doesn't have to be in a police station, but nor am I going to wherever he's living, bearing in mind that he's still an illegal immigrant. In any case, I'll take a couple of heavies with me, just to be on the safe side. We'll meet again the day after tomorrow.'

The next morning, in a hotel a few miles off the M4, with a room booked for the purpose, Bellamy shook hands with Haidar Alwan. As if meeting up for a vital international summit, the two men sat at either end of a table, its computers and notebooks conveniently moved away to the sides of the room. Standing behind Haidar were his son Kassim and his adviser Ahmed; behind Bellamy stood two burly constables.

Bellamy decided it was most appropriate for him to start the proceedings.

'Mr Alwan, my feeling is that we might be able to talk more easily if we are the only people in the room. I will ask my constables to wait outside the room if you will do likewise with your accompanying gentlemen.'

Haidar looked at the younger men behind him and whispered something to Ahmed.

'Sir, Ahmed here is my adviser and sometimes interpreter. My English is not always as reliable as I would wish. I would be grateful if he could remain by my side. My son Kassim will withdraw.'

Bellamy nodded at the younger of the two constables, and he and Kassim left the room.

'You don't need me to tell you, Haidar – may I call you Haidar? – that at the moment your status is that of an illegal immigrant to this country, and while I have every sympathy with your problems in your native country, you do rather put yourself in the wrong when you enter Britain by illegal means.'

Ahmed whispered in Haidar's ear for a moment. Haidar nodded solemnly.

'I do understand that, sir, and the fact that I am here shows my willingness to submit to British justice, though, as Ahmed will tell you – he has evidence to support what he says – my life and that of my son, the only young man to survive our experience – will be severely in danger if I am sent back to Iraq. The officer, Captain Norwood, who approved of my efforts, is now Major Norwood, and we know that he has written evidence of my work. But that is no longer the most important issue, sir. It is our belief that our young countrymen were murdered by a plot involving Lord Railton—'

'It is a very serious business to accuse an English peer of the realm of murder, Haidar,' Bellamy said.

'I realise that, sir. But you will forgive me if I say that Ahmed and his contacts in England have been investigating this case for some time now; years have passed since the supposed accident, and it seems that no one here has as yet even realised that a crime was committed. We have some evidence from local contacts to suggest that someone linked to the man Irwin did talk to the owner of a boat for hire and told him that a well-paid job was available for them concerning an incoming dinghy. We have no evidence that these men were known to Lord Railton, but we know that Mr Irwin has briefed local men to do things for him in the past.'

'That is a lot of surmise and suspicion, Haidar; none of it is proof.'

An awkward pause; Bellamy was used to awkward pauses in investigations, and generally saw them as potentially revealing. During this one, he saw Haidar and Ahmed clearly exchanging odd glances, as if trying to make a decision by telepathic means. Whatever decision needed taking, Haidar appeared to take it, and he turned back towards Bellamy with determination in his voice.

'I know from my experience, sir, that senior English police officers are not easy to convince. My English is usually up to the task after my time of working in your country, but on this issue I feel it might be better for Ahmed to explain the situation. Ahmed, please.'

Ahmed appeared to reluctantly accept his role, perhaps his idea of seemly modesty, but the way he then launched into his explanation was in itself an indication that Haidar was probably right.

'What I have to say now, sir, you may also dismiss as surmise, but I would most strongly recommend you not to. We have information that the case of these ten drowned men has reached the ears of a man known to us only as Khaled, though we believe the American authorities have another name for him. The Iraqi war had disastrous consequences for many men, sir, and as you probably know, it was instrumental in bringing about the organisation known as the Islamic State, or ISIS. Most men prefer to work with comrades rather than strike out on their own, but there are a few clever and resourceful individuals who emerged from that conflict not only traumatised but determined to wage their own personal war. To come to the point, sir, Khaled is known as what you would call a hit man, a professional hit man. He has used his experience of weapons and forgery to provide himself with several aliases and passports, and while he is generally concerned with making his own fortune internationally, he does sometimes take on personal cases, directed against people who have committed crimes against his countrymen. There are strong rumours – and yes, sir, I cannot say that they have yet got beyond that – that Khaled heard about the case of the ten corpses in the grounds of Cavelcombe House and the far-right multimillionaire who lives only minutes away from that shore. He could hardly fail to hear about it, given the national and international media coverage following the excavations at Cavelcombe House. We don't know where he is at the moment – no one knows where Khaled is at any time – but the Iraqi international grapevine, I think you would call it, sir, is saying that he is "on the case". Khaled is frequently referred to in Iraqi circles as "the Scorpion" because of the way he creeps into the life of his victims and suddenly contrives a way to slaughter them.

'You might, with your well-known Western scepticism, dismiss the whole thing as the fancy of a superstitious and resentful people, but I would suggest to you, sir, that Khaled may well already be known to your own secret service – in fact, I would be surprised if he wasn't. He has at least eight victims we know about in his record so far, most of them rich industrialists, but also including a couple of ex-Allied administrators of the Iraqi occupation. You will, I hope, heed our warning, sir, whatever contempt you may feel for the conspiracy theories which haunt all our affairs now. We also suspect that the man Massiter, who at the time was very publicly against the Iraqi war, may have died because of his opposition to what he suspected were the plans of the man Irwin and his superior, Lord Railton. Not at the hands of the Scorpion, of course – the Scorpion would not hit at known opponents of the war – but by agents of Irwin or Railton. Please believe, sir, that we are trying to help, not hinder. This man Khaled is very dangerous; we have watched your conscientious pursuit of this case, against the interference of the criminal individuals responsible, with admiration. It would be very wrong to find your career damaged by events beyond your control.'

Bellamy had to move himself away from the other people in the room. This, he knew, could be a careful and well thought out ruse to make him identify Railton as the main force behind the drownings, while also providing him with a neat resolution for the Massiter case. Yes, he could remember Bill Massiter being quoted as being against British intervention in Iraq, but so were a lot of people, though few of them allowed themselves to get directly involved. And concocting a suicide scene was certainly not beyond the wit of Eric Irwin, though bringing it about himself was improbable; the relationship between Massiter and Irwin had been close for years. Irwin had been influential in ensuring the success of the Cougars.

As he gazed out of the window, seeing nothing but several anonymous buildings – seeing them, but only half registering their existence – Bellamy could hear some shuffling and coughing behind him. They were already nervous about his reaction, which could either be sincere people genuinely anxious that what they were saying would not be taken seriously, or conspirators recognising that they were on the edge of success or failure.

Such is this job, Bellamy thought; however much thinking, however much information, it still tended to come down to the gut feeling, the hunch, the best shot. Ahmed was not necessarily the man most likely to convince; he spoke concisely enough, but his whole manner tended to be apologetic, verging on the servile, and Bellamy could hardly fail to notice the unsubtle flattery at the end, calculated, perhaps, to appeal to an English ego. Haidar was a solid military man; reliable and intelligent in his way, but certainly not an inventor of conspiracies and probably not usually inclined to believe in them.

He returned to his seat and fixed them with a steady gaze.

'Thank you, gentlemen, for being prepared to confide in me about this. You are right, Ahmed, to say that a man with a record like Khaled should be known to our secret services, and it would be in my power to find that out. But I ought to point out that this man Khaled is likely by now to know quite a lot about the British, following the war and his experiences since, and therefore, he is also likely to know that the assassination of a British peer is guaranteed to bring the whole machinery of British security, both national and international, down on his head and make his future life and career difficult, if not impossible. Whatever you think of the British class system, and I will keep my own opinions on that to myself, an attack on the aristocracy can be taken very personally indeed. Whether he would be prepared to put such a burden on himself on the basis of a suspicion, even a strong suspicion, I rather doubt. You must also know that what happened on the sea that day could fairly easily be portrayed as an accident by any lawyer worth his salt, and they would make the case that, at worst, it could be seen as an attempt to intimidate future refugees from making such a crossing. The deaths, they would argue, were largely a result of the adverse weather conditions and the impact of the boats colliding; no murderous intention was involved. And they would also maintain, of course, that the fact that two of the men were able to swim to shore meant that the others could quite conceivably have done the same, thereby once again denying any premeditated murder intentions. What is just as criminal, in British eyes, would be the clandestine way in which the men's bodies were abducted and buried, naked and without ceremony, without any regard to their religious identity and the feelings of their families and friends.'

Bellamy saw the men in front of him nodding vigorously, and for once, he had an idea on the spot which he was prepared to put to them.

'I would like you and me to look on a map, Haidar, perhaps with the aid of Ahmed, who I suspect probably knows that section of coast better than either of us, since it was Ahmed who met you when you swam to shore. I want us to plot, as exactly as possible, where it was that you and Kassim landed. When we know that, we should be able to identify, without too much trouble, where the collision between the boat and the dinghy happened. You will also be able to tell me the date, so we can calculate, also with reference to the Met Office, the light and conditions prevalent on that day. Many a police officer has fallen foul of clever lawyers by not properly knowing a crime scene. We will also then be able to estimate the chances of an accident happening at that point, which will get us closer to being able to discard the idea that it was an accident at all.'

The men in front of him seemed to be exchanging uneasy glances. Bellamy didn't need to think for very long before he worked out why, but Ahmed started speaking first.

'I think the general opinion, sir, is that the boatmen on that section of the coast, who we understand include some who have previously worked for Mr Irwin, are likely to try as much as they can not to incriminate any of their friends. They are likely to firmly deny that any of them were on the sea that day, and if an incident did take place, which they are also likely to deny, the boat which collided with the dinghy wasn't one of theirs. The people in that area are very protective of each other, sir, and resent the interference of others.'

'Two things to be said to that, Ahmed. As a senior police officer, I have powers, and they could include forcing every boat on that section of the coast to remain in harbour until evidence becomes available. I don't want to do that, but I will if necessary. And the fact that Haidar and Kassim are here, and were met by you on the coast, indicates quite clearly that something did happen on that day. It would be enough proof for most courts, I think, and when the locals there realise that there were survivors, it will be difficult for them to deny that something happened. And please don't misunderstand the people of that area. I don't doubt there are a few bad eggs amongst them, there are among every group of people, and I suspect the local men know who they are. We have to now put enough pressure on them to ensure that the decent men, and most of them will be decent men, come forward. They will know who has accepted jobs and money from Mr Irwin in the past. If Railton is involved, it will emerge in due course; it is well known that Irwin often works for him.'

Exchanged glances again, but this time, it seemed to be about who was to sum up on behalf of them all, and of course, they all looked towards Haidar.

'You give us confidence, Mr Bellamy. If any of us can help with your investigation in any way—'

'Well, to begin with, Haidar, you and Kassim could probably supply me with the clothes you were wearing on that day. Of course, you will have washed them since, but I don't doubt, in the confines of that dinghy, that evidence of the DNA of the men around you may still be traceable. I should also perhaps assure you all that if I tell the Home Office that you are essential to my present investigation, no proceedings to expel you from the country will happen until at least my investigation is finished, and that will give us more time to gather information and witnesses about your interpreting help during the war.'

The sense of relief and relaxation in the room was now almost tangible. But Ahmed, of course, continued to wear the look of controlled anxiety which seemed to be a constant with him. Bellamy glanced towards him, and the question in his eyes was so obvious that Ahmed responded.

'I am very concerned about the Scorpion, Mr Bellamy. I know it sounds rather childish, I suppose, these dramatic nicknames, but our information is that there is nothing remotely childish or adventure story about this man. He is an efficient and totally ruthless cold-blooded killer, and I think you know as well as I do, Mr Bellamy, the likely conclusions your police colleagues will come to if Lord Railton is suddenly shot to death by a man from our country. They are likely to think we are all in it together, and the result will be not only the end of Haidar's and Kassim's chances of remaining in the country, but also the end of any chances we have of giving our countrymen a decent burial and making whoever caused their deaths pay for it. It is well known that Khaled does not delay for very long when he has decided on a target; the kind of people who employ him don't want him to, and when he's aiming at a personal target, he will want to do it quickly because he is not earning anything from it. It is low, immoral, depraved; it is all of those things, but all past experience suggests that, not long after rumours emerge of his next target, he will act so as to ensure the rumours don't start putting people on his tail.'

'I suspect Railton will have security guards employed on his estate. He's not a man who will deceive himself into believing everyone loves him,' Bellamy said, and the men around him became suddenly restless as a result.

'Khaled has killed very rich men living in mansions bristling with security measures. I will name no names, Mr Bellamy, in case I make accusations that will cause him to come after me, but on more than one of his cases, the scene after the killing included a number of security people tied tightly in restraint or knocked unconscious, taking hours to recover. The only saving grace, if it can be described as such, is that it is usually only his target who actually dies; if anyone else does, it is because they have shot at him or tried to assault him.'

Back in his office, Bellamy had made the necessary arrangements with his chief constable and could now only wait for some anonymous voice from Spookland to contact him.

'They will know your name and rank, Max, but you won't know theirs,' Jack Henshaw had said. 'They come to us like taciturn angels from on high, if generally angels with British public-school accents. They don't tell you who they are and they don't give a shit who you are, though they will always have checked on you from their damn files. And if they don't want to tell you anything, they are just as likely to tell you to go fuck yourself. Best of luck, but if they decide to clam up on you, come back to me and I'll have a go myself. I have a few buddies in amongst them, which can be very useful at times.'

As the appointed time approached, Bellamy had started to get the odd mixture of excitement and dread which usually presaged times of action and sometimes desperation.

He had rarely known a case where the death of one man had proved to have such widespread and potentially damaging repercussions, and the longer it continued, the more nuanced and remarkable had become the revealed character of Bill Massiter, for whom even the exalted description of "pop star" seemed somehow inadequate, for all the background catalogue of a broken marriage and drug problems.

It took several seconds for him to realise, in his reverie, that the phone was buzzing, an insidious noise like a mechanical wasp. He picked it up.

'Hello. Am I talking to Detective Chief Inspector Bellamy?'

Expecting a languid southern drawl, Bellamy was surprised to hear a quiet Scottish accent, probably from the Edinburgh area.

'Yes, speaking,' he said.

'Good. You guys often seem to have layers of minions to wade through before reaching your rarefied personages, and I rarely have time to fuck around, like yourself, I suspect. What's your name?'

'Bellamy.'

'No, your first name. I'm not a fucking Etonian talking surnames all the time.'

'Max.'

'Good. So, Max, you want to know about Khaled, the so-called fucking Scorpion, though in his case, it's an appropriate enough name. Do we know of him? Yes, we certainly do, and of course, we blame your colleagues largely for the fact that he's still in circulation. We've proposed stake-outs on several occasions when he'd practically sent us a postcard – he's an arrogant fucker, and he likes to pull our chains. But you lot will hum and haw about available personnel and should they be armed, and by the time you've had your committees and made your bloody minds up, he's off and away like the fucking invisible man.'

'I'll take your word for it. I know nothing about any of that, but I do know he has a peer of the realm in his sights now, and if he succeeds, it will create additional problems for people whose co-operation I need in a murder case, possibly eleven murder cases.'

'Peer of the realm? Yes, well, I suppose you could call Railton that. He's a peer mainly because he brown-nosed a certain British politician when they were both college boys, so said politician made him a lord later on, probably because he saw it as a jolly jape. He's really the most appalling shit; he spends his time blasting his mind out with old heavy rock like a bloody overgrown adolescent, and we've been hoping we might get him eventually for being a member of an illegal organisation; to all intents and purposes, he's a fucking Nazi.'

'Meaning, presumably, that sooner or later someone is going to have to do something about him, and that can only be either you or us, unless we're going to leave Khaled to do our dirty work for us.'

'Exactly, Max. A masterful summary of the situation. I'm glad I'm talking to a police officer with a brain in his head. You used to be a journalist, didn't you?'

'Yes, I did, but I don't see what that's got to do with it.'

'Public perception, Max. It's not just a question of what happens, it's about how what happens is perceived, especially in a democracy. We can say we'd like Khaled to do the job for us, but the great British public will be shocked and stunned at the murder of a British milord, however much of a shit he is. What I'm going to suggest is the nearest thing we can think of to an ideal solution; there is no such thing, of course, but we're in the business of trying to get near. When you go to see him, tell him we know the Scorpion is after him because of his role in killing those men on the dinghy; he'll deny it, of course, but then you make him understand that it's not ultimately what we think which is the dangerous factor here, it's what Khaled thinks, and Khaled isn't going to stop and argue the toss. Tell him we can't afford to give him twenty-four-hour protection, because there are plenty of other demands on the public purse, and in any case, he can afford to protect himself. Therefore, the best thing for him to do is make himself scarce for a while. Take himself off to some God-forsaken hole where he can amuse himself with the local girls and surround himself with cheap local hoods. Then he's out of our hair for a while, which gives us time to get rid of Khaled and gather evidence about the things Railton's been up to, including his escapade with the dinghy; we can do Irwin in the meantime, because if Railton sanctioned it, you can bet your bottom dollar that Irwin had his oar in somewhere. It's our belief that Irwin was mainly responsible for the death of poor Bill Massiter, but that's your baby, Max. He wouldn't have done it himself, that's for sure; he's a big mouth, but most of it is piss and wind. Any comments so far?'

'Only one. It rather depends, doesn't it, on whether Khaled is going to give us time? Haidar and his friends think that he usually acts very soon after rumours start, because the more the rumours spread, the more he's likely to have people waiting for him.'

'Oh, yes, Haidar, while I remember. He was useful in Iraq and he's already being useful in this country; he'll get asylum, whatever the fucking Home Office think about it. He would have already got it, if the Home Office didn't work at the pace of a crippled snail. Anyway, Max, you've got the number. Keep us in touch. We're not in the business of telling you what to do, DCI Bellamy, but we did want to give you a few pointers in the right direction.'

Two days later, Bellamy sat alone in his temporary home, listening, once again, to a few of his favourite Chopin pieces. There was something exultant, consoling, life-affirming about much of Chopin's music, and he found it useful to get himself in the right frame of mind to do something which could well turn out to be dangerous. There were situations which he had faced in journalism as well as police work. Criminals generally hated the idea of their real names appearing in the media as much as they hated the police having useful information on them, and the more seriously criminal they were, the more they hated it. Whistle-blowers, sometimes in the lower ranks of very large organisations, were also very vulnerable to those in the higher echelons of those organisations whose criminality was undiscovered and who were very keen on keeping it that way. In his journalistic days, Bellamy had been threatened, both publicly and privately, with everything from a beating or being thrown off cliff tops to being hanged in the street or shot in his own home. Such episodes had continued in his police career, and the further up the ladder of promotion he went, the more frequent they seemed to become.

He considered that, in the case of the murder of Bill Massiter, the people he was dealing with, most obviously Railton and Eric Irwin, were the very people who would have constituted a very real threat to him at one time, though Bellamy knew from past experience that the nearer he got to the guilty people, the more likely they were to panic and jump into activities potentially harmful to their interest.

The plan agreed, under Bellamy's orders and with the tacit approval of the secret services, though only Bellamy knew that, was for him and three armed police officers, all firearms-trained, to mount a raid on Lord Railton's home. If there was no sign of Khaled, the so-called "Scorpion", the raid could be justified on the grounds that a visit from Khaled was anticipated and the police were taking the threat seriously enough to discourage him if he was still thinking about it. When Railton was told that police budgets would not allow the protection to become permanent, he could be panicked into a confession concerning the deaths of the men in the dinghy, so that he could be taken into custody awaiting trial. At the very least, he would be encouraged to use his considerable resources to ensure his home was fully protected. But the idea that this was now the way he would have to live for the foreseeable future might also encourage him to be clear about his previous actions, including the hiring of people to launch attacks on Bellamy's wife and home. This last item rankled with Bellamy particularly; for most of this difficult and at times dangerous case, he had had to deal with it without the company of the wife he loved and who gave a particular meaning to his life. In Bellamy's book, someone had to pay for that, and that someone, he was now as sure as he could be, was Lord Railton. Irwin, for all his arrogance and menace, was a bagman, a gofer, who did as he was told; His Lordship, crazy or politically on the edge, however it was interpreted, was the main villain of the piece.

Privately, Bellamy faced the prejudice in him, that Railton was the kind of man who would not be a loss to the world, and if the Scorpion got him, the killer would probably be doing everyone a favour, but Bellamy was a professional police officer, and foreign gunmen could not be allowed to rampage around Britain killing peers of the realm, however morally dubious the peers of the realm might be.

For a few minutes, Bellamy was able to lose himself in the wonderful patterns and cadences Chopin could conjure up. An imperious knock on the door, which Bellamy registered as meaning one of his party was suitably assertive to be at least a sergeant, took him drastically away from the music.

The next five minutes were the kind of completely silent prelude to action common to professional law agents about to confront an equally professional member of the criminal classes. The two front seats were occupied by a young, trained driver in the front passenger seat and a not quite so young, trained driver actually driving the car, while Bellamy and the sergeant, a man called Ellis who Bellamy knew from earlier cases, sat in the back. The car's back windows were shaded and all the windows were bulletproof.

A few minutes after they departed, Bellamy turned to the man beside him.

'Sergeant Ellis, let me make clear to you and your colleagues that no one must shoot without my explicit instructions. If we are in a situation where any of you are visible to me and I am not in a position to speak, one simple nod will authorise you to fire on whoever the gunman might be. If I can speak, only when I say "fire" will you shoot. I say this clearly in the hearing of all of you, so you know exactly when you can claim to have been given instructions to fire. If you fire at any time without having been given instructions, it will mean a disciplinary hearing at the very least. Is that clear to everyone?'

'Yes, sir,' said Ellis, and the two younger men in the front seats echoed him.

An inspection of Railton's property had revealed a side entrance about halfway down a long street leading down to the sea. Bellamy ordered the car to stop about 200 yards short of the entrance on the landward end of the street. As the four men emerged from the car, Bellamy noticed a long black vehicle similar to their own, and he suspected also with bulletproof windows, which was parked at the top of the ramp leading down to the sea, and it was turned to point inland. Bellamy noted that the car must be close to the rear door of the house, meaning a quick exit for Khaled if it was his car, and it was easy to imagine that such a car would be placed there if it was intended to be an escape car. There didn't appear to be anyone in it, but Khaled was a professional, and he was more likely to place any backup men outside the house at the rear, to cover his escape.

'PC Nicholson,' Bellamy said quietly as he emerged from the car, addressing the older of the two constables. 'I want you to get as close as you can to that car and find somewhere where you can't be seen. If it has to be someone's front garden and they're at home, show them your police warrant. If I want you to shoot, I'll tell you by communicator; if you don't hear from me, don't shoot. Is that clear?'

Entering the house was easy; a door at the side had been left open. Careless, possibly, but just as likely to make escape from the house easier. Bellamy and his two companions found themselves in the large and luxuriously equipped kitchen of the house, and by the look of it, someone had left rapidly only a few minutes earlier; something was still slowly simmering on the hob. As he was turning the gas off beneath it, a shot resounded through the house, and even allowing for the silencer obviously attached to the weapon, it made noise enough for the two men he was with to look at Bellamy expectantly. Bellamy noted, gratefully, that neither of them shouted or made any noise at all.

'PC Moyes,' whispered Bellamy. The young man's eyes were as wide as they could go. 'Cover the front of the house; again, don't shoot until I say so.'

Gratifyingly again, Moyes said nothing, but moved rapidly away with the speed and agility of his youth.

'Sergeant Ellis,' Bellamy whispered again. 'I'm going up there. I want you to position yourself somewhere at the back of the house where you can clearly see into the rooms; I believe, having looked at the plans of the place, that there is a fire escape at the back going right up to an upstairs entrance. I'm going upstairs to see what's happening.'

'Are you sure, sir? Senior officers' lives are not usually put at maximum risk,' said Ellis.

'Senior officers don't get paid more for nothing, Ellis. Do as you're told. If you cover me properly, there shouldn't be too much risk.'

'Sir.'

Bellamy edged his way up the stairs. Fortunately, the carpet covering them was luxuriously thick, meaning he could make minimal noise. As he remembered the layout of the house from the diagrams he'd seen, the stairs turned directly left halfway up and Raiton's main living area, covering the entire first floor, would then be in front of him.

He slowed right down as he approached the top of the stairs, and allowed himself a brief look when his eyes could see into the room. Railton was tied very thoroughly and securely to a chair, his hands behind his back and his mouth gagged. His eyes widened as he saw Bellamy's head appear, but he still had enough presence of mind not to cry out. Beside him lay the shattered pieces of what Bellamy suspected had once been a precious vase. Khaled, it seemed, was making a simple mistake for a professional killer – making a meal of it, rather than striking quickly and getting out. Perhaps he saved this sort of approach to killings he did for personal rather than professional reasons.

'I want you to see your death coming slowly upon you, you piece of shit,' Khaled said, without raising his voice. 'Like men floating on a dinghy and watching your murderous fucking boat descending on them.'

'It wasn't my boat, whoever you are. I don't own any fucking boats,' Railton said, and even though his voice was shaking, there was spirit and defiance in his tone.

'You lying English cunt,' Khaled said.

Bellamy found time to wonder at his almost complete lack of a foreign accent. With a spasm of frustration, he suspected this man must have been operating in the US and the UK for some time, and still without being caught. Perhaps that's why he had started getting a little careless.

Another shot, and another object to Railton's right, beyond Bellamy's vision, shattered loudly.

'That was also worth a lot of money. You're basically just a fucking vandal, aren't you?' Railton's voice was now shaking uncontrollably, but the note of challenge remained.

'Well, the next one's going to take out two objects worth nothing at all, Your Lordship. As in your balls.'

Bellamy grabbed his gun tightly and walked into the room. He instantly noted Sergeant Ellis on the fire escape platform behind Khaled on his right.

Khaled was encased almost entirely in black; only his eyes and nose were visible. His eyes were flashing with anger; this was clearly a very personal mission. He was tall, with the height of a long, lean build and probably very developed standards of athleticism.

Bellamy chose his moment.

'Mr Khaled, the house is now surrounded. Your methods of exit are all covered by my men. Please put your gun down slowly now, and I can assure you that you will be given a fair trial. If you attempt to kill anyone, we will kill you.'

The eyes, now almost insane with anger, also registered a moment of doubt.

'You are a brave man, Police Officer. What makes you think I haven't got men of my own with their guns trained on you? But I have no fight with the British police. I will spare your life if you get out and let me deal with this reptile as he deserves. Put your gun down, Police Officer, or I will shoot your hand off with your gun in it. Then I will kill the scum in the chair.'

Bellamy made to start putting his gun on the floor. At the same time, he placed his hand on his right thigh and nodded at the watching torso of Sergeant Ellis. Almost immediately, a shot thudded into Khaled's right leg. He spun round, and the gun flew out of his right hand. Bellamy moved quickly to grab it, and at the same moment, Ellis crashed into the room from the fire escape and pointed his gun directly at Khaled, whose thigh was now bleeding profusely.

'Cover him, Sergeant,' said Bellamy. 'And well done.'

'Thank you, sir. But congratulations are due mostly to you, sir. You know who we've got here; one of the most notorious serial killers on even the spooks' books. They're going to love you, sir.'

'I think I fear their love almost as much as I fear their disapproval,' Bellamy said. Ellis grinned.

'Just shoot the bastard, why don't you?' said Railton, still tied up in his chair. 'He damn near murdered a peer of the realm. What more do you want?'

Bellamy's patience stretched to its limit and snapped.

'Be quiet!' he shouted at Railton.

Regaining control of himself rapidly, he spoke into his communicator, summoning Nicholson and Moyes to him. He grabbed a chair and sat in front of Khaled, with his gun trained on him.

'Ellis, call an ambulance, and tell them we mean now, not tomorrow.'

'Sir.'

'Do you know Muqaddam Haidar Alwan, Khaled?'

'I know of him,' Khaled said, his voice reflecting the pain he was in. 'A collaborator, as far as I know. A shame; he was a good soldier.'

'As were you, once upon a time, weren't you, Khaled? But unlike Haidar, you didn't try to stop bloodshed, you revelled in it.'

Moyes and Nicholson burst into the room. Khaled groaned and Bellamy registered that the professional killer had still thought escape might be possible, until the full numbers of the police were revealed.

'OK, Sergeant, I want you, Nicholson and Moyes to stay with Khaled, at least until the ambulance comes, and you must warn the hospital that we will be mounting a security operation there for as long as Khaled remains in their care. Nicholson, release Lord Railton from that chair. Lord Railton,' he said, turning towards him, 'please accompany me to the other end of your generous living lounge, or studio, whatever you call it, because I think we need to have a chat.'

As Railton moved towards the other end of the huge room, rubbing places on his torso where the tightness of the ropes binding him had left their marks, Ellis returned.

'Fifteen minutes, sir; they say that's the best they can do.'

'OK, Sergeant. Now I want you and your colleagues to search that man for weapons, and when I say search, I mean strip him naked; give him the full works. He's a professional killer, and I don't want him to suddenly produce a gun he's kept tied in his pants or up his arse or something as soon as there's a lull in the proceedings. And tell Nicholson to find some cloth somewhere

– tea towels would probably do – to put a makeshift bandage on his leg.'

Railton was now sitting near to the huge screens he used to scan the stretch of coast outside his home; below and to the right were the two gigantic speakers which would blast his heavy metal out, a strange habit for a man in his sixties, but then Railton, Bellamy considered, was a strange man in a number of ways. However, at the back of his mind, a large question mark still lurked concerning whether he was strange enough to murder ten men in cold blood.

His Lordship's arms and legs were now shaking, and Bellamy realised he must still be in a state of shock.

Ignoring Khaled's protests behind them as he was being stripped and searched, Bellamy decided that a sympathetic approach towards Railton, difficult as it might be to bring off sincerely, might be the best move at the moment.

'You probably need a shot of brandy, Your Lordship,' he said. 'Tell me where it is.'

Railton pointed to a cupboard only a few feet away from him. Bellamy found the brandy and a couple of glasses. The brandy was very rare and very old.

For a few minutes, he let the tension subside while he and Railton sipped their brandy, and realised himself that he was still on edge.

'Now, Lord Railton, let me make myself abundantly clear as to the position. This killer' – he pointed vaguely in the direction of the already almost naked Khaled – 'obviously and very definitely believes that you are responsible for the deaths of ten of his countrymen, none of whom has, as yet, had a decent burial. I suspect he may not be the last man to seek vengeance for that. And we don't yet know what will happen to him.'

Railton looked up sharply.

'He will be imprisoned for life, surely? He is guilty of attempted murder.'

'Not necessarily, sir. You see, he is considered to be largely the province of the secret services. If he is put on public trial, his lawyers will no doubt want all of his killings to be considered rather than going through a trial for every single one, and that will not show the secret services in a good light. And I suspect there will be those within the services who would consider that a professional gunman of his pedigree could be very useful to them, if they make a deal whereby he becomes an agent of British intelligence rather than spends long periods in prison, which does no good to anyone and also costs the state a considerable amount of money. Prison is expensive to begin with, and prison for a man like him would involve a huge security operation. "Turning him", as I believe the spooks would call it, could be easier and much less expensive.'

'That's disgraceful,' Railton said, draining his glass. 'That doesn't sound like the British way at all.'

Bellamy refilled both of their glasses.

'The British way? What would that be, My Lord? Conniving with a few impecunious local boatmen to sink a dinghy with twelve desperate men on it, and then stripping them of their identity and burying them naked in hotel grounds so their bodies don't drift onto the shore? Is that the British way, My Lord?'

Railton's eyes settled on him, and Bellamy was surprised to see that there was no apparent hatred there – perhaps he could even detect a note of admiration.

'Don't keep on with that "My Lord" stuff. I made a lot of money, using what my father left me, and I donated some of it to a political party so they made me a lord. It means nothing, it means less than nothing, especially at the moment. You saved my life, Bellamy. I've never seen courage like that, walking straight into a room where you knew a ruthless gunman had me prisoner. I cannot, I never will, forget that. I may be a shit, Bellamy, but I'm not a stupid shit. I know a brave man when I see one. As they constantly remind me, I didn't actually fight in the Falklands, all that time ago, when I was little more than a boy. When I went in, the fighting was already over; the only thing they wanted me for was to make some deals to get supplies to the island. My father had Argentinian connections, the kind of men who didn't give a damn about who won as long as they made lots of money. They needed supplies and I got them supplies, but in the meantime, I got to drink and talk with some real men, brave men with more balls than I will ever have. There is no pattern, no justice in life. It's the shits who have all the money. I blast my mind out with devil music to try and forget the fucking absurdity of it. But I know brave men when I see them.'

Bellamy was momentarily dumbfounded.

'Ambulance arriving, sir,' Ellis said.

Bellamy got to his feet.

'Please remain where you are, sir. I will be with you again in a few minutes.'

In fact, it was the best part of forty minutes. Bellamy used his secret service contact to arrange for Khaled to be taken to a hospital ward attached to a high-security prison. It would mean a journey of 120 miles, with a police escort, but the paramedics had confirmed that Khaled was not dangerously ill; the bullet had skimmed off part of his thigh and caused the loss of a lot of blood, but it had not lodged itself inside him and he was not going to die.

The "spook" man was unstinting in his praise.

'Fucking hell, Max. We've been after that bastard for years. You take him and one of your guys puts a bullet right where we can catch him without killing him. When he starts singing for his supper, which the bastard will, he could clear up a whole file of cases.'

'And you will make use of his services, presumably.'

'What a cynic you are, DCI Bellamy. Yes, we probably will. Set a thief to catch a thief, Max. Works for gunmen, too. He's no use to us, stuck in a prison, probably being remorselessly buggered by every guy who wants to tell everyone when he gets out that he once fucked a big-deal gunman. Great work, Max. You might even get a gong for this.'

Eventually, Bellamy went to continue his conversation with Railton, while Sergeant Ellis remained, ready to drive Bellamy back to the station.

Railton's heavy metal was already blasting out. Bellamy walked in and turned it off. The equipment reminded him, incongruously, of his own, last used for playing Chopin.

Railton didn't protest. He had filled his glass again. This, Bellamy knew, was the kind of atmosphere when results could come.

'Let's get down to basics, sir,' he began. 'You know as well as I do that with the kind of lawyers you can afford, you might well get away with a large fine, or a suspended sentence. They have to prove that you intended to kill those men. Did you?'

The silence was beginning to last too long for Bellamy to feel comfortable, but at last, Railton spoke.

'I take it you've heard of Thomas Becket, Mr Bellamy.'

'Yes, I have.'

'Killed because the King, Henry II, announced to a group of his enthusiastic but not very bright followers that someone should rid him of this turbulent priest, meaning Becket. So four of them galloped off and murdered Becket in his own cathedral. In my case, the enthusiastic but not too clever guy is called Eric Irwin. I saw that dinghy approaching on my screens. It's always been my dread that, even though the journey is much longer, it will occur to some of these asylum seekers, or whatever you want to call them – parasites, I call them – that the south-west coast is not so policed and watched as the south-east, and this beautiful retreat of mine will become the first stop for gangs of young men, some of them quite possibly armed, and I will become a prisoner, or worse, in my own home. If and when I see them coming – which

I can do, with my equipment – I want to at least do something to discourage them, or send them somewhere else. Irwin knew that, and broadly speaking, he shares my views. He is just not a subtle or hugely intelligent man. What arrangements he made, I don't know, and I mean that. Irwin knows various disreputable individuals who will do just about anything for a bit of money – I don't know who they are, and I don't want to know. I wanted them to deflect those men – a dozen pretty desperate-looking specimens they seemed to me – so that their dinghy headed off in another direction or they were picked up from the sea by a coastguard ship which would take them away to one of the south-coast cities and out of my neck of the woods. I had no intention of killing anyone, Mr Bellamy, and if I was stretched out on some fucking rack having my fingernails pulled out, I would say the same thing – I never wanted to kill anyone. And then I heard that two of them had actually managed to swim to shore, which just shows what tough characters they would have been and what short work they would have made of my home and me if they'd made it to shore.'

'I can tell you now, sir, that one of those two men was an ex-lieutenant colonel of the Iraqi Army, who had spent some time in this country when younger, and who put himself in danger by acting as an interpreter to avoid misunderstandings between Iraqi civilians and Allied soldiers. He was waiting for a decision on his application for asylum, but had he waited for much longer, so-called Islamic State fighters would have killed him and his entire family. He managed to get his wife and daughters into Jordan, mainly because his wife is Jordanian, but his beloved younger son and several of his wider family drowned when that dinghy was overturned, most of them knocked unconscious by the impact of the collision.'

'None of that was ever my intention, Mr Bellamy. I will swear to it on whatever you want me to.'

'You want to pass the buck fully on to Eric Irwin?'

'I was never holding the buck in the first place. If Irwin says, at any point, that I instructed him to kill those men, he will be lying through his teeth; I did no such thing. Like I didn't tell him to arrange someone to shoot at your wife, or to attack your home.'

Bellamy sat up, and couldn't stop himself from clenching his fists. Louise, his beloved wife, was still exiled in Scotland; he missed both her body and her mind like an almost unbearable and perpetual ache. He looked at Railton with narrowed eyes.

'Yes, all your training is about to go out of the window, isn't it, Mr Bellamy? You've found who you think is the culprit for the heartache of the recent weeks, and you want to kick the shit out of me. Well, go ahead, I won't resist, as if I could at the age of sixty-six. But am I worth you losing your job and your integrity? Is Irwin?'

Bellamy's voice came out in something like a feral growl. 'So what exactly did you tell Irwin to do, Railton?'

'Firstly, to get and keep the initiative in the case, and keep you and your colleagues wondering exactly what they were up against. His interpretation of that was his affair, as it always is; he is my assistant, not my puppy dog. His methods seem to have been unsubtle and even a little idiotic, even by his standards. Secondly, I wanted him to get it across to you that there would be a price to be paid for what you would call success in this case. And thirdly, distract you away from the Massiter case.'

Bellamy could feel the anger rising within him, but controlling his anger was a lesson he had learned over the years, if very gradually and sometimes very painfully, and even this case was not going to send him hurtling back into the impotent rages of his youth.

'Now, why did you want to distract me from the Massiter case?'

For a long and awkward pause, Railton seemed to be somewhere else, his eyes, still alight from too much brandy, flickering towards his big screens, empty as they were, as if they would provide him with some kind of inspiration. At long last he spoke, as if to himself. 'What the hell. It's all over now, anyway.'

He turned, very deliberately and with an obvious effort, to Bellamy.

'I will make it clear from the outset that I did not, at any time, give Irwin any instructions or even suggestions concerning Bill Massiter. Their relationship was no business of mine, and I preferred it that way. You will already think of me as a shit to throw my assistant under a bus, and I probably am, but this business was nothing to do with me. Nevertheless, I think Eric was somehow involved in the death of Bill Massiter. Don't ask me how; Eric is an odd combination of independence and reliance. He needs some kind of figurehead over him to act as a kind of ultimate justification for things which he would probably do anyway. Bill had talked to Josie about the deaths of those men, which is not surprising – Josie is his wife. But the hints coming across to me, and they are only hints, Mr Bellamy, I have no hands-on proof, said that Bill had passed on some vital evidence to Josie about the involvement of Irwin in the deaths of those Iraqi men. Bill had been poking about among the boat owners along the coast and paid for information about Eric having hired some of them in the past, including the strong possibility that he had hired someone the night that dinghy was overturned. Josie, as I understand it, wanted him to drop it. I think that might have been partly because she was finally fed up with the thing between Eric and Bill. Ever since Eric more or less took over the affairs of the Cougars – and it's as well he did, because Bill never did have any head for business – Bill has resented him and questioned his methods.'

'And what about Tony Richards?'

Railton looked puzzled. 'Yes, what about Tony Richards?'

'Didn't he consider himself effectively the leader of the Cougars?'

'He may well have done, but nobody else did. Orestes and Lane didn't take a blind bit of notice of him. And he himself was interested in only one thing; boys' bums and bits. But if he thought he could manage without the rest of the Cougars, he was badly mistaken; his so-called solo career was a joke. Eric had his number from the start. Whatever Eric's faults, he was more than a match for Tony Richards. Bill Massiter was different. Bill was a handful for Eric from the start.'

At this point, Bellamy's phone sounded.

'DCI Bellamy,' he said.

Seemingly, in present circumstances, like a voice from the past, Elaine's voice sounded, and Bellamy found himself extraordinarily pleased to hear her.

'Hello, sir. Hope all is well with you. If you didn't realise you were a legend to start with, you can be sure you are now. The man who faced down the Scorpion—'

'Oh, God, is that what's going on now?'

'It seems so. How the hell this has got around, God knows. The spooks have taken Khaled under their wing; they've whisked him off to a safe house, where they'll get a doctor they can rely on to keep schtum about it to patch up his leg. They didn't like the idea of him going to even a high-security hospital because the media are going berserk. I would advise you to get both yourself and Lord Railton out of there as soon as possible, sir, because the place will be under siege. Social media is going berserk on the subject of Railton, sir; the far right think he's a hero and everyone else thinks he's – well, whatever the opposite of hero is.'

'OK, Elaine, it's good to hear from you. I want you to send a team out – three armed officers, it will need to be – to arrest Eric Irwin on suspicion of murder. Put him in a cell and let him stew for a bit. I've still got Sergeant Ellis here; I'm going to talk to Josie Massiter, or whatever she calls herself now. I will also arrest Lord Railton and bring him in first, for his own protection.'

Bellamy's eyes rested on Railton for the last sentence. The man seemed deflated, as if he no longer had the strength to argue.

Bellamy called Ellis up to him and then turned back to Railton.

'You heard what I said, sir, I take it? We need to go. I will do the necessary arrest and caution on the way.'

Even as the three men hurried into the car, men and women were gathering on the other side of the road and shouts were directed, mainly to Bellamy, about what was to happen now. A few began to run across the road and cameras were already flashing as the car drove rapidly away.

In the car, Ellis was summoning police cars to him to escort them to the nearest secure station. Bellamy turned to Railton who was now pale with the impact of the recent hours.

'Why on earth, when you knew what you knew about Eric Irwin, did you continue to use him as – whatever it was – an aide-de-camp, a bagman?'

Railton sighed. 'One, I was afraid of him. He is a very determined and potentially violent man. When he first came to me, both he and the Cougars were in deep financial trouble; Bill still needed his cocaine and expected the Cougars' funds to pay for it. He thought the Cougars were still rolling in it, and they would have been, but for Eric's various adventures and investments. I saw him as a kind of tame gorilla with a brain in his head, who could be useful to have around and would keep the intrusive media off my back; the ones who love me are every bit as bad as the ones who hate me. He looked like, and in some ways he is, the classic number two, equipped to do as he's told without bothering me too much with it. But what he wanted, I came to realise when it was already too late to get rid of him, was someone to legitimise him, like a favourite uncle who would pat his head and tell him how well he was doing from time to time. I thought, even then, that at worst he would be an amiable blunderer – he was a blunderer all right, but there was nothing amiable about it.'

Bellamy came, at last, very near to losing his temper altogether. He leaned in closer to Railton, his eyes flashing. Ellis's eyes flickered at him in the car mirror.

'I haven't seen my wife for three fucking weeks for your amiable blunderer. A journalist was shot. My wife, Louise, could have been killed if we hadn't had a police marksman with us. I'd like to kick the fucking arse of both you and your amiable blunderer.'

Railton shrunk from him, his eyes suddenly terrified.

'I'm not answerable for what Irwin does,' he said quietly.

Bellamy regained control as quickly as he'd lost it. As the car sped on, he made himself think of the conversation he would shortly have with Louise, and the homecoming that would follow, and the love-making – especially the love-making – that would follow that. And the awareness that the worst was over was now flooding through him like a healing medicine. The strength of the opposition had been destroyed. Yes, he still needed to establish exactly what had happened to Bill Massiter, and perhaps especially so now, since Bill, for all his drug taking and ineffective leadership of the Cougars, was emerging as one of the few decent individuals in the case. He had always suspected that someone his father had liked couldn't be all bad, and it was gratifying to have that assumption vindicated.

That same evening, Bellamy sat in the familiar surroundings of his home and on this occasion, he did not choose to play music to avoid the silence, because he knew the silence would not now last for very long. He had agreed to have one police officer stationed outside the house until "further notice", reflecting Jack Henshaw's anxiety that one of his senior officers should not be felled with the winning post in sight.

Louise was on a returning train and Bellamy was looking forward to the reunion while not attempting to deny to himself that his anticipation was carnal as well as emotional. His sexuality was one aspect of the control he had finally managed to establish over himself, after the relative turbulence of his youth which had at times involved keeping more than one girlfriend at a time. His parents had always been partly amused and partly concerned about his increasingly promiscuous activities with the opposite sex from his late teens onwards. But Louise had changed all that; she was as attracted to him as he was to her, and she had made very clear from the start that monogamy was what she had in mind for both of them.

Eric Irwin had been arrested and cautioned for several offences, including conniving at the deaths of ten Iraqi men, conspiring to murder Bill Massiter, conspiring to murder a police officer and his wife and obstructing police officers in the execution of their duty. He had protested with his usual volume and emphasis, and demanded to see a lawyer. By now, Bellamy estimated, he was probably talking to one, and that was no bad thing as far as Bellamy was concerned because the lawyer might manage to get through to him how precarious his situation was and how this was one situation he would not be able to shout and bluster his way out of.

Mary and Dean had joined forces and were working along the Devon coastal towns to get closer to whoever had been hired on the night of the dinghy's destruction. Mary, with her considerable natural ability to get people talking to her, had already gathered a few leads from the men, and Dean, who was old enough to be able to turn his good looks to advantage, was getting some positive feedback from the women. The dogged silence which had surrounded that night and the collision between the boat and the dinghy was loosening by degrees, by the dual use of stick and carrot. Bellamy had authorised his investigators to make plain that sanctions could be placed on the movements of all the boats if information was not forthcoming, and the local people were, in any case, largely in sympathy with the investigation. Yes, there were a few of the "who cares what happens to foreigners?" brigade, but Devon people were fair-minded and not prepared to collude in cover-ups where the deaths of ten young men were concerned. The fact that Irwin had been arrested was also concentrating the minds of those who had worked for or with him in the past. Bellamy lived in hope that whoever had been hired that night, even if they weren't directly hired by Irwin, would do as Railton did and cut their potential losses by admitting to an accident happening without murderous intention.

As for Josie Massiter, which, to Bellamy's surprise, is what she still called herself, an appointment had been made to see her in the morning. Leaving her to stew overnight made sense as far as Bellamy was concerned; the very clear suggestion now was that Bill had discussed the night he had seen the bodies coming in to Cavelcombe House with her and he may have discovered some incriminating information and confided in her about it. In any case, Bellamy's very powerful suspicion, as a result of their first conversation, that Josie was keeping something important to herself remained with him. He had experienced, both as a journalist and as a police officer, people being deliberately evasive or dismissive; he knew both the physical and verbal signs of it, and Josie had been showing both.

The opposition, which had once looked so powerful and all-controlling, had crumbled. Max Bellamy had already been credited with capturing a notorious professional killer who had managed to elude the security services for years. He felt well up to confronting both Josie and Eric Irwin and closing down both cases.

In the meantime, he remembered Railton and his heavy metal passion, and suddenly, he wanted more than the silence around him. His own old guy music was classical, quieter and more melodious and thoughtful. But on this occasion, it also needed to have an easy high-spiritedness about it. He decided on Chopin's "Mazurkas", beginning with No. 1 in B-flat major, which always sounded to him like a casual, dismissive wave of the hand at supposedly difficult reflections.

PC Nicholson, keeping watch on the street outside, was remembering Sergeant Ellis holding forth in the station.

'He stood there, cool as a fucking cucumber, facing that killer; not so much as a bead of sweat on his brow. I was shitting myself, and I was outside on the fire escape. I tell you, he's the Ice Man. So-called fucking Scorpion melted in front of him.'

Nicholson's reflections were interrupted by Chopin. For an Ice Man, he thought, he has some dainty tastes in music.

PART SIX

Resolution 2

In the sober atmosphere of his office, Max Bellamy was feeling more relaxed than he had been for weeks, even if a little tired. The reunion with Louise had been everything he would have wanted it to be, but it had taken a good while before either of them got to sleep, and aching as he was in certain areas, Bellamy felt more laid back than he had done for weeks. It was probably just as well, because he had three interviews already arranged for this day, and all of them would probably prove to be demanding.

He'd deliberately chosen his office as the venue for them all, to underline to his interviewees, in the order of Josie Massiter, Eric Irwin and Lord Railton, that they no longer had the initiative and were no longer calling the tune. Even with the satisfaction of resuming the company of his wife, Bellamy had a deep-seated irritation at the way these three people had conspired against him. Getting rough with suspects did not come very naturally to him. He could usually understand why people did what they did, and he had long since disciplined himself not to take their lies and evasions too personally, but this case had at times been very directly personal, and he knew it would take all the resources of objectivity he had to keep his temper and bring everything to a close as dispassionately as possible.

Josie was shown into the office. She looked more tired and distraught than she had the last time Bellamy had seen her, but that was understandable. In the way she'd no doubt acquired in dealing with egotistic pop stars, she tried to seize the initiative from the start.

'My goodness, you do nicely for yourself now, don't you, Mr Bellamy? Or perhaps I should just call you Max. I don't know why I've been summoned here and threatened with an interview room, but I agree this is probably a nicer setting, though I don't know what it is I have to say to you which I haven't already said—'

'When did Bill tell you about the evidence he'd gathered on the death of the men in that dinghy?'

She was taken aback at the abruptness of the question, presenting an opportunity for Bellamy to add further impact.

'And how's Bryan? Or do you have another boyfriend now?'

'Let me answer one question before you ask me another—'

Bellamy leaned forward.

'Certainly, Josie, and maybe this time you won't tell me a pack of lies.'

'Oh, God.' Flustered, she attempted a winning smile, which faded almost immediately. 'Lies? What lies?'

'What did he tell you, Josie? Ten young men were fished out of the sea, stripped of everything which might give any clue as to who they were, and buried without the proper dignity or observances of their religion. That's a mass killing, Josie. That's mass murder. Your husband saw them bringing those bodies into Cavelcombe, didn't he? What else did he do? What did he tell you about it? When did you pass it on to Eric Irwin?'

Josie rose out of her chair.

'I don't have to do this, with you shooting questions at me like I'm some sort of criminal…'

She made her way to the door and opened it. PC Nicholson, young but well built, was standing there, and clearly he wasn't going to move.

'Sit down, Josie. You're not going anywhere.' Now he had control, he could resort to "good cop". 'OK, then, Mrs Massiter. One at a time. How's Bryan?'

'Oh, I got tired of Bryan very quickly. Quite a respectable shag, but not much else going for him. Thick as a plank.'

'Bill wouldn't let it go, Josie, would he? After he saw those men in the night—'

'No, he bloody wouldn't.'

Josie suddenly looked alarmed with herself. Bellamy changed his tone.

'You loved him, didn't you? Most of the time. But he didn't like Eric, did he?'

She sighed, long and hard, as if recovering from a blow.

'No, he didn't. He resented Eric ever since Eric took over the band. It's as well somebody did take it over, because otherwise they would have gone bust long ago. Bill didn't have much of a head for business. Mind you, Eric always paid himself generously; he didn't lose on the deal.'

'And paid for Bill's cocaine supplies?'

'Well, yes and no. Bill thought he was getting top-quality South American stuff, but Eric was buying crappy stuff from Portugal, where the price has dived since they de-criminalised it. Eric just put some South American print on the boxes, making it look like coffee—'

'And you knew Eric was swindling your husband, taking the extra money for himself? Why didn't you tell him? Who were you most loyal to, Eric or Bill?'

Josie went on the attack.

'Eric made sure some of that money got back to me. It's all very well you being so fucking holier than thou, Mr Fucking Police Officer, you didn't live with a junkie for years, watching him sniffing all the Cougars' money up his nose and thinking he was some kind of upstanding moral citizen while his wife had to go short of decent clothes and everything else. Not to mention a non-existent sex life because hubby's too stoned to get it up.'

Bellamy let the pause lengthen, and eventually spoke into it.

'You must know that if this comes to trial, Josie, as it inevitably will, you are highly likely to be summoned as a witness, and perhaps as an accessory in the death of Bill?'

'Oh, God,' Josie said again, seemingly talking to no one in particular. 'I knew it would come to this. I knew he would land both of us in the shit before he finished. I don't know why I agreed to marry him in the first place—'

'Well, what first attracted you to his estimated £20 million of Cougar wealth, I wonder, Josie?'

Josie's eyes daggered across at him.

'Yes, alright, you can make me out to be some gold-digging tart if you like, but I loved Bill then, I really did.'

Tears were starting now. Bellamy felt a wrench inside. He was accustomed enough to tears, in many different circumstances, but women's tears were always a problem. Yes, some women could do it without meaning it, but he thought there probably had been a time when Josie had meant it, or at least thought she did.

'I don't know how Bill died, Mr Bellamy, and that's the truth. I know Eric was there, with two other men, but that was just an argument; Bill died later than that.'

'But Bill knew something, didn't he, Josie? About those men in the dinghy?'

For a long moment, Josie stared blankly out of the window. Then she spoke again, and her voice had suddenly deepened.

'He had the names of the men who owned that boat, the one Eric hired. He'd been down there, throwing money about until someone told him. Not many of the men on that shore have much time for Eric Irwin, or Railton, for that matter. Two of the men on that list were with Eric on the night Bill died. It had got back to Eric that Bill had been asking around, as Bill must have known it would.'

'So Eric murdered him?'

'I don't know. I wasn't there. I doubt it very much. Eric always had a soft spot for Bill. He recognised that Bill was the real inspiration behind the Cougars. As your dad did. Bill was really cut up when your dad died. You must have known that, Max.'

So, at the crucial moment, she plays the personal card, Bellamy thought, like making a quick and unobtrusive grab at his balls. Bill must have struggled to win any arguments with his missus.

'Yes, I knew that, Josie. But that isn't what we're talking about now, is it? My father knew Bill; he liked and respected him. Bill invented the Cougars and was responsible for much of their material. Even if he wasn't so good as a money man, he was a music legend. He knew that. So did he really kill himself, Josie? Did such a man really kill himself?'

She was staring down at the floor.

'You didn't know him like I did. Yes, he knew he was special. But the Cougars were over. Bill and I were spending most of our time arguing. I could believe that he didn't want the Cougars any more. But it seemed he didn't want me any more either.'

A long, loaded pause.

'What did you do with that list of names he gave you?'

'Oh, I put it away somewhere. It's probably still there. I thought, well, I don't want to know this now, but it might give me – what should I call it – a bit of leverage with Eric? To stop him getting too snotty with me.'

'Good. Your place is being searched as we speak.'

Josie sat up and almost launched herself across his desk.

'You bastard! You can't do that without a search warrant.'

'I got a search warrant. Cleared this morning. You are a possible accessory to eleven deaths, Josie. I could have got a warrant to search you if I'd wanted to. It's not just the police force who want to know what went on here. It's the spooks as well.'

For the first time, she seemed to be genuinely surprised.

'Spooks? What's it got to do with them?'

'Ten dead foreign men. International incident. Islamic State. International drug dealers. British peer. Attempted shooting of British MP. Far right. All in there, Josie. When that amount of shit is being thrown around, it can stick to all sorts of places.'

She sat staring at him for a while.

'I just want to go home, Mr Bellamy. Max. If your lot haven't wrecked the place, that is. Couldn't you have just asked me for it?'

Bellamy laughed.

'You would never even have admitted you possessed it, Josie, never mind giving it to me. You can go home, but I wouldn't try to leave the country, if I was you. Withholding evidence is also a crime. We'll have someone watching you, for the time being.'

She stood up, and shooting a final poisonous look in his direction, banged out of the room.

Two hours later, having taken in a generous dose of the filtered black coffee which he favoured on long interview days, Bellamy was ready to face His Lordship. His sense of slowly placing the final pieces of the jigsaw was growing. The search of Josie Massiter's flat had revealed the document he sought without too much difficulty; placing it in a drawer of clean underclothes may have represented a cunning hiding place as far as Josie was concerned, but it was never going to fool professional searchers. The piece of paper was a simple printed advertisement for the Penrose brothers, Mike and Stewart, and a sizeable "cargo or passenger boat" available to hire. Written on it in what looked like feminine handwriting was a date, which Bellamy estimated was almost certainly precisely the night that the boat went out to confront the dinghy, and a sum of money. It beggared belief for him that Irwin would hire the boat personally; that, he thought, was certainly not the way he operated. He and Railton would put someone, if not several people, between them and the actual hiring.

Bellamy guessed it would be a friend of a friend of Josie's who happened to live in the same coastal town as the registered boat; possibly someone known to her boyfriend of the time. Some conversation, with Josie herself or a local contact of Irwin's, would have explained to the Penrose brothers what was expected of them. Bellamy had already sent out a car to bring in the Penrose brothers.

Railton entered with breezy nonchalance which Bellamy guessed was probably his normal attempted approach to potentially difficult conversations. He still looked pale, but he was neatly turned out in a well-cut blue suit, immaculate white shirt and sober dark blue tie.

He offered his hand, and after a moment's hesitation, Bellamy shook it. There was no reason why the normal standards of civilised behaviour shouldn't be observed, for the time being at least. His personal anger against this man would have to wait.

'Let's get the issue of how I address you out of the way first, sir, if we can. Last time we met, you were not happy at being addressed as "My Lord".'

'No, well, that probably still applies, Chief Inspector. "Railton" is what everyone called me at school, long ago and far away; that or sir would be fine, especially from a man who saved my life on our last meeting.'

Upper-class manners or aristocratic condescension? To the pragmatic Bellamy, it made no difference, as long as it minimised the barriers between them.

'I'm hoping it might simplify matters, sir, if I summarise what I believe, on the evidence of the proof we already have, happened on the evening of...' He looked at the date on the piece of paper in front of him, and quoted it. 'You may disagree with some of the detail, but I would ask you to wait until I've finished the summary before you express your views.'

Railton, he noticed, was already disturbed by Bellamy's precise naming of the date from the paper in front of him, but he was doing his best to retain the indifferent attitude he had adopted for protection.

'On the afternoon of this day, you had a conversation with Eric Irwin concerning the approaching dinghy, with twelve men on it, which you could see on your surveillance screens approaching the shore and, as you saw it, your land. You instructed Irwin to find some way of stopping those men from landing, uninvited and unwanted, on your land. You will no doubt emphasise to me that you did not tell Irwin to bring about any fatalities but simply to divert the men from their course or somehow force them to ask for help from a coastguard or other boat in the vicinity. You will presumably tell me that you didn't instruct Irwin, in so many words, to upset or capsize the dinghy.

'Irwin then did what Irwin has done for you in the past when interpreting ideas or projects of yours which could be in danger of breaking the law. He got someone else, and it looks at this stage that the someone else might have been either Josie Massiter or an associate of Josie Massiter, presumably with the idea of getting one over on the increasingly difficult Bill Massiter. This person, perhaps with prior knowledge of that section of the coast, contacted the Penrose brothers and passed on the instruction that a boat was needed to stop the men in the dinghy coming ashore on Railton land. I don't, at this stage, have any relevant knowledge concerning the attitudes and working practices of the Penrose brothers, other than to say that the mission they were on, by definition, was dangerous and more than likely to break some aspects of the law.

'The brothers set off to intercept the dinghy. They received a radio message from whoever was Irwin's agent to say the dinghy was drifting closer and closer to the shore and action was needed quickly, if not instantly. By now, the daylight was fading, and presumably one or other of the brothers decided that if they rammed the dinghy, it could quite feasibly be described as an accident in the poor visibility. Ramming was agreed, but perhaps something wasn't quite right; perhaps they meant to nudge the end of the dinghy and simply topple the men into the sea. Perhaps they misjudged the speed of the approach. In any event, they hit the dinghy bang in the middle with considerable force, thereby destroying the dinghy and causing several of the men to be instantly knocked unconscious or fatally wounded. Panic set in on the boat. Was it panic, sir, I wonder, or was it some kind of gratification? After some delay and discussion – a fatal delay for most of the men in the water – the boat worked to pick up as many of the men from the dinghy as possible, to find that most of them were already dead. Haidar Alwan and his son Kassim had managed to avoid the main collision, I suspect because they were both at the front of the dinghy. The incoming tide helped them to swim to shore, but the prevailing wind which had driven the dinghy further and further west drove them further away as they swam and they came to land two or three miles west of Railton land.

'The men on the boat discussed, if that's the right word in such a situation, whether to call a coastguard or some other kind of boat. One of the Penrose brothers themselves, I understand, is a qualified diver so they decided that rather than contact any other boat, which might trigger police investigations or a RNLI lifeboat, they would take on board as many men as they could and head back to the shore, picking up any remaining men when they reached the shore. I suspect they picked up six or seven dead bodies from the water around them. The bodies of the others they would have picked up from the shore. Consultations with, I suspect, a furious Irwin or whoever was acting for him, went on while the bodies remained hidden in the bottom of the boat. Irwin – by now it must have been Irwin, I would think, as Cavelcombe House was used – instructed that the bodies should be taken under cover of dark, stripped naked and buried in the grounds of Cavelcombe House. However, even though they were moved at the very dead of night, Bill Massiter, who was staying at Cavelcombe at the time with his wife, did see something of the bodies coming in and, much as Josie tried to divert him to other subjects, he became obsessed with finding out what had happened, so much so that eventually, some years later, Irwin and his agents arranged what looked like a suicide, with everyone knowing the Cougars were finished and Bill had increasing financial problems, not least because he had, for some time, been fiddled out of the Cougar money due to him by Eric Irwin.'

Bellamy came to a halt, realising that the Massiter part of his description was not directly relevant to the affairs of Lord Railton and he had, to some extent, been thinking out loud. Nevertheless, he had been referring to the actions of Eric Irwin, who was widely known to be a leading lieutenant of Railton, and His Lordship's next words confirmed that the connection had registered with him.

'I must emphasise, Chief Inspector, that whatever Irwin has done at any time in relation to Bill Massiter is not connected with me in any way, and if you have included his actions in your account because you think they may rebound onto me, I must stringently deny that I had any knowledge of anything involved in the relationship between Irwin and Massiter. The whole area of the ex-Cougars was one I kept out of altogether. There were some odd things, both personal and financial, going on there which I knew nothing about, nor did I want to.'

'Except,' Bellamy ventured, 'when it came to bailing Irwin out of his financial mess. That's why he came to you in the first place, wasn't it, sir? You've already hinted as much.'

'Yes,' Railton said impatiently. 'But that was entirely between Irwin and me. All in all, Mr Bellamy, the parts of your account which are relevant to me are largely accurate, but I must stress the point, as my lawyers will do as and when any of this comes to court, that I did not give Irwin any reason to believe that I wanted any of the men on that dinghy to die. As a highly experienced police officer, can you make some kind of prediction as to where all this is going?'

'I'm a police officer, not a lawyer, sir. What decisions the director of public prosecutions may make can and often do baffle me. But I would be very surprised if they do not go ahead with some kind of prosecution in this case. I think a charge of murder or even attempted murder might be too extreme for them, but charges of manslaughter would not surprise me. This is a case with international implications, sir, and they need to be seen to have done something. And I haven't yet spoken to Mr Irwin. His version of the instructions given to him may differ somewhat from yours, sir.'

A single look at Railton's face was enough to convince Bellamy that his words had presented His Lordship with an aspect of the case he had perhaps overlooked. Acting under orders was a familiar defence for those accused of heinous crimes of one kind or another; it was a defence heard often enough in the Nuremberg trials of the leading Nazis after the Second World War.

Railton was suddenly looking furtive and vaguely guilty, as if an idea had just occurred to him. Bellamy knew his chances of preventing Railton from getting bail were slim; "Lord" in front of the name still had a lot of clout in English courts.

'Lord Railton,' Bellamy said, and the look his interviewee shot back at him suggested that his suspicions were not far from the truth. 'I don't doubt you have useful international connections, but I must caution you not to try and flee the country. The stations and airports will, in any case, be closed to you. I am also warning you for your own safety, sir. The so-called Scorpion may not be the only one to see you as a criminal to be brought to justice in some arbitrary way. There is no shortage of disgruntled Middle Eastern ex-soldiers on the continent.'

Railton sighed and put his head in his hands.

'What a mess. What a bloody mess.'

'I can keep you in custody, sir, for your own protection. You will be treated considerately, I do assure you; you haven't yet been charged with any crime, let alone convicted of one. The jackals of the media are waiting for you, I'm sure, and with the scent of blood in their nostrils, there isn't much they wouldn't do to get access to you. I know; I used to be one of them.'

'So I believe. I do my homework on people I come into contact with, especially people who have saved my life. I will stay in your custody, Chief Inspector, and if you or those people we so often refer to as "spooks" – not a flattering term – can manage a safe house, or even a safe flat, so much the better.'

'I will do my best in that respect.'

Bellamy stood up. But there was to be no concluding handshake.

'Thank you,' Railton said, and left immediately.

Bellamy checked quickly through the notes he had made following his interview with Lord Railton, and turned to inspect the information which had now been gathered on Eric Irwin. There was at least three times as much of it as there was on Railton, mostly contributed by Sergeant Mary Stanhope, but also with some interesting additions from Dean Matheson. He suspected also that Irwin had never fully realised who was actually "keeping tabs" on him. Perhaps he had conveniently managed to forget the individual who shot an entirely innocent young journalist. The organisation which employed that particular young man did not care very much for their personnel being indiscriminately shot at, and his colleagues had been given generous resources to aid in bringing whoever it was to justice.

They had tracked down both the person concerned and the agent used by Irwin to hire him. The individual who had held the gun had since left the country, but there were a number of clues as to where he was and it remained an investigation in process. The hiring agent had been offered quite a considerable amount of money by Irwin to keep quiet about his involvement, but he was maintaining that Irwin lied to him about what was required and the whole incident was a kind of misunderstanding. Bellamy estimated that not much more pressure would be needed to make him tell the full story.

Mary Stanhope, who had contacts in Inland Revenue, knew Irwin was under investigation for tax issues, and Dean had discovered that Irwin's drug dealings were also being looked at by the police department which handled drug offences. Not only was he under suspicion of importing illegal drugs but it was increasingly clear that not all of the substances imported were going to Bill Massiter; Irwin, they thought, was using some of the stuff himself, poor quality as it was, and selling some on.

Max Bellamy had come across Irwin's kind of man before, in both his journalistic and police careers. A would-be master criminal, already insecure because of his apparent psychological need to find a boss figure above him. A would-be master criminal without the essential strategic planning and creative-thinking talents to make him a master criminal, who tried to compensate for those shortcomings with fear, making himself, he hoped, such a threatening figure in people's lives that they would opt not to interfere in any way with what he was doing. Unfortunately, the older he got, the less reliable these tactics became. Age had destroyed Eric Irwin's menace.

Richard Bellamy had never had much to say about him, which Max remembered as typical of his father. If he couldn't record anything positive about someone, he probably wouldn't record anything at all.

Thinking back on his childhood memories of the Cougars, Bellamy recalled that, when visiting their rehearsals with his father, Irwin was nowhere to be seen. In those days, the Cougars, in particular Bill, ran their own affairs, and even Rory Blaze's eccentricities were easily absorbed into the general goodwill. Perhaps Bill had been against Irwin becoming involved in the first place, and he had been consistently undermined by Irwin. Bellamy was entirely convinced that Irwin was responsible for Bill Massiter's death; how exactly it had happened, he still didn't know, but Irwin was undoubtedly behind it.

He could hear Irwin and his escort approaching long before they actually arrived. Irwin was doing what he did; throwing his weight around and making his presence loudly felt.

'I can see your number, Constable whatever your name is, and you will be on the charge sheet when I sue the arses off the lot of you. Don't so much as touch me, let alone grab my arm like that – you'll come to regret it—'

'Yes, sir. Whatever you say, sir.' Bellamy recognised the voice of PC Nicholson. The young constable's phlegmatic temperament had registered with Bellamy on the visit to Railton's house. He would make a good officer before much longer.

Eventually, Irwin banged into the room. As usual, he made a lot of noise to try and gain the initiative from the start.

'Manhandling by two boys not old enough to wipe their own arses. You're lucky I don't sort the pair of them out, Bellamy.'

Moyes, the younger constable, was red-faced and clearly trying hard to control his anger.

'Sit down, Mr Irwin,' Bellamy said.

'Tell me the names of these two first. They give me hassle, they'll get hassle. One more item in the law suit that's coming your way, Chief Inspector.'

'Sit down, Mr Irwin,' Bellamy said again.

'You tell them. You're responsible for your officers—'

Bellamy sprang to his feet. 'Sit down, or I'll have wasting police time added to the long list of charges coming your way. Sit down there, now.'

Irwin snorted and clattered down into the chair facing Bellamy's desk. The two constables, with obvious relief, left the room to stand outside.

'Big man, aren't you, Bellamy, in your plush office with big boys running around after you? You won't be so comfortable when my lawyers have finished with you. I want my lawyer here in this room with me.'

At that exact moment, a tall, bespectacled man tapped lightly on the door. Bellamy glanced at him and felt a moment of relief himself. It was John Fennell who could be as slippery as any of them but he knew the rules and generally played by them. Fennell was known to like taking on cases which interested him. Bellamy wondered what aspects of this case had excited his interest.

With Fennell settled beside his client, Bellamy started saying what he had to say.

'It is my duty, as you know, to explain to you in detail why Mr Irwin has been detained and what exactly the charges against him will include—'

'You can forget the lot of them, Bellamy. None of them will stick.'

Bellamy raised his voice.

'If you interrupt me again, Mr Irwin, before I ask you to reply to what I'm telling you and your legal representative, I will send you back into custody and I will conduct this conversation entirely with Mr Fennell, who I gather is familiar with most of the details.'

Irwin subsided into silence, and sat with a sardonic smile on his face, staring directly at Bellamy.

'Firstly,' Bellamy began, 'we believe Mr Irwin used Josie Massiter or someone she knew to approach the Penrose brothers, who owned a boat for hire, and instructed them to stop a dinghy with twelve young Iraqi men on it from coming to shore on Lord Railton's land. How they were to do this was not specified.'

Bellamy moved remorselessly through the list, including the shooting of the journalist, the actions taken against him and his wife, including the threatening phone call, the imports of banned substances, the manipulation of accounts, the murder of Bill Massiter, made to appear like a suicide, and the illegal abduction and burial of ten Iraqi men. As he progressed through the charges, making references to the detailed discoveries made by his team, Irwin made two further efforts to interrupt, until his own lawyer advised him, with an emphasis Bellamy could not help but admire, to keep quiet. When Bellamy concluded by saying that Lord Railton denied categorically giving Irwin any instructions regarding doing harm to the men on the dinghy, the stuffing seemed to go out of Irwin. Bellamy then referred to the incident regarding the Scorpion, which Irwin clearly knew nothing about, and it was this which finally seemed to break Irwin. The knowledge that he might well be on the kill list of at least one Middle Eastern hit man was the aspect of the case which barged into the whole situation like a battering ram.

'Lord Railton, I may say in conclusion, has made it abundantly clear that he will not wish to avail himself of the services of Mr Irwin in any capacity at all in the future.'

An odd noise, half sigh and half moan, escaped from Irwin. 'Getting out from under,' he murmured, half to himself.

Bellamy nodded to the two constables waiting outside. He stood up. 'I think that's as far as we can go this morning, gentlemen. We will have a break until two o'clock this afternoon. You will be able to avail yourselves of a meal if you choose to do so. Mr Fennell, may I have a word before you go?'

Irwin glared belligerently at the two constables escorting him, but neither of them reacted in any way, and it did seem that a lot of the fire had drained out of him.

Bellamy turned to the lawyer.

'I am not intending to say anything which you won't be able to repeat to your client, Mr Fennell, and I'm not the one who should be deciding what is and isn't in your client's interest, but you are and it might be worth your while and his if I make a few points. With the weight of evidence we have, your client may be facing a lengthy custodial sentence. It cannot fail to be in his interests to co-operate with the police as much as possible. If Mr Irwin did not kill Bill Massiter, and I am not convinced of that – he is loud and assertive, but in the habit of using others to do his dirty work – it is still my belief that he knows how Mr Massiter died, and making clear to us how it happened could be of assistance to him when the judge determines the sentence. Now, if you will excuse me, I have been talking a great deal today, something I rarely do, and a drink has become an absolute necessity.'

'I cannot make any coherent response to that, Chief Inspector, until I've discussed it with my client. But we will definitely bear it in mind.'

Bellamy made himself have a decent lunch. Fatigue from an inadequate calorie intake was not the best preparation for an interview which could lead to the conclusion of a murder case. His feeling was that the afternoon session should be less confrontational; Fennell would have managed to at the very least get across to Irwin that he was in a very serious situation which would not be helped by him trying to throw his weight around.

He found confrontational interviews tiresome. They tended to simply prolong the length of time it took to settle the case and increase the workload needed to do it. He was not afraid of Irwin; he had dealt, in both of his careers, with men, and women for that matter, who would make Irwin seem like the local vicar by comparison. No, Irwin was not the criminal mastermind he longed to be, but he wasn't a stupid man either, and if he hadn't realised yet that the game was effectively up for him, Bellamy thought Fennell would get that across. Fennell certainly wasn't stupid either. He could be slippery, evasive and secretive, as were most lawyers in Bellamy's opinion, but he didn't care much for cases dragging on past their sell by date either.

Irwin managed to take his place in the office that afternoon with nothing more than an occasional glare at the escorting constables. Nicholson had taken to smiling brightly at him and Nicholson was young and good-looking enough to have a smile which could potentially disarm even the hardest cases.

Bellamy glanced at his watch. His interest in how long this would take was mainly academic, but he knew Louise was likely to be returning home early today; her schedule had deliberately been kept light until this case had finally been settled.

'Now, Mr Irwin,' he began, 'are you prepared to tell me how Bill Massiter died?'

Irwin glanced at his lawyer, who nodded.

Irwin sighed, a long sigh of resignation.

'Bill persisted. He was like that. From the moment I took over the band, which was more the wish of the other three Cougars than it was Bill's, he would pick up on some detail and worry it to death. He saw the bodies being carried into Cavelcombe House, and from that time onwards, he was on it like a dog after a bone. I'd done my best with Bill. Yes, I was getting him inferior stuff to what he was used to, but that was because of the disastrous state of the Cougars' finances. I took my whack, yes; nobody works for nothing, and if a top band wants a top manager, they need to be able to pay for it. The record sales had been tailing off for some time, and once they stopped doing gigs, it became much more outgoings than incomings. Cavelcombe House itself cost a lot of money just to maintain.

'Josie tracked down the name of the boat, and used someone she knew to hire it and sign the papers. I knew the Penrose brothers; they had a decent-sized boat, which was their only way of making a living, and there wasn't much they were not prepared to do with it to make money for themselves. But they were not, and I want to make this point with as much emphasis as I can, instructed by me or anyone else to drown or do serious damage in any other way to the men on that dinghy. Mike, the older brother, is a level-headed guy, and he was in overall charge of the operation, but he'd put Stewart on to steer the boat so he could keep an eye on what was happening. The original idea was to place the boat near to the dinghy and allow the wash coming off the bigger boat to cause the dinghy to drift away from a landing place on Railton land, and when the dinghy got close enough to the land to enable the men to wade ashore, fix a reception party for them. But the nearest coastguard boat was a long way away; more results of so-called austerity.

'Stewart, the younger brother, who always has been hot-headed – Mike's had to dig him out of trouble more than once – was getting impatient. He shouted to Mike that the light was fading, they could overturn the dinghy by nudging it at one end and everyone would think it was an accident. They could then pick the men up and take them in to the police. Mike shouted to Stewart to nudge the boat; he should have known better than to trust Stewart to do something as tricky as that. According to Mike – there were only the two of them on the boat – Stewart got that mad gleam in his eyes and by accident or design, he didn't just nudge the dinghy on the end, he ploughed the boat right into it. At least five of those men must have been knocked unconscious before they entered the water.

'Mike panicked and phoned me, something I'd specially told him not to do. I told him to pick up every man and bring them in as quickly as they could. The brothers worked on picking them up, but it took them ages; some of them had sunk right down. Mike is a qualified diver, but it must have been over three hours and dark by the time they'd heaved in all of them; six of them were already dead, and four more were washed up onto an isolated beach by the time the boat got back to the shore. They must have been in a pretty bad way, I might mention, before that boat hit them; they'd drifted way off the original course and they'd been in that dinghy for ages without food or drink. Now we know two of them swam to shore, but we didn't know that then; we thought we had all of them. Nobody thought to count how many were on the dinghy.

'They landed at a secret cove we know, where I'd agreed to meet them. The two swimming lads were in another one not more than two miles away, I reckon. Under cover of dark, we took the bodies of ten of those men to Cavelcombe House and buried them.'

'Having first stripped them naked,' Bellamy said quietly.

'Most of them were near naked, anyway. The water had soaked the clothes off them. Most of the clothes had drifted off, and they were ruined. We didn't have any clothes to put on them.'

For the first time, Bellamy saw on Irwin's face something which looked like regret, though whether it was regret at the failure of his strategy or regret at ten unnecessary deaths, it was difficult to tell. From his previous experience of "hard" men, he knew that a whole morass of different emotions and insecurities often lurked not far below the surface, and sometimes it was those which had made them hard men in the first place.

That, for the moment, seemed to be as much as Irwin wanted to say. Whether a court would believe such a version of events, Bellamy doubted; the argument that someone could deliberately ram a small dinghy in the near dark without really meaning any harm to the people on it would be seen as thin at best. It wouldn't need the most talented prosecuting counsel in the world to make the most of it. All of them – Railton, Irwin and the Penrose brothers – were guilty of manslaughter at the very least, as far as Bellamy was concerned, but he was not the prosecuting lawyer and for the moment, Irwin's rather qualified admission would do.

The only person who seemed to emerge with any credit from this was Bill Massiter, and Bellamy was prepared to spend the rest of the afternoon, and the evening as well, in getting a clearer understanding of Massiter's fate if he had to. It wasn't just about professional pride; it had a definite personal element to it. He owed it to his father. Massiter, whatever else he was, had been his father's friend.

'Thank you, Mr Irwin. I imagine Mr Fennell will want to go over that with you a number of times before it gets to court.'

'It will definitely get to court, then?' Irwin said, and his voice was almost subdued.

'That is not my choice to make. But I would be surprised – staggered, to be honest – if it didn't. There is a media frenzy going on, with international dimensions, and any government would want to be seen to be putting it to bed properly. But now, we really must turn to the death of Bill Massiter. You know and I know, Mr Irwin, that Bill's death was not a suicide, and you also know that I can prove that in court very easily. If you want to do something to protect your position, you really must give me your version of how Bill died.'

Irwin got up out of his chair and Bellamy glanced towards the two constables outside. But it seemed all his interviewee wanted to do was go and stare out of the window. The closest sight available was the station car park, but beyond that, the view stretched across the river to the countryside beyond, and Bellamy had sometimes stood there himself, looking for inspiration or, occasionally, solace.

Fennell started to get up as well; Bellamy shook his head towards him, and after glancing at his client – Fennell was in a position to see Irwin's face – he nodded and sat down again.

After a pause of several minutes, Irwin turned and when he spoke, it was as if the fire in him had gone out.

'It's all over for me now, I know that. Even if I don't get banged up, no one's going to employ me, and no doubt there will be a few more nutters like the so-called Scorpion around – nobody's talking about banging him up, it seems, even if he is a known killer – queueing up to have a go at me. But it's true; Bill deserves more than he's had so far. I kind of knew Bill would get me one day. After the burial of those men from the dinghy, he wouldn't leave it alone. He plagued me and he plagued Josie – we knew she was looking for a way of finishing it with Bill. If you were being kind, you'd say it was a married couple finally finding themselves incompatible; if you weren't, you'd say Josie was more interested in having a good time than trying to save her marriage after the Cougars' gravy train had run out. She went on at me to give her something to shut Bill up about those men who died, and eventually I gave her the names of the Penrose brothers, thinking Bill would go to them and ask them, and I would get to them first and tell them to keep up the story that it was an accident, a collision in the dark. When all's said and done, it will be difficult to prove it was anything but, clever lawyers or not. The Penrose brothers are good liars; they've been doing it all their lives. They've used their boat for all sorts of stuff in the past, most of it either against the law or on the edge of being. They had been Cougar fans; I hoped they would flatter and soft-soap Bill out of it, make him accept that the whole thing was an accident. At the same time, I told Josie to never admit that she'd told Bill about the brothers; it looked like conspiracy.'

'Which it was,' Bellamy said.

'Maybe. But she was his wife, and he was going down the drain fast after the Cougars had ended. No more than a trickle of money coming in, no celebrity status, just one more ageing junkie. I thought, well, if he did top himself, not many people would be asking why.

'I took the brothers with me and went to see Bill in that great spreading camp thing which he called home, which had once been a recording studio with lots of people having a lot of fun. Now it looks like an abandoned prisoner-of-war camp.

'I did not go there to kill him, and I'll say it again, in case it didn't register the first time, I did not go there to kill him. I wanted to talk to him, first of all to persuade him to concentrate on saving his marriage and getting his life back together after the Cougars. You'll probably find it difficult to believe, but I was quite fond of Bill. But I've let no one else wreck my life after both my parents died when I was sixteen – that's another story – and Bill bloody Massiter wasn't going to do it either.

'We took a rope – I knew how to really frighten him – and wore gloves so we wouldn't leave our prints all over it.

'I tried talking to him. He wasn't having any of it. I was a crook, he said; I'd taken over the Cougars and wrecked the whole business. I ran after Lord Railton like a puppy dog and I'd brown-nose him and do anything for him, and I'd deliberately set out to kill the men in the dinghy just to stop their foreign feet daring to step on Railton land. He said all sorts of things; all the resentments and hates he'd ever had towards me came out.

'I took as much of it as I could stand – it was all I could do not to put my hands round his throat and finish him there and then. Eventually, I'd had enough. I signalled to the brothers to take the rope over to him. They tied a noose around his neck and hung the other end off one of the roof beams. Then they held the rope, ready to pull him up. He grabbed at it to try and loosen it, which was good, I thought, because now his prints would be all over it.

'At last, he'd shut up. Now then, Bill, I said, you're going to co-operate and be nice for once, or you're going to top yourself. Now that the Cougars are over, and you're broke and you can't pay for your little comforts any more, you've decided you want to die young, like all the great pop stars. "I fucking haven't," he said, though he didn't find it too easy to talk by then. "You have, Bill, if you don't stop going on about those foreign bastards in that dinghy. You think about it, or we'll come back and make sure you do top yourself."

'He retched, and then he spat at me. I signalled to the brothers and they hoisted the rope up. "You'd better make your mind up, Bill," I said.

'He couldn't speak any more. Then one of the brothers said some kid had just come over the fence and entered Bill's land. I looked at them, they looked at me. For a while, none of us knew what to do, but this kid was getting closer all the time. The brothers didn't stop to think; they were out of there. Bill's place has a concealed side entrance; that's where he would park whenever the press were around or the fans were after him. The brothers had gone, and I knew very well they wouldn't wait around too long for me.

'I stood wondering what the hell to do. By the time I'd cut him down, that kid would be peering through the window. He'd stopped to go behind the pool house for some reason, but there he was again. I looked up at Bill.'

Irwin stopped. His eyes closed, and when he opened them again, they were moist.

'I saw it was already too late. I didn't realise how bad a state Bill had been in. He must have died in about two minutes. I thought, well, the kid is bound to find him, but then I realised that everyone would assume that he'd topped himself, wouldn't they? I could hardly reckon with a smart-arsed police officer who happened to know Bill was left-handed.'

Silence poured over them like a kind of benediction. Bellamy glanced to his right. The two constables outside were seemingly entranced; their instincts were telling them something significant was happening.

For some seconds, everyone froze, as if caught by a snapshot. When Bellamy broke the silence, his voice sounded intrusive to him, like a sudden noise in a church service.

'I think that's as far as we can go now. Mr Fennell, do you wish to add anything?'

'No, I don't think so,' Fennell said. He was looking at Irwin with a kind of resignation. 'I think my client and I need to talk in private, Chief Inspector.'

'Yes, of course.'

Bellamy watched them go, Irwin now walking between the two constables with his head bowed and his arms hanging at his sides.

Bellamy crossed to the window, thinking he could perhaps work out what Irwin had been looking at. Before the countryside took over, a school playing field was in view, with twenty-two boys, looking in the region of fifteen or sixteen years old, strongly contesting a game of football, while the boys with the excuse notes stood by the side, shivering. One of the taller players looked familiar, even at a distance. Bellamy wondered whether it was Raymond Oswald, the kid who suddenly appeared to the men trying to frighten the life out of Bill Massiter, the kid who would now almost certainly be called as a witness in a murder case. Bellamy wondered what Raymond's mother would have to say about that; quite a lot, he suspected. Oddly enough, if the boy had wandered onto Massiter land ten minutes earlier, he might have saved Bill's life.

Had Irwin been remembering schooldays, times when the world was a great deal simpler and the future loomed ahead like a great big adult fun park?

Bellamy turned and left the office, in search of a cup of coffee.

PART SEVEN

Aftermath

Ten Months Later

Chopin again. Bellamy was in his study, having one of the reflective pauses which made him able to do his job. The whole Massiter imbroglio was beginning to fade from his mind, but there were still occasions when moments of it came back to him very powerfully. His main cases now had returned to familiar ground; the ongoing and often vicious struggle between big drug dealers to either protect their patch or move onto someone else's. Few people, in his experience, were all evil, and in some cases, the reasons why they had become evil became obvious with a greater knowledge of their background, but occasionally, individuals came along who appeared to have no mitigating factors at all, and quite a number of these people seemed to feature in his knowledge of drug dealers.

The loose ends of the Massiter affair had been largely tied up. As Bellamy suspected, the jury at Eric Irwin's trial did not swallow his explanation of events. He had been convicted of manslaughter in the case of the Iraqi men and murder in the case of Bill Massiter, as had both of the Penrose brothers. Irwin had also been convicted for conspiracy to murder, in the action taken against Bellamy and his wife and the shooting incident which wounded a journalist. Tracking down the gunman who had actually pulled the trigger on that occasion was now a matter for international police organisations, and Bellamy suspected the spooks were probably also on the case. The fact that the gunman clearly did not intend to kill anyone made the search more casual than it might otherwise have been.

Irwin had been sentenced to a total of twenty years in prison; Stewart Penrose, who had been driving the boat when it collided with the dinghy, to twelve, and Mike Penrose to nine. The brothers asked for a number of other offences, mainly concerned with smuggling, to be taken into account in order to avoid having to go through another trial as soon as they'd served their sentence. Josie Massiter had got away with a suspended sentence.

Lord Railton, with his squads of clever lawyers and references to mental health problems, had also received a suspended sentence, with the proviso that if he was even associated with any further deaths in the future, he would also go to prison. His Lordship had left the country for somewhere on the continent, where rather than going to prison, he had effectively imprisoned himself with so many layers of security he never spent more than five minutes on his own.

What exactly had happened to Khaled the Scorpion remained indefinite. As Bellamy had suspected, the secret services had made his fate their business, meaning they were probably employing him as a human killing machine to dispatch troublesome terrorists at home and abroad. Putting him on public trial was never going to happen since he had been associated with so many killings that his public exposure would put the secret services on trial as much as Khaled himself. Bellamy's secret service contact had told him that, if he was worried that Khaled might regard the police officer who captured him as a target, he need not concern himself, as Khaled had been told that the murder of a senior police officer would put him in prison for the rest of his life.

'In any case,' the spook man had concluded, 'he got on his high horse and told us he doesn't kill brave men. He kills crooks, cowards, thieves and murderers.'

The remains of the ten men on the dinghy had been re-buried in a Muslim cemetery after a Muslim commemorative service, their ten names, as told by Haidar, placed on the gravestones. What was left of their bodies was buried with their right side facing towards Mecca, according to Muslim practice.

Haidar and Kassim Alwan had been granted asylum and they were both now involved in translation work with the police and the border services. Haidar was negotiating a publishing deal for a book describing his working life in England and his experiences during and after the Iraqi war.

Louise had not wasted her Scottish exile, having written and published a number of articles regarding her views on what professional politicians should be and do, and now a certain momentum seemed to be growing for her to be found a place on her party's front bench.

Elaine Price's connections with the media had developed to such an extent that she had accepted a post as a senior media officer, an area of work which occasionally caused crossovers between police personnel and journalists, because without a fairly exhaustive knowledge of the media, candidates for such a job were unlikely to be successful. After working with Elaine for so long, Bellamy felt rather deprived at losing her and felt he had been instrumental at throwing her at the media, but the experience had clearly suited her and opened up new career paths.

Raymond Oswald was called as a witness in the case of Bill Massiter's death. He was now a sixth-former, and he managed the experience well, insisting that he only ventured onto Massiter land because he saw the hanging figure in the window. He had a moment in court when the defence lawyer questioned whether he could really have seen the figure at such a distance.

'I think those with normal eyesight, including me, I have to say, would have struggled to see such a thing from the very edge of Mr Massiter's land.'

'Well, my eyes are rather younger than yours, aren't they, sir?' said Raymond, and even his mother allowed herself a smile.

The Cougars had embarked on a "nostalgia tour", with a lead guitarist called Ed Jones taking time out from his own band, standing in for Bill Massiter. Tony Richards had dropped the Rory

Blaze and the solo career and now performed with the Cougars in his own name; he wore suits and ties these days to cater for what he called "our more mature audience". He had also formed a civil partnership with one of his long-standing fans called Mark Welland, and he no longer entertained young male fans in his dressing room – Mark, who was no one's fool, had seen to that. "The Cougars and Ed Jones", as they now called themselves, were now contemplating putting together some new material.

'It might be old guy music,' Manny Orestes was reported as saying, 'but there are a lot of old guys around, and their money's as good as anyone else's.'

The meditative "Nocturne" in C-sharp minor came to an end. Some people might think of Chopin as old guy music, Bellamy thought, but he couldn't yet classify himself as an old guy, and in any case, everything Chopin ever wrote seemed to him to be imbued with youthfulness, even when it was sad.

Somewhere, he thought, in some forgotten corner of France or Italy, Lord Railton continues to blast his mind out with heavy metal, which is now so long past its heyday it probably also qualifies as old guy music. Perhaps, in His Lordship's addled mind, some virile young adventurer is still trying to believe in himself. Perhaps he believes, as so many other old guys might well do, that when his music stops, so will he.